Johnnie Alone

ELIZABETH WEBSTER lives with her husband in a rambling old Gloucestershire house which overflows with books, manuscripts, costumes, instruments and young people wanting help with anything from housing to university interviews, from poetry to a new job. Musician, critic, stage director, teacher, writer and composer, Elizabeth Webster has worked with young people all her adult life, and raised three children of her own. Her concern for children in distress began in the early years after the Second World War, when she ran a small residential nursery school for children whose parents were in difficulty.

She founded The Young Arts Centre of Cheltenham and today divides her time between the Centre, her work as a music critic, and writing and composing.

D0610872

ELIZABETH WEBSTER

Johnnie Alone

FONTANA/Collins

First published as a serial in *My Weekly*
under the title *Johnnie Dumbo* 1982

First published in hardback in Great Britain
by Judy Piatkus (Publishers) Ltd 1984
This edition first issued in Fontana Paperbacks 1984

Copyright © Elizabeth Webster 1982

Made and printed in Great Britain by
William Collins Sons & Co. Ltd, Glasgow

PART I

The Park

Johnnie was looking at clouds. They lay upside down in the lake, pure and white on the brown water. Like swans. Trees with wide arms met in the lake, too. They leaned down to each other, standing root to root at the edge. The water was dark, but the clouds shone with light.

He loved light. He could sit for hours just watching the reflections. Their shapes fascinated him. Sometimes he would move his hand as if he wanted to touch them and feel their shifting contours under his fingers. Or as if he wanted to draw their shapes on the air.

Monday was Park Day. That is, it usually was. But sometimes other days were Park Days too. It depended on Big Joe. Johnnie's calendar was governed by Big Joe.

Saturday was Thumping Day. Weekdays were sometimes Thumping Days too, but Saturdays were worst. Then the bells in Johnnie's head rang louder than ever. He usually waited till they stopped ringing and then crept away somewhere and hid.

On Sunday Big Joe lay in bed all day, sleeping it off, and Johnnie was safe. In the evening when Big Joe got up, lurching about and swearing loudly, Johnnie was out. He stayed out until he saw Big Joe shamble off to the pub, and then he crept in again and went up to bed.

His mother, Julie, got very quiet when Big Joe was in a thumping mood. In Johnnie's mind she was like a child somehow, with her long hair and her wary eyes. Just like the other kids – quiet and scared. She tried to keep Treesa and the baby, Benjy, out of Big Joe's way, but Kevin who was older sometimes dared to stand up for Johnnie, and then Big Joe got really angry. He didn't thump Julie or the kids as hard as he hit Johnnie because they were his, and Johnnie – as he frequently told him – was not.

If the thumping was bad, Johnnie didn't go to school on Mondays. He lay in bed till Big Joe had gone to work, and then he went to the Park. He loved the Park. It was empty in the daytime on weekdays. And quiet. Wonderfully quiet. Nobody spoke to him. Nobody shouted at him. Nobody bothered about him at all. The trees and the sky accepted him and asked nothing of him. He was not clumsy or dumb or stupid to them. He could sit there, curled up on the edge of the bank by the lake, and dream the day away.

He wasn't lonely. There were animals in the Park to talk to – especially dogs. He knew most of them by name – the ones with owners and the ones who didn't seem to belong to anyone. They all came to talk to him – particularly one very thin scruffy little dog he had christened Get-Lost.

It used to sidle up to him where he sat by the water, and thrust its cold wet nose into his hand. Scrawny town cats came and went too, but they were indepen-dent creatures usually intent on stalking birds, and they didn't stay long. Sometimes even a squirrel would come down out of a tree and sit looking at him. . . . He felt more comfortable with animals than with human beings. Nothing was required of him except a kind of affectionate quietness, and he had plenty of that. . . . His hand would linger on the not-very-silky head of little Get-Lost, and he would think: he only wants a bit of attention, he's probably lonely.

The squirrel wasn't lonely, though. It was just inquisitive because he sat so still.

But above all, it was the trees and the water that drew him. He could not get enough of their beauty and stillness into his battered mind. Sometimes he used to put his arms round the smooth trunk of a tree and just stand there, embracing it, feeling its strength and its calm slow growth seeping into his own frail body. If he stood there long enough he almost felt he was a tree, growing quietly and steadily in the sun and rain, with its roots deep in the earth. . . . But then the Park Keeper, who was a grumpy man much plagued by children, would come along and shout at him: 'Don't you dare vandalise my trees!' and push him away.

Johnnie didn't know what vandalising was, and anyway he couldn't hear him clearly – but he recognised shouts. They banged in his head and hurt him. So he moved away, reluctantly letting go of his tree, and wandered off along the path by the lake.

That was how he found the Painting Man. He was sitting on a little stool, with a kind of small white blackboard propped up on legs in front of him. (Johnnie had never seen an easel.) He had a box of tubes of colour beside him on the grass, and a whole stack of paint brushes, and he was painting trees. Trees and water, and the long, curving arch of the bridge over the lake, with dark shadows and a second reflected curve underneath.

Johnnie stopped to look, fascinated. He stood there

for a long time, just watching the man's brush strokes, and the magical way water reflections and tree branches and light and shade grew on the empty canvas.

The man took no notice of him at first, but just went on painting, absorbed and quiet. But he was well aware of the small, enthralled figure beside him. He thought he would probably get tired of watching and go away. But Johnnie didn't get tired. He just stood there, gazing and gazing at the miracles that paints and brushes could do.

At last the man stopped painting and looked at Johnnie. He saw the beautiful curve of his blond head and the strange dark blue eyes, black-fringed and visionary, and the curious anxious attention and puzzlement deep inside them. . . . A flawed beauty, he thought – and then wondered why he had thought 'flawed'.

'Do you like painting?' he asked, smiling a little at the boy's rapt expression.

Johnnie did not answer. He did not even hear the question. But he was aware that the Painting Man was trying to communicate. He lifted his hand and traced the line of the tree on the canvas, keeping his fingers away from the wet surface, but near enough to feel the shape of that curving bark in his own fingertips.

The man looked at him intently, seeing something still and ecstatic in the boy's face. He was not troubled by his silence. In fact he was rather pleased by it. People talked too much anyway. This enraptured, silent appreciation was much better.

Presently a thought struck him, and he got out a piece of charcoal, tore off a sheet of paper from his sketching block, and silently handed them to Johnnie. The boy turned the charcoal over in his fingers, looking at it carefully. Then he made a tentative stroke on the paper. The man nodded approvingly, and waved a hand at the trees and water before him.

'That's it. Draw! See what you can do.'

Johnnie looked at the tree, following its solid, graceful curve with his eye. Then he began to set down what he saw. He worked swiftly, in total concentration, and the tree grew, black and beautiful, flowing up out of the white page.

The man watched him, half incredulous. This extraordinary, beautiful, silent child could draw. He could draw like an angel!

Johnnie went on until the tree was finished. Then he stood back to look at it, head on one side. At last he turned to the Painting Man and shyly offered the drawing to him.

The Painting Man hesitated. 'Wouldn't you like to keep it?'

Johnnie heard that. When he was drawing, the noises in his head subsided and went quiet. A wonderful silent peace came into his mind. After that, for a little while, he could hear quite clearly.

He shook his head and held out the drawing again. 'For you,' he said. He tried to keep his voice small, but even so it seemed to boom and echo in his head and spoil the silence.

The quiet artist smiled and accepted the drawing. Johnnie smiled back. The man looked as if a squib had gone off in his eyes. For a moment he sat looking at the boy in astonished compassion, seeing the knowledge of pain, the patience and acceptance in that tired, radiant smile.

My God, he thought, what is this? What is it about this boy? He's like a. . . . What is he like? Lucifer before the fall? Full of light, yes, but not proud. . . . No, there's no evil there. . . . Untouched, some-

how. . . . More like a star-child on the wrong
planet. . . . No, he's human all right. . . . That burning, sorrowful beauty . . . and that puzzlement and
longing to communicate. . . What have people done to
him?

Aloud he said: 'Tomorrow?' And then, speaking
slowly and carefully, looking full at him: 'I will be
here . . . tomorrow.'

Johnnie nodded. Then he looked up at the sky and
cast a practised glance at the position of the sun. He
would have to go. They would be coming out of school.
He would be due home any minute. Mom would expect
him to get tea for the kids. She would want to go out to
bingo soon. He would have to get it all done before Big
Joe got home. And then there was the paper round to
do. He liked that. He borrowed the shop bicycle and
rode round the streets shoving papers through letter
boxes. It never occurred to him that he was not safe on
a bike, or that he might never hear the car coming
round the corner. . . . It was a job. He got paid. He
had to hand over the money to Big Joe, of course, but
sometimes he gave him ten pence back to buy sweets.
He didn't buy sweets though, he bought a pencil and
some paper usually. Lately, though, Big Joe had been
crosser than usual and hadn't given him any. . . . He
could always pinch some from school, he supposed . . .

'Here,' said the Painting Man. 'Take these. . . . See
you tomorrow.' And he gave him two sticks of charcoal
and four whole sheets of the sketching block.

Johnnie's eyes grew round with delight. Stammering
with pleasure, he got out 'Thank you!' and carefully
tucked the paper away inside his jersey. Then, cradling
the charcoal in his hands, he ran off down the path.

The man watched him go. Something about the boy's

fragile radiance pierced him. At length, sighing, he picked up his gear and went in the opposite direction along the shady path by the lake.

Johnnie went home. He knew he had to, and anyway, the kids needed him there. When he got in, Treesa put skinny arms round his neck and said in her breathless five-year-old voice: 'You're back! What's for tea?'

Seven-year-old Kevin, brown-haired and thin as a reed said: 'The baby was sick but I mopped it up.' He gave Johnnie a brotherly push and a gap-toothed smile. 'Where you been then?'

Johnnie shook his head. He was a silent boy. The bells in his head made it difficult for him to take in what people said to him. And his own voice sounded strange and booming in his head – echoing round his brain like a shout. He hated shouts. People always seemed to be shouting at him. Big Joe shouted. His mother shouted back: 'Don't hit him, Joe.He hasn't done nothing to you! Have you, Johnnie?' And, when he failed to answer: 'HAVE YOU, JOHNNIE?'

Thump.

'Answer when your mother speaks to you!'

Johnnie would look at him, bewildered, wondering what he was supposed to say. 'No,' he would mutter. But the sound seemed to shout and echo in his head, exploding into a thousand fragments of noise, and all of them hurt him. Silence was best.

'I can't stand him sitting there, never speaking. Always looking at me with those big cow's eyes!' shouted Joe. 'Why can't he say something?' A hand would come out and start shaking him by the shoulders. 'Hey, you! Johnnie! Why don't you say something?'

What did they want him to say? He didn't know.

Anxiously, he would search Big Joe's angry face for a clue. The noises in his head were like a fog between him and other people. He couldn't quite reach them. He couldn't explain. He would look at Big Joe in despair.

The trouble was, he had one extraordinary handicap in Big Joe's eyes. He was too beautiful. Blond hair falling in a straight swathe over eyes that were too large and too expressive with their deep, arresting blue. A pure, clear young profile that was much too vulnerable – and that incandescent look of burning attention while he strained to understand. . . . It hurt Big Joe somehow, and because it hurt him, Big Joe hated it and got angry. The boy disturbed him . . . he had no business to look like that . . . those anxious, seeking eyes bothered him. He wished they would go away. They tried too hard to understand him, and Big Joe didn't want to be understood at all.

'Stop staring!' Big Joe would shout.

'Sorry,' he would mutter, flinching at the booms in his head. 'Sorry, Big Joe . . .'

'I'll give you sorry!'

Thump.

His ears sang. His head rang with sound. It was too loud. Too loud to bear. He put his hands over his ears and rocked to and fro to escape the pain. But he couldn't escape. Not ever. Big Joe's hand came down again, hard.

Even so, something cool and calm inside his head said to him over and over again: It doesn't matter. . . . Hurting doesn't matter. . . . The Park will be quiet . . .

When he got back from the Park on Mondays, he longed to go back there. Especially if it was a shouting evening.

But this time, after he met the Painting Man, it was not so bad. The children were glad to see him. He got them their tea. The baby, Benjy, allowed Johnnie to spoon custard into his mouth and then fell asleep. Julie, his mother, pushed the long blonde hair out of her eyes, put on a shiny dress and went out to bingo. Big Joe had won something on the horses, so he was in quite a good mood. He ate his tea and went out again to celebrate.

Johnnie put the other children to bed and sighed with relief. When he was quite alone, he got out the Painting Man's charcoal and paper, and began to draw . . .

On Tuesdays, they always asked him at school where he had been. They shouted at him, too. But he had learnt to be evasive and vague.

'Wasn't well,' he muttered, trying to stop his own voice from booming.

'You should bring a note.'

He looked blank.

'A NOTE, Johnnie.'

He nodded. 'Forgot.'

It happened nearly every week. Sometimes, he missed Tuesdays as well because he was afraid of the questions. Then there were questions on Wednesday instead. No-one ever seemed to think seriously about the cause of those absences. Johnnie was a dead loss in school, anyway. He didn't seem to listen or to learn anything. Mostly, he sat and drew things on scraps of paper. He never paid any attention to the teachers, except when they wrote things on the blackboard. Then he copied things down carefully, but failed to respond to any questions. They tried getting angry, but he just looked blanker than ever. They tried coaxing. He didn't respond. They were busy and rushed. There was never time to bother much about one silent, apparently sullen boy. In the end, they left him alone and went on trying to force knowledge into the unwilling heads of some thirty less unrewarding kids. They got used to seeing him sitting there with his blond head bent over his desk and his hand moving in long, decisive strokes on the paper. Occasionally they would look to see what he was doing, and were surprised at the accuracy and vigour of his drawing. . . . And once, to their intense astonishment, they caught him reading quite an advanced book.

'What are you reading, Johnnie? JOHNNIE! What are you reading?'

He looked up, puzzled. Then, seeing the questioning face above him, politely held out the book for their inspection.

'*Scott of the Antartic?* You can't read that, can you?'

Still puzzled, he held out his hand to take the book back again.

'Where did you learn to read books like that?' asked the teacher, for a moment stirred out of his habitual tiredness.

Johnnie looked vague. 'Words . . .' he said dreamily. 'Words . . . make shapes . . .' He looked up at the teacher's uncomprehending gaze and tried vainly to think of a way to explain. But there was no way.

For a moment a glimpse of understanding seemed to flash between them, and then it was gone. Sighing, the teacher handed back the book and went on with his class. Johnnie bent his blond head and went on reading.

So, mostly they let him alone and took the easy way out. 'That Johnnie Cass, can you do anything with him?' one would ask.

And another would shrug and answer: 'Not a thing.

12

Dumb as a coot, I fear. Best let him alone. He's no trouble.' That was his form master, Dave Stephens. He wasn't unkind. Just rushed and tired.

The rest of the school week was all right, except when the questions came. Some teachers just droned on, or wrote things down to be copied. Johnnie could copy anything. As long as it was that kind of lesson he could keep out of trouble. But questions were different.

He could see the teacher's face turned enquiringly in his direction. He knew he had been asked something. But he had no idea what it was.

'Johnnie Cass?'

Silence.

'JOHNNIE! Are you listening?'

Silence. What was the question? What was he supposed to say? He never knew.

'You'll have to stay behind and write it out. Do you hear me?'

He didn't. But despairingly, he nodded. He stayed behind.

Sometimes they showed him what to write, and he wrote it – beautifully. He had strong, well-formed writing, fluent and easy. He had taught himself to write, from endless blackboard copying which was supposed to be a punishment. But it was like drawing. He enjoyed it.

But if they didn't tell him what to say, how could he write it? He didn't understand education. It seemed a mystifying process. What exactly did they want him to do? He never found out.

All the same, he quite liked staying in. It was better than going out. The playground was terrifying. The shouting got louder and louder. His ears hurt like fire. Gangs of boys set on him, chanting things at him. He could see their red mouths opening and shutting. Yapping at him, like dogs.

'Johnnie Dumbo! Johnnie Dumbo!
Hasn't got a single Crumbo!'

The circle of faces bounced round him, advancing like a wall of pale balloons.

'Johnnie Dim
Hasn't got a glim!

Johnnie Moo (That was those eyes again)
Hasn't got a clue!

Johnnie Cass
Bottom of the class!

Pea-brain Johnnie,
Flea-brain Johnnie!
Johnnie Dimbo
Lives in limbo!'

Limbo. Johnnie caught that. Limbo, he thought. I know what limbo is. It was in that book about myths. Limbo is a place of twilight. A place of shades. A place of silence. I think I would like limbo.

He smiled.

The circle of faces hesitated. Before that blinding, seraphic smile, they were abashed. They didn't know quite why, but it shook them.

Johnnie didn't know why they paused, either. But he was glad. The closing circle of noisy mouths terrified him.

But before they could begin again, a girl pushed her way through and scattered the circle with one rough swing of her arm.

'Leave him alone!' she said. 'Piss off!'

The group of tormentors retreated, but one of them turned and chanted:

'Johnnie's a hoot,
Dumb as a coot,
Poor old Johnnie Dumbo!' as a parting shot.

The girl lunged at him and caught him a swingeing blow on the side of his head. He ran off, bawling.

Then the girl turned quite cheerfully to Johnnie and smiled. Cautiously, Johnnie smiled back.

'You don't need to listen to *them*,' she said.

Johnnie watched her anxiously. Sometimes if he watched carefully enough he could see from the shapes their mouths made what people were saying.

'Here,' said the girl, 'have half my sandwich. It's peanut butter today.'

She put a sticky piece of bread into his hand. Johnnie looked at it in surprise, then back at the girl.

'Go on,' she said. 'Eat it. Won't bite you!' She put her own piece into her mouth and chewed.

Johnnie was looking at her with his seeing, artist's eye. He saw shapes and colours very clearly and with brilliant intensity. People's faces told him a lot about the people themselves without them knowing it. He could usually tell who to trust, and who to avoid.

This one before him intrigued him. She was tall – as tall as he was for nearly twelve years old, and her hair was dark where his was fair. It framed her face in a wild, unruly tangle of almost black curls that looked as if they never got brushed. Her eyes were wide apart, and grey. They seemed to see things a long way off, like his own, and they looked at you straight. Her face was pale and a bit thin, but there was something about it that attracted him. . . . Heart-shaped and delicate, but strong. And her mouth was kind when it smiled, but a bit stern, too. It could laugh, though – and it could fight.

He lifted his hand suddenly, as if he wanted to curve

it round the shape of her face – to draw it in one sweeping line on the air. But he saw something that made him pause. When he lifted his hand, she flinched.

He recognised that look. He understood it. To him it was unmistakeable. She was a fellow sufferer. There was a Big Joe in her life, too.

'Sorry,' he muttered, and smiled with more shyness than before.

'What're you sorry about?' she said.

But he couldn't tell her. Instead, he offered her the only precious thing he had – a stub of black pencil he had saved from the classroom.

'No,' she said, closing his fingers over it. 'You keep it. I've seen you drawing. You're good.' She looked at him, head on one side, considering. 'Tell you what. You do me a drawing, see?'

He looked into her face, desperately trying to understand. She saw his mind struggling with the effort to reach her, and tried to make it easy for him. She took out a grubby piece of paper from her pocket and showed it to him. 'You –' she said slowly, pointing to his hand still clutching the pencil, 'draw – for me!' and she pointed to herself.

Delighted, Johnnie nodded vigorously, and the vivid, sweet smile broke out again. 'Yes,' he growled, disregarding the boom his voice made in his own head, 'I – will – draw – you – a – picture.' It was a long sentence for him. He was pleased with it.

The girl grinned at him then, and skipped away. He didn't even know her name. But he resolved to pinch a bit of classroom paper and make her a wonderful drawing. Or he could ask the Painting Man for a bit of real drawing paper, if he was there tomorrow . . .

*   *   *

He was there the next day. Johnnie ran up to him joyously. He didn't say 'Hello,' but squatted down beside him to look at his work.

The Painting Man looked up and smiled, and Johnnie smiled back. Once again the man looked slightly stunned, but he said nothing. Instead, he reached out and tore off a sheet from his sketch-pad and handed Johnnie some charcoal again. Johnnie's smile got even more luminous. This time, remembering his promise to The Girl, he began to fold the paper, meaning to tear it in half.

But the Painting Man said swiftly: 'No. Don't do that. It'll make the trees too small. . . . Always draw big, if you can . . . big and bold. . . . If you want two pieces, have another one . . .' and he handed him another piece.

Johnnie looked into his face questioningly for a moment and then settled down to draw. But he didn't draw trees this time. He drew the man hunched over his easel, painting, his brown face absorbed and quiet. . . . Johnnie had eyes that saw clearly, too, and he began to put down what he saw. . . . A squarish, rough-cut sort of figure, wearing a shapeless, thick brown pullover and shabby, paint-stained jeans . . . a head that reminded Johnnie of a lion's – shaggy, with thick grey hair, and a strong, calm, watchful look about it . . . a broad, highish forehead, very bright eyes under bushy grey eyebrows, and fine crowsfeet lines at the corners, especially when he smiled or when he was concentrating. And his hands – squarish, like the rest of him, but clever and sensitive, light on the canvas, the fingers ending in flattened pads that could feel and touch and set down everything they knew in glorious lines and curves and washes of colour . . .

When the drawing was ready, Johnnie carefully

printed: 'The Painting Man' underneath, and shyly offered it to him.

This time the man did not hesitate to accept it. He almost seized it in his excitement, and when it was in his hand, he gazed at it in astonishment and delight.

'But that's splendid!' he said. 'Simply splendid! Is that how I look to you? Rather an old rag-bag, eh?' His eyes were full of laughter, and something very like admiration. 'Study in concentration, though, isn't it? Look at the set of my head . . . determined, aren't I?' He laughed.

Then he turned and looked keenly into Johnnie's face, and said slowly: 'You are going to be an artist, you know. An artist must always sign his work!'

Johnnie understood that. Carefully, he wrote in smudgy charcoal: 'Johnnie.' He did not add any more.

'Is that all?' asked the man, smiling.

Johnnie nodded. He could not explain to the Painting Man how he felt about names. Cass was his mother's name. Big Joe's name was Harman. Johnnie's wasn't either, really. But deep down in his mind he remembered a big laughing man who had been his father, and who had been an engineer. . . . He went away, or Julie, Johnnie's mother went away, he couldn't remember which exactly. But he thought somehow that his drawing came from that tall, happy, laughing man he had known when he was small.

'Just Johnnie?' persisted the man. Then, seeing Johnnie's look of stress, he added quickly: 'Well, never mind . . . sit down by me and I'll show you how to put light and shade in water . . .'

The two heads drew close together, side by side, absorbed and quiet. Johnnie was utterly content.

*   *   *

18

The day after that, Big Joe went to a football match. When he came back, he was very drunk and in a foul temper. His side had lost, and he felt it was a personal affront.

Not expecting Big Joe home early, Johnnie was in the house giving the younger children their tea. His mother was down at the bingo hall again – at least, he supposed she was. That was where she usually went to as soon as he got home from school.

He was standing with a saucepan full of hot baked beans in one hand and a spoon in the other, when Big Joe lurched through the door.

'Well?' shouted Big Joe. 'What the hell are you doing with that saucepan? Baked beans again! Where's my proper tea!'

He lunged at Johnnie, who sidestepped neatly and tried to put the baked beans down on the table.

In the oven, thought Johnnie desperately. Big Joe's tea's in the oven. Mom said so. I must get it out before he gets any madder.

He turned to open the oven door. Big Joe was swaying on his feet right beside him, and the saucepan full of hot beans caught him on the elbow, flew out of Johnnie's hands and fell in a sticky, scalding mess on Johnnie's feet. Some of them fell on Big Joe's, too, and he roared with rage.

Johnnie stood petrified. He didn't try to run away. He couldn't.

Big Joe advanced on him, unbuckling his leather belt with the metal clasp and bellowing like a bull. . . .

He woke up on the floor. His mother was back and was hastily putting the other children to bed. She didn't glance in his direction. That meant Big Joe was still about somewhere. Kevin tried to hold back and come over to him, but his mother pushed him upstairs, saying in a hushed, tight sort of voice: 'Not now, Kevin, not now.'

Johnnie lay still. He hurt everywhere. But it was better to keep still than to protest. Presently he felt the mood of the house lighten, and he knew that Big Joe had gone out again.

His mother came over, looking more like a dishevelled frightened child than ever. She bent over him, tearfully, and said: 'What did he do to you? Oh, my God, I'd better bathe your back. . . . There now, Johnnie, he's gone out now . . . he won't be back till closing time. . . . Can you walk? Get you to bed, that's best . . .'

Vaguely, he heard her talking to him. The sound boomed and clattered round his head, but it was soothing. . . . His mother meant well. It was just that she was weak and was afraid of Big Joe. And she couldn't cope with the kids very well. There was always too much washing, and too much cleaning. She never caught up somehow – even though Johnnie did most of it. And as for cooking – she mostly left that to Johnnie, too. He wondered, in a muddled, anxious way, what the kids had eaten after he dropped the beans. . . . Were they still hungry?

When he tried to walk, all sorts of agonising pains assailed him – especially on his feet where he dropped the hot saucepan. The room swam mistily as he struggled to keep upright. In front of him were the stairs, steep and bare and forbidding, going on for ever . . . he didn't think he would ever get up those. . . .

Somehow or other he got to his bed. He shared it with Kevin, who was small for seven and did not take up much room. He was already asleep, sprawled out across it, looking innocent and unguarded. Johnnie couldn't describe to himself what he felt about the others – but he minded what happened to them, and he knew he had to protect them from Big Joe if he could. When they looked like Kevin did now – asleep and open to any hurt – he felt a kind of knot inside him that he couldn't undo.

It was not quite the same with his mother, Julie. She was grown up – well, sort of – she could look after herself. Or she ought to be able to. But of course she couldn't. She was as helpless as the kids in the face of Big Joe's violence.

Treesa, being only five, slept on a small camp bed with the baby's cot beside her, at one end of her mother's and Big Joe's room. Mostly, Big Joe didn't get angry in bed, except when Benjy cried – which he did quite a lot, especially in the early morning. Treesa was quite good at rocking the cot to stop him, but when it got bad she would slide out of bed and go to fetch Johnnie.

Strangely, Johnnie could always tell when Benjy was crying. He didn't know if the thin sound penetrated his damaged ears, or if he just felt it. But he always knew, and he came padding in on bare feet to pick up Benjy and take him away before Big Joe woke up and got angry . . .

Now, a dark wave of anxiety overcame him. What would happen to the others if he couldn't get out of bed to help them? It was awful to think about . . .

'Mom,' he began, trying to make things clear.

'Yes, Johnnie, yes. There, now . . . better in the morning . . . go to sleep now . . .'

'But Mom,' He couldn't manage it. Talking was agony. It made his head explode with pain.

'Yes, Johnnie? My poor baby, what is it?'

He heard that with sudden clarity. I'm not your poor

baby, he thought. I'm nearly twelve. I'm a boy on my own, and your man Big Joe beats me up every time he sees me.

Faintly, he remembered a time when his ears didn't hurt. When no-one beat him. When that big, brown, laughing man called Danny who was his father used to come home and swing him aloft on to his shoulder, saying: 'How's my boy? Riding high, up in the sky!' and he would laugh again, and Johnnie would laugh with him . . .

A strange, fierce anger took hold of him. He couldn't just lie here! His mother was hopeless. Hopeless. Like the kids. Young and frightened and hopeless. He was the only one who could cope. It was up to him. 'The kids . . . ' he said.

'They'll be all right, Johnnie. Don't you worry.'

He watched his mother run her hand through her long, dishevelled fair hair and look helplessly round the untidy bedroom.

He struggled to move. '. . . get up . . . ' he muttered.

'No, no. You lay there. I'll see to things.' But the tears dripped out of her eyes, and she said in a sudden, strangled voice: 'Oh, my God . . . what am I going to do?'

He couldn't hear her. But he saw her tears, and put up one hand to her face in a kind, tired gesture. She was just like the kids, after all. . . . She only needed a bit of comforting – like Benjy when he cried . . .

'Sorry . . . ' he murmured. 'Sorry.'

When Johnnie failed to turn up at school for over a week, the staff reported it to the Schools' Attendance Officer, who called in the Health Visitor from the Welfare Department and Maggie Fraser from Social Services for a conference.

'Any indication of home difficulties?' asked Tom Ellery, the Attendance Officer.

Maggie Fraser, social worker and incurable optimist, known to many of the kids as The Welfare Lady and to their parents as That Interfering Busybody, sighed. 'Plenty of indications. Nothing positive.'

'What kind of things?'

'Well – he's very withdrawn. The teachers report that he does nothing constructive at school, though I don't believe he's altogether a half-wit. Doesn't answer when spoken to. Jumps at loud noises. And he's away nearly every Monday.'

'*Is he?*' Tom Ellery sounded as if he recognised that pattern.

There was a pause while he considered. Ellery was more experienced than Maggie Fraser, and even more aware of the awful problems involved. He was a grizzled, weary, sardonic looking man. He had heard every truancy excuse under the sun and believed none of them. But he wasn't really cynical. He still cared about the kids – whatever the little blighters did. Maggie cared about the kids, too. But she was young. Rather pleasant to look at in a muted kind of way, with her urchin-cut soft brown hair, those observant, clear hazel eyes and that warm-hearted friendly smile. . . . Probably a shade too kind-hearted for this job. It didn't do to get involved.

'Sounds a familiar pattern,' he said. 'Some kind of violence at home. . . . Fright can often make children appear extremely stupid. Is there anything he *can* do?'

'I believe he can draw. His form master says he's talented. But can't get through to him.'

'I see. . . . Have you been round to the house?'

'Not yet. I haven't had any excuse.'

'Well, you have now.' Tom's voice was as grim as his expression.

Maggie nodded. 'You're right. I'll go round tomorrow.'

'Today would be better,' said Tom.

Maggie agreed.

When she knocked at the door there was a wail of children's voices within, but no-one came.

She knocked again. The wails increased, but still no-one came.

After a time she walked round the side of the house and found the back door. It was unlocked and – grimly admitting to herself that she was overstepping her duties as a social worker – she walked in.

The kitchen was indescribable. Dirty plates piled high, half-eaten fish and chips still in their greasy paper, milk gone sour in half-used bottles, and babies' nappies – clean and unclean – all these lay indescriminately heaped on the table, the chairs, in the sink and even on the floor. Beyond the inner door, there was the continuous sound of a baby crying and another small voice saying in tired desperation: 'Oh, do be quiet, Benjy, *Shut up*, Benjy, do!'

Maggie left the chaotic kitchen and went through into the living room. A small girl of five stood staring at her, finger in mouth, eyes wide and alarmed. Beside her, Kevin was frantically bouncing the baby up and down in its pram in a vain attempt to stop it crying or shake it into sleep.

"Who are you?' said Kevin.

'I'm Maggie. The Welfare Lady.' She was used to trotting out this phrase and watching the children's reaction.

Kevin froze. 'Mum's out.'

'So I see. . . . Actually, I came to see Johnnie. Is he anywhere about?'

There was a silence. The children looked at one another. Their faces closed like flowers in the frost.

'Come on,' said Maggie, coaxingly, 'I won't hurt him, you know . . . I came to help you.'

Kevin continued to stare at her in silence. But he suddenly seemed to recognise something like an ally in Maggie. Maybe she really could do something. Though grown-ups mostly only talked, or shouted.

'He's upstairs.'

'Can I go and see him?' Maggie was already moving to the stairs.

'S'pose so,' said Kevin, in an offhand manner. But he was longing for her to go up and see for herself. Johnnie was bad. He lay there and didn't see them. His feet were all black and swollen where the beans had burnt them, and his back was too sore to lie on, so he lay on his front. He made a funny noise when he breathed, and Kevin was frightened.

Maggie went upstairs. Kevin followed. Treesa just stood there, like stone, finger in mouth, still staring.

Johnnie lay in a kind of dream. He didn't hear anyone or notice when they came and went. It hurt too much to move, so he didn't try to turn over. Somewhere he could see trees behind his eyes, their branches waving gently above his head, and his sore, burnt feet were standing in cool water while he looked up at the sky.

'Sky?' he said, and bells rumbled in his head as he spoke.

'Yes, Johnnie,' said Maggie gently, 'we'll get you some sky. . . . Don't worry.'

She was very angry. She didn't remember ever being so angry. After she had got Johnnie to hospital, and the three other children had been put into temporary emergency care, and the police and the doctors and the social service officals had all stopped talking, she was still angry.

Big Joe was angry, too. He was to be prosecuted for something he considered to be a basic right. What kind of life was it for a man if he couldn't beat hell out of his wife and kids if he liked? A man had to show them who was boss. Anyway, that cow-eyed idiot son of Julie's deserved all he got. It was very good of him, Big Joe himself, to father him at all, considering. And then there was all the publicity, and his mates all glared at him in the pub and wouldn't speak to him. Unfair, that's what it was. He wasn't supposed to touch the boy again, but by God he'd get back at him somehow.

Julie Cass wept at everyone and protested that she loved her boy, Johnnie, even if he was a bit dim, and she loved her other children, and Big Joe, too . . . and who were they to think they could take the children away from her? The Social Services people sighed some more – they had met her and Big Joe before – and someone asked her quite kindly if she would attend housekeeping and mothering classes before she was permitted to have the children back. She said she would, if Big Joe would let her. But he wouldn't hear of it. No-one was going to interfere with his home and his way of life. So that was that. Until the police indicated to Big Joe that it would be a good idea if he would cooperate – or the sentence might be worse than he thought. So he gave in. A bewildered Julie went to classes. But they did not do her much good.

Meanwhile, Johnnie lay in a white hospital bed while his burnt feet and his cracked ribs healed. Everyone was frighteningly kind to him. He couldn't hear what they told him, but he smiled at them when they did things for him, and obediently ate what he was given and lay still and dreamed. . . . Once he tried to ask about the children, and even attempted to get out of bed to look for them. But they told him several times over that his brothers and his sister were all right, they were being well looked after, and he was to be a good boy and lie still. So he did.

He could still see trees in his head. And he could still hear water falling. . . . It sounded cool . . . cool and clean. . . . He would have liked to draw it. But he hadn't a pencil or any paper, and he didn't think he could get enough words out to ask. . . . His ears were much fuller of bells and whistles than usual, and trying to speak made them worse . . .

He was thinking of trees one drowsy afternoon, when the Welfare Lady came, and with her was The Girl. There was something in the Girl's hand, and she came up to his bed and handed him a big drawing block and a whole case full of pencils and colours.

'Look!' she said. 'The class was sorry, see? We bought them for you! Now you can draw me a real picture.'

His eyes grew huge. He couldn't believe it. His fingers stroked the block of paper in amazement. He opened the case full of pencils and colours and fingered each one in turn.

'For . . . me?' He got out the words, though the echoes hurt his eardrums painfully.

'For you.' She pointed to a corner of the block cover. 'We wrote your name on it.'

He bent his head over it and read the scrawled message. It said: 'For Johnnie. Get well soon. Love from Dessie and IIIb.'

The Girl was smiling. Johnnie smiled back. 'Dessie?'
She nodded. 'That's right! Dessie!'

Johnnie's smile grew even more radiant.

Maggie Fraser, seeing those strange, communicating smiles, blinked and drew back a little to leave them together.

But Dessie seemed to know that Johnnie did not need her any more at the moment. She stooped over the bed and wrote something else on Johnnie's pad. Then she turned quite cheerfully to Maggie and said: 'We can go now. He'll be all right. Can I come and see him tomorrow?'

'Of course,' agreed Maggie. Looking down, she saw that the Girl had written: 'Drawing is better than words . . .' on the top of the block of paper.

Johnnie's blond head was bent over it gravely while he considered the remark. Then he looked up again and nodded at Dessie, without saying anything more.

'Right then,' she said briskly. 'See you tomorrow, Johnnie!' She tossed the wild hair out of her eyes and waved a careless hand.

Johnnie lifted one of his, dreamily, and waved back.

Together, Maggie and Dessie turned and walked out of the ward side by side.

'You know,' said Dessie, 'Johnnie's not dumb. He's just deaf.'

'*Deaf?*'

Suddenly, the whole thing fell into place. Maggie was appalled at her own stupidity. And at the carelessness of the school. How had they missed it? But of course that was it! The boy was deaf. Not stupid, not recalcitrant, not sulky. Just deaf. He couldn't hear them – not even when they were trying to help him. No wonder Dessie had written 'Drawing is better than words' on Johnnie's carefully chosen present. The girl Dessie was far more observant and far kinder than she was.

'How did you find out?'

Dessie looked at her with faint contempt. 'Obvious. . . . He's been knocked about a lot, hasn't he? Even before this happened. I expect Big Joe did it. If you box people's ears enough they're bound to go wrong, aren't they? Big Joe's always hitting Johnnie. Everyone knows that.'

Everyone except me, thought Maggie. She was full of shame at her own blindness. How could she be the Welfare Lady to these kids and not recognise a deafened, battered child when she saw one?

The girl was looking at her with a kind of mocking tolerance. 'It isn't your fault,' she said. 'But . . . you kind of get to recernize it. . . .' There was a world of knowledge in her voice.

Maggie, who really was a very conscientious and concerned young woman – too concerned, some said – felt even more inadequate. 'Are you saying?' She hesitated, and then abruptly asked the forbidden question: 'Who?'

The girl shrugged. 'Oh . . . it's not like Johnnie. . . . Big Joe's too tough to get away from. . . . With me, it was my auntie. But I'm getting too big now.' She sounded very casual about it. But Maggie was not deceived.

'What about your Mum?'

'Oh, she went off. . . . I been in care on and off most of the time since then. But my auntie, she thought it was her duty to bring me up proper. . . . Then she used to overdo it, see?' A grin touched the edges of Dessie's mouth. 'So . . . back I went into care . . .'

'Did you mind that?'

Dessie's grin got wider. 'No. It's usually a rest!' Then she added flippantly: 'Sometimes I think she did it on purpose to get rid of me.'

'Dessie!'

29

'Well – I was a nuisance, see? She was always telling me.' She kicked idly at a Coca-Cola tin in the road as she walked. 'Anyway, they told her – next time it would be for keeps. . . . So now she lets me alone and just . . . doesn't speak.'

'Doesn't speak?' Maggie sounded puzzled.

'S'right. Not for days. . . . Pretends I'm not there. Suits me all right. I can look after meself!' She gave the tin another deft, hard kick.

Maggie was silent for a moment. Then she said slowly: 'How old are you?'

'Twelve . . . nearly thirteen. Johnnie's nearly twelve. He'll be too big to hit soon, too. It gets better when you're older.' She smiled at Maggie's anxious face. 'When I'm older . . .' she repeated softly, and her voice was as full of dreams as Johnnie's head . . .

'Yes? When you're older? What will you do?'

'Leave home. . . . Get a job miles away. . . . I'd like to see the sea . . . and lots of different places. I'll be all right when I can work . . . she won't be able to get at me then. . . .' Her glancing smile flashed out at Maggie again.

Maggie didn't altogether trust that smile. It was somehow perilous. 'Dessie, do you have a case-worker looking after you?'

The girl stared. 'Who?' Then she shrugged. 'Not now . . . I did. . . . But that was a long time ago . . . when things were bad . . .'

'Then,' Maggie took a deep breath, 'if things get bad again – mind you come to me.'

Dessie stopped in the street in mid-stride and turned to look at Maggie in a summing-up kind of way. Then she tossed back her tangled mane of hair and grinned. 'OK, I will.'

*　　　*　　　*

30

But she didn't. For three days she came to see Johnnie in hospital after school. She sat by his bed while he drew pictures, and though neither of them spoke much, the bond of understanding flowed peacefully between them.

Sometimes she decided to chatter away companionably and let Johnnie pick up what bits of it he could, and on those occasions she talked a lot of cheerful nonsense so that it didn't matter whether he listened or not. But on the third day she brought him a present and decided to talk seriously. It was a glass snowstorm with a little silver man inside dressed in a gleaming space-suit. Johnnie was enchanted.

'Armour, Johnnie,' she said. But she was pointing to the glass ball, not the shining silver suit.

Johnnie looked at her enquiringly. She took hold of his hands and curved them round the little glass sphere.

'Armour,' she said again, insistently. 'He's safe in there . . . behind the glass . . .'

Johnnie nodded. He understood that very clearly.

Then she took a pencil and put it into one of his hands and pointed to the drawing block 'Your armour,' she said. 'See?'

He looked at her searchingly for a moment. Then he smiled. He took the pencil and pad and he drew a beautiful glass bubble full of reflections, and inside it, two small figures – a boy and a girl – hand-in-hand. Outside, he drew thunder clouds and lightning, and a drifting haze of faces looking down at the bubble, all of them with open mouths – shouting. But the boy and girl inside the bubble were smiling.

He understood her perfectly.

The next day, she did not come.

Johnnie watched the door, but she was not among the troop of visitors who came in the afternoon, or at night.

Or next day. Visibly, he faded as he watched the door. By the third day, he looked quite pinched and ill again. The nurses began to worry.

Maggie Fraser had not been able to visit Johnnie every day either. Other work was pressing, and now that he was so much better she did not feel justified in neglecting other claims on her time. . . . But she had some good news to tell him, so she came in on the fourth day after Dessie's absence.

'How is he?' she asked the sister at the end of the ward.

'A bit down, I think. . . . His ribs are healing, but his feet are still a bit of a mess . . . and I think he misses his girlfriend.'

'What girlfriend? Dessie, d'you mean?'

'Yes.' The sister was smiling. 'The little dark girl who is so bossy!'

Maggie laughed. 'That's Dessie. Hasn't she been in?'

'Not for three or four days.'

Maggie's heart went cold.

She went back to the school to check. Yes, the girl was away, with no explanation. No, no note or telephone call. . . . Yes, it had happened before . . .

Alarmed, Maggie went round to the house. The aunt let her in. She was a tidy-looking woman, neatly dressed and very polite. No, Dessie wasn't very well. Yes, she'd be back at school soon. No, really, it wasn't necessary to see her.

But it was. Maggie's back was up. She was not within her rights, but she insisted. The woman blustered and refused and finally stood in stony silence while Maggie marched upstairs.

The door was locked – on the outside. She demanded to be let in. When the door was opened, a furious Dessie, frozen, hungry and dishevelled, glared at her from the bed.

'I locked her in,' said the aunt coldly, 'because she kept

32

staying out late . . . going to see some boy.'

'But,' protested Maggie, 'that was Johnnie. . . . A sick boy in hospital . . .'

The woman's lips were one thin straight line. 'That's as maybe. I won't have it! Chasing boys at her age! Just like her mother!'

There seemed to be no point in explanations. 'Where are her clothes?' asked Maggie. For Dessie was wearing nothing but a skimpy vest and pants under the thin sheet . . . and the room was perishingly cold.

'I took them away,' said the aunt.

'Fetch them,' commanded Maggie. 'When did you last eat, Dessie?'

The girl shook her head defiantly. 'Doesn't matter. . . . Not hungry.'

'*When*, Dessie?'

But Dessie only tossed her head, – the mutinous mouth obstinately closed. So Maggie rounded on the aunt. 'When?'

The woman stood there, holding Dessie's neatly folded clothes, and stared back at Maggie. 'Rebellious girls have to be tamed,' she said.

Dessie began to cough. It sounded ominously harsh and bubbly.

Maggie thought, appalled: Oh God, it's five days since she last came to see Johnnie. . . . *Five days?* 'Get dressed!' she said to Dessie. Then, seeing the child fumble with cold and shaking fingers, she went to help her, bundled her into her car and took her straight round to the hospital for a check-up.

There, the doctors pronounced a mild case of bronchitis and a not-so-mild case of malnutrition, and kept her in overnight for observation.

Sick and angry, Maggie went back to her office to invoke the law and all the authorities once again. . . .

But for Dessie the pattern was changed at last. She would stay in care now. They would never let her go back again.

All the same, she tried to be fair to the aunt. But when she went to see her, the cold, ungenerous eyes did not waver, and the mouth that was thin with distaste did not soften.

'She's like Madge,' she said. 'Like her mother. Young and sort of – *ripe*. Bound to lead to trouble.'

Maggie shook her head in disbelief.

The woman went on stonily. 'I'm Joyce, see? Good old Joyce. She'll look after the baby. She hasn't got a man, she doesn't need to go out. While Madge – there was a different man every night – and then off she went and never came back. . . . So when Dessie looks like her – kind of *promising* and knowing . . . I can see how it's going to end!'

'But you can't!' said Maggie. 'Dessie isn't like that. She's loyal and kind – and strong! Not a bit flirtatious.'

The aunt's face was still grim. 'That only makes it worse.'

Maggie sighed. 'Well, you've lost her now. The decision this time is final.'

The woman stared at Maggie, and for a moment something struggled in her face. 'What – will happen to her?'

'She'll stay in care – unless she is fostered – until she is old enough to support herself.' She added in a softened tone: 'I'm sorry.'

The aunt turned away, once more impassive. 'It's probably for the best.'

'Yes,' agreed Maggie firmly. 'It is.'

But even so, she felt somehow that she had failed. She knew what to do for Johnnie and Dessie though. How to give them a little respite.

'Johnnie,' she said, when she visited him in hospital next day, 'you are going to the sea. And Dessie is going with you.'

Johnnie looked up and smiled.

She drew a picture for him and wrote THE SEA under it, – and then as an afterthought put in some clouds and a seagull and wrote SKY.

Johnnie's smile grew positively radiant.

'Sky?' he said, and looked out through the hospital windows. 'Sky?'

So Johnnie and Dessie walked by the sea together and looked at waves and sky. They had neither of them seen the sea before – except on the telly or in a film-show – and they were overcome by its unexpected hugeness and grandeur. A riot of new colours and shapes and scents assailed Johnnie. He was dazzled. . . . He had never imagined such riches . . .

The convalescent home where they were staying was run by a group of friendly nuns and helpers who were used to all kinds of sick, injured and frightened children being sent to them to make well. They did their best to heal their bodies, but their scarred and battered minds took somewhat longer. They could only surround them with kindness and affection, and a sense of security they had never known before – and wait to see them blossom. Often, the time came for them to return to the world long before this could happen, and the blossoming they had waited for never got a chance. . . . It made some of the helpers very frustrated – particularly Sister Ruth, who was a young nun and had not yet learned to obey every order without question. . . . She questioned quite a lot, and nearly always got answers she did not like – and nearly always had to let her children go back home too soon . . .

But Johnnie and Dessie didn't think ahead. They didn't think about going back at all. They walked by the sea and they were happy.

Once, long before his ears got damaged, Johnnie had been able to hear music clearly. He remembered it now, vaguely, as a kind of wonderful ache that made you want to laugh and cry at the same time. The waves seemed to him to be part of the same music . . . they had a rhythm in their strange, wild singing. . . . He watched them drawing back and crashing forward in ceaseless cascades, in heavy chunks of blue and green and silver and gold, in dark valleys of purple and indigo and high crests of curling white. . . . Almost, almost he could hear their music. . . . It seemed to wash into his head and heal the hurts inside with its gentle, endless flow. Even the dazzle of sunlight, breaking the surface into a myriad sparks, seemed to sing its own firefly-dance kind of tune . . .

'Scintillating . . .' he said aloud. He knew what it meant, but he pronounced it 'skintillating . . .' and his voice came out hoarse and rough with excitement.

'Skinty-what?' said Dessie, puzzled.

He translated it into her terms of reference. 'Milk bottle tops!'

'Silver and gold,
Silver and gold,
Never been bought
And never been sold!' she chanted, and did a little pirouette on the sand and skipped round Johnnie, singing it over again.

He turned his head and watched her, delighted. Sometimes, he thought, Dessie behaved as if she was as young as Treesa . . . dancing about the sand and laughing. . . . And sometimes, when she talked to him, she sounded older and wiser than – than Julie, his mother . . . or even Mrs Fraser, the Welfare Lady. . . .

But sometimes Dessie talked to him just for fun – like she did in the hospital – not bothering to make herself understood. She knew now that he liked the companionable feeling of conversation, and he followed most of it one way or another, so she just chattered on, knowing that more than a few words got through. Sometimes, too, Johnnie came out with these strange long words – like skintillating. . . . She supposed this was because he was used to reading lots of books, but he never talked much with ordinary people. So his words were like the books – long and serious.

'You could paint the sea, Johnnie. . . . It'd be hard, though. All those chunks of green glass . . . curling and pouring over . . . and lots of sparkle. . . . How would you paint sparkle? And you'd have to put in the white bits. . . . When the sun dazzles like that on the water it looks like thousands of gold coins, doesn't it? Is that what you meant by skinty-whatever-it-was? Look, Johnnie, there's a seagull on that rock. . . . No, it isn't . . . it's black, with a long neck . . .'

'C-cormorant,' said Johnnie, distinctly.

She stopped and looked at him. 'How did you know that?'

But Johnnie just smiled his seraphic smile and went on gazing at the sea.

When the weather got warmer, Sister Ruth said they could go in the sea and swim, so they were even happier. They were both fitted out with swimming gear, and told by the smiling sister that they could splash in and out as much as they liked, but not to go out of their depth.

Dessie explained 'depth' to Johnnie very seriously, and led him into the water by the hand.

Johnnie stood up to his waist in swirling green and

37

blue water and gazed downwards at the sandy sea-bed. Shadows and sunlight flickered on the watery floor. Even his feet had ripples on them. They looked pale and shimmery and far away . . . pebbles gleamed like jewels in the sand, and feathery fronds of green and ruby-red seaweed floated by. . . . It was a miracle, this new, quiet, slow-moving world beneath the water. . . .

He didn't splash about like the other children all laughing and squealing at the edge of the waves. . . . Instead, he waded further out, and then let himself sink slowly until only his head was above the surface. He was part of this new world now . . . he could feel the movement of the sea all round his body, gentle, caressing, lifting and falling. He wondered what would happen if he went underneath the water altogether. . . . Could he live entirely in that beautiful, enclosed, untroubled world?

He sank under the water and looked down. . . . But then, almost at once, the air bubbled in his lungs and his breathing hurt and there was a piercing agony in his ears. He opened his mouth to breathe deeper, and the sea rushed in and choked him.

'Hey!' said Dessie. 'What the hell are you trying to do? Drown?' And she yanked him up by his hair and held him, spluttering and gasping, till the breath came back into his lungs. 'You can't breathe under water, you know,' she said, smiling. 'You're not a fish!'

But she looked into his face and saw such desolation in it that she stopped scolding him. She fancied that there were even tears in his eyes – and not from the sea-water, either.

'What is it?' she said, her voice all at once quite gentle and adult. 'What's the matter?'

'Pure . . .' said Johnnie, while the tears spilled over and ran down his cheeks. 'Not . . . spoilt . . .'

Dessie understood. She too lived in a world that was mostly ugly and rather squalid. All this unsullied beauty was new to her, too. So she left him in the sea and went back to ask Sister Ruth if she could get a snorkel mask for Johnnie.

'You can hire them from the hut on the beach,' she explained, sounding eager and pleading all at once.

Sister Ruth looked doubtful. 'I don't know if – '

'I can pay,' said Dessie, swiftly. 'The Welfare Lady gave me some pocket money . . .'

'But why for Johnnie particularly?' asked Sister Ruth, 'we can't get one for every child.' She felt curious about this little dark girl's championship of the shy, blond boy . . .

'Johnnie's different,' said Dessie. 'He sees things different. He says it's all pure out there . . . under the sea. . . . Not spoilt . . .'

Something changed in Sister Ruth's placid face. It was almost as if Dessie had hit her. She seemed to wince. 'Very well,' she said. 'But I'll pay for it. . . . Run along and get one right away. But be sure to show him how to use it . . .'

'I will,' said Dessie, running. 'I will!'

Johnnie's watery world flowered then. He was in it. He was part of it. Quietly, he moved among the rocks and floating strands of weed and small, silvery fish that darted away, making shadows on the sand. Before long, he was really swimming . . . But he remembered the sense of choking, and Dessie's words: 'You're not a fish, you know!' and he stayed where he was safe. Even so his ears hurt under water. But he was so used to them hurting that he took no notice. . . . The only trouble was, he didn't want to come up at all . . .

But Dessie wouldn't let him get cold. After a while she hauled him up and towed him back to land.

'It'll be there tomorrow,' she said, and rubbed at him vigorously with a towel. But she was careful not to rub his back. She knew about that . . . hers was still sore, too. . . . Only, the green-and-gold sea made her feel strong and clean again . . .

'Tomorrow?' said Johnnie, getting it out slowly to avoid the bells. His head still felt cool and quiet and full of the gentle swell of the sea. . . . He didn't want to spoil it . . .

'Tomorrow,' said Dessie firmly. 'Lots of to-morrows . . .'

'Pure,' said Johnnie, and sighed.

In the evenings, Johnnie spent a lot of time drawing, while Dessie chattered round him. But if she really wanted to talk to him, she just turned him towards her so that he could watch her mouth and spoke slowly and clearly, watching the understanding grow in his eyes.

'Do you remember your Dad?'

Johnnie nodded.

'What was he like?'

Johnnie considered. 'Brown . . .' he said slowly. 'From the sun . . . tall and brown . . . and he laughed. . . . He was always laughing . . .' His own voice sounded slow and harsh in his own ears. It boomed and rattled, and the noise of it hurt. Words were useless really, to describe how he felt about that far-off figure. He put up both hands to his ears and covered them with his palms, holding his own head steady. It felt as if it was flying off.

Then he remembered something. He fumbled in the pocket of his jeans and brought out a small crumpled photo. It was a coloured snapshot of three men in safety helmets, arms round each other's shoulders, laughing in the sun. The central figure was tall and brown, with wisps of bright gold hair escaping from his helmet, and very bright blue eyes looking straight at the camera. He stood there, laughing, feet wide apart, astride some kind of metal structure attached to a long, snake-like pipe, and the sea was behind him. All of them were wearing thick parkas with furry hoods, and their helmets were red with a white name stencilled on them, but their upflung heads tilted the tin-hats so that Johnnie couldn't read the word. . . . He had often tried. It seemed to end in 'o' – but lots of words ended in 'o'. On the back of the photo was written in a vigorous, sprawling, educated hand: 'Me, with my mates Tom and Nick. All my love, Danny.'

Dessie examined it with attention. 'Is this where he worked?'

Johnnie nodded.

Both of them peered at the metal superstructure. . . . Was it a ship? Or some machinery on a dock? There was a faint name stencilled on one of the thick metal struts, too – but they couldn't decipher it. Was it something like '– isk?'

'What is it? A pylon?'

Johnnie thought hard. 'No,' he said doubtfully. Then he got out his paper and pencil and drew a curious tall structure with wide stilted legs. It looked almost like a fantastic metal man . . .

'Not a pylon . . . or a crane?'

Johnnie shook his head. Then he drew a spout of dark pencilled liquid going up into the air.

'Oil!' said Dessie, excited now. 'An oil-rig. . . . Is that it?'

Johnnie was nodding vigorously, smiling with triumph at being understood.

'Where, Johnnie?'

He looked vague. Then he thought hard again. He remembered the tall brown man coming home and laughing, laughing, and lifting him up on to his shoulders. . . . He had on a waterproof jacket with a furry hood, like the ones in the photo. The fur was spiky and tickled his legs as he rode on his father's shoulders. 'Oh Johnnie boy,' his father sang, laughing, 'your Danny-boy is home again . . .' and his mother, Julie, had laughed too. 'The parka . . .' he muttered. 'Furry, and thick . . .' He pointed to the photograph again, and to the dark sea behind the men. 'Cold?'

'Not Iraq, then,' said Dessie positively. 'North Sea Oil. Obvious.' Laboriously, she drew him a map of England and Scotland, and put a cross by the North Sea. 'Up there . . . that's where he is . . .'

Johnnie smiled at her and drew a little thin man standing in the North Sea. He was wearing a parka with a furry hood.

Neither of them seemed to realise how big the North Sea was, or how wide and far it went.

'When you're older,' said Dessie kindly. 'you can go and find him.'

The trouble was, she was never quite sure what words Johnnie heard or guessed at, and what he missed. Sometimes, she knew, sounds were all blurred and muddled. Sometimes, for no reason, they were crystal clear. . . . Johnnie never knew when it would happen either . . . he couldn't explain it to her. . . . But those last words of Dessie's he heard – quite clearly.

While Maggie was wondering what kind of a battle she was going to have with the Social Services Department about Johnnie's future, she had a visitor.

He came into her office where she was wrestling with

42

other case-work papers, and stood in front of the desk in calm silence, waiting for her to finish.

'Yes?' she said, looking up. 'Can I help you?'

'I don't know,' replied the man. 'Maybe I can help you.'

He was tallish, she saw, with a thick thatch of grey hair, penetrating, deep-set eyes, and a long, mobile, humorous mouth. He was dressed in a brownish elderly pullover and faded jeans, and his hands resting on her desk were brown, too, spatulate and competent.

'Could I ask you – about the Johnnie Cass case?'

She glanced at him sharply. 'What about it? I'm not supposed to discuss cases with strangers.'

He smiled. 'I'm not a stranger . . . at least, not to Johnnie.'

He had her attention wholly now.

'I think I'm right . . .' he said. 'They put his picture in the local paper. . . . And he signed his drawing "Johnnie". . . . Is he very fair, with dark blue eyes and an absolutely ravishing smile?'

'Yes,' said Maggie, smiling herself. 'That's Johnnie.'

'Well,' the man was looking at her in a steady, friendly way that was full of reassurance, 'I don't suppose he spoke of me? I'm the Painting Man.'

She looked doubtful. 'Johnnie never speaks much about anything.'

'Didn't he ever show you his drawings?'

'Yes,' she said slowly. 'Yes, he did.'

'Charcoal ones? Of trees?'

She nodded. 'Yes . . . I wondered where he got the charcoal.'

Patiently, the man related all that he knew of Johnnie. 'I thought there was something wrong . . . but I couldn't put my finger on it. . . . He was so silent . . . and so beautiful,' he added, almost under his breath.

43

'And that . . . haunted smile of his . . .' He paused. 'He used to come every Monday . . . and sometimes other days as well. . . . I suppose I ought to have wondered about school . . . but he was so happy, drawing. . . . It can't have been wrong. . . ?'

'No,' said Maggie. 'Of course not. Probably the only respite he ever had, poor little boy.'

'I don't think you should pity him,' said the man slowly. 'He is too strong for that.'

Maggie looked at him. Yes, she thought. You are right. I don't know why you saw it and I didn't. Johnnie is too strong for pity . . .

'What I came to say is –' he hesitated. 'My name is Hamilton, by the way, Bill Hamilton. . . . I really am an artist by profession . . . I make quite a respectable living, painting trees and things that people want in their living rooms!' He laughed, and then began again. 'Is there anything I can do to help? I've got a bit of money. . . . The boy can really draw, you know . . . he should have proper training . . .'

'Did you realise he was deaf?'

'*Deaf*? Was that it? I knew there was something . . . of course, that explains a lot.' Then he looked puzzled. 'Not from birth, though, surely?'

'Oh no!' She hesitated. 'Since it's all in the press, I suppose I can tell you. It was probably caused by a beating – or several beatings, more likely.'

'Can the doctors do anything?'

'They don't know yet. . . . So far they've been concentrating on getting him well enough to go and convalesce somewhere safe. . . . We only found out about the deafness by accident.'

'By *accident*? You mean – they didn't pick it up in the hospital?'

'No. They treated broken ribs, weals from a leather

44

strap with a metal buckle, burns on the feet and shock. . . . That seemed to them enough . . .'

Bill Hamilton's face was grim. 'But, good God, shouldn't they have looked?'

Maggie shrugged. 'They x-rayed for skull fracture. . . . I suppose it takes a special kind of diagnosis for damaged ear-drums . . . and he was scarcely conscious at first. . . . Anyway, thank God little Dessie told me . . . now they will really look properly and see what can be done.'

'Who is Dessie?'

She told him about Dessie. She could feel him getting as angry as she was.

'Do you have this sort of thing happening all the time?' he asked at last. 'How can you bear it?'

Maggie sighed. 'Not all the time, of course. But quite often. . . . A lot of our cases are quite different problems. But this – you know, I have an awful feeling we don't even touch the tip of the iceberg. We only see the cases that get found out. . . . What about all the other kids in this town? In this country? In the world, come to that. . . . Where do we begin?'

Bill Hamilton, who was a mild man by nature, swore.

'Well,' he said, after looking into Maggie's face rather searchingly, 'we can start right here – with Johnnie. Tell me what I can do?'

Maggie was looking at him, too, trying to assess what kind of an ally he might be. He had a strong face, with a kind of rough, sturdy good sense about it, and the careful long-term patience of the good craftsman. But his eyes were like Johnnie's – visionary and strange and absurdly idealistic. They had not seen the kind of squalid, incurable horrors that she had . . . nor tried to deal with the helpless, incompetent, lazy and slovenly folk she tried to help . . . nor fought the kind of endless

45

battles with unbendable officialdom that she was forced to engage in, time after weary time. . . . All the same, Bill Hamilton looked like a good ally – and she felt herself curiously drawn to this kind, forthright man.

'You could talk to the doctors,' she said. 'They might like a little outside support when the time comes. . . . And you could back me up when the Committee decide to send Johnnie back home.'

'Back home? To Big Joe? They *can't*!'

'They can! They will say the mother has a right to look after her own children. . . . A mother's rights always gets the woollier men councillors! If she applies to get them back, they'll agree.'

'They wouldn't dare!'

'Oh yes, they would! Some elderly, sentimental councillor will start waffling on about maternal love and family ties . . .'

'What utter b-' began Bill, outraged.

Maggie laughed. 'I know. They never learn. It happens time after time. I get kids settled in a happy foster home . . . they begin to relax and even to love someone . . . then back comes mother, demanding their return. . . . Home they go, and three months later there's another beating, worse than the one before – or an even worse tragedy. . . . Then the Committee get all flustered and upset and blame everybody else for being shortsighted and taking the wrong decision. More often than not, I'm the one who gets blamed for not taking more positive action to protect the child . . .'

'That's outrageous!'

'Yes. Except that they may be right. Sometimes it does work to send them home . . . we always have to consider that. Sometimes it is really a once-in-a-lifetime thing and the child will go home to real love and affection. We can't ignore the possibility, can we?

Only, in this case, I know Julie Cass – and I know Big Joe . . .'

'Can't you persuade them?'

Maggie's shrugged. 'My hands are tied. I can do nothing without the Committee's consent. Unless I act as a private individual and blow my whole future career.'

'Would you do that?'

Maggie's mouth went stern. 'Yes,' she said. 'But, remember, I might be wrong!'

'But you'd do it for Johnnie?'

'For any child at risk,' she said. 'If it came to the point – and to hell with committees!'

But, even so, when the Committee discussed the Johnnie Cass case, she found herself powerless to prevent the wrong decision.

'The mother has already asked for them back,' said the plump local councillor. 'We have to respect a mother's rôle in the family.'

'Even if she's totally incompetent?' asked Maggie.

'She has been having some courses in domestic management, I believe.'

'Yes, but will that be enough?' asked Maggie, despairingly. How can you change a helpless, hopeless slut in five easy lessons? 'And apart from coping with the children – can she protect Johnnie from Big Joe?'

'The man's got a suspended sentence. That should deter him from further violence.'

'I doubt it,' Maggie's voice was dry. 'He just loses his temper. He doesn't think about the consequences.'

'I feel sure he will have learnt his lesson,' said the plump councillor blandly. 'We mustn't be too hard on him, must we?'

47

Why not? thought Maggie. Why not be hard on a man who can beat a little boy into almost total deafness? Who can break his ribs and mark him for life with the buckle of a leather strap? Why not? She shivered.

'Can't we recommend that the children stay in care a little longer?' she begged. 'They seem very happy.'

'It's expensive,' said the councillor.

'Fostering would be cheaper,' said another voice.

(And better for them, thought Maggie, longingly. Wouldn't it be lovely if – ?)

'Yes, but that's a more permanent arrangement. The mother has asked for them back . . .'

'Just a bit longer?' pleaded Maggie.

'What about the boy, Johnnie?'

'He could stay on with the nuns at Bournemouth.'

'Not indefinitely. Besides, don't the doctors want to do tests about his ears?'

'Yes,' agreed Maggie, seeing a gleam of hope. 'Could he go back into hospital, then? While they find out what's wrong?'

There was a doubtful silence.

'There's a great shortage of beds . . .' began the councillor.

'No, there isn't!' contradicted a voice from the other side of the table. It was the doctor who had first treated Johnnie when Maggie found him and called for help. He had his own welfare scheme and was often called upon by the Social Services Department, particularly when children were at risk. 'The children's ward isn't full at the moment. He could stay there while the consultants have a look. I'm sure I could fix it.'

'*Fix* it?' said the councillor.

'*Arrange* it,' amended the doctor smoothly, and winked at Maggie.

'That sounds promising,' Maggie sounded relieved.

'Then – we let the other children return to their mother, providing the court agrees. . . . Is that the general opinion?'

'I suppose so,' said Maggie sounding even more doubtful.

'You'd better make frequent visits,' said her ally, the doctor. 'Keep tabs on that woman, Julie. And on Big Joe.'

'I will,' agreed Maggie. 'Don't you worry!'

'That's settled then,' said the Chairman. 'We'll make that recommendation to the court. Shall we move on?'

'What about the Dessie Morgan girl?'

'Yes. That is the next case on the list . . .'

The same blankness of procedure took place. But here there was a difference. The aunt had been cautioned twice, convicted once, and put on probation with a suspended sentence after the last time. . . . This time, it was clear, the girl would not be sent back. She would stay in care.

'How old is she now?'

'Nearly thirteen.'

'That's at least three years till she leaves school. . . . What about fostering?'

'It's usually difficult with a girl as old as that,' said Maggie uneasily. 'But we can try.'

'Who was on her case before?'

'Mrs Fielding. But she left.'

'I see. . . . So no-one has been keeping an eye on things?'

'No,' said Maggie. 'Not till I stepped in . . .'

('Stepped in is right!' muttered the doctor.)

'It was out of order,' said the councillor, severely.

'I know.' Maggie tried to sound humble. 'I'm sorry.'

It seemed to her all wrong that they should even contemplate sending Johnnie back to Big Joe, while cheerfully assigning Dessie to care for the rest of her child-hood days. She supposed it would be out of order to say so.

'The aunt is having psychiatric treatment, I believe?'

'I believe so.'

'The reports were encouraging . . . though of course she can't have the girl back. She may, however, find some other outlet . . .' said the woolly councillor vaguely. 'The doctors say a loving relationship is what she really needs.'

'*Don't we all!*' said Maggie, aloud. They looked at her in surprise.

'Do I take it, Mrs Fraser,' it was the councillor again, 'that you don't *approve* of help to the woman in question?'

'Oh yes, I approve' said Maggie wearily. 'But that doesn't help Dessie, does it? Any more than sending those children and Johnnie Cass back to their mother will help them. It may help the mother – I don't know – but who is more important? The parents or the children?'

'They are both important, Mrs Fraser.'

'Yes,' said Maggie. 'But my job is with the children. Parent are adults – or supposed to be. (Though I doubt whether Julie Cass is one!) They are responsible for their actions and their behaviour. . . . But the children didn't ask to be born . . . they didn't ask to be beaten and bullied. . . . I think they have a right to expect a decent life where they are reasonably safe and well-treated. And, above all, *they* need a loving relation-ship, too!'

She was a little astonished at her own outburst, and so were the other members of the committee, who looked a trifle shaken.

'Bravo!' said the doctor.

'I mean –' persisted Maggie, 'children aren't parcels to be pushed around from place to place according to how we decide. They've got wishes and preferences, too. . . . We fall over backwards trying to help the offending parents. But do we really consider what the children themselves would like?'

'I wonder,' said the councillor suavely, 'if that would be entirely *wise?*' His small red eyes flicked a spark of animosity at Maggie. 'I doubt if a child would really know what it wanted.'

'*It?*' snapped Maggie. 'Have you ever asked him – or her?'

There was what is known as a pregnant pause.

'I can see your point, Mrs Fraser,' said the councillor. 'And I'm sure your championship of the children is very laudable. . . . But child battering is, as we all know, usually a *symptom* of some deeper problem. . . . It is not our place to judge, you know, but to *help*. . . . And as regards the offending parents, we've got to try, haven't we?'

'At the expense of the children?' cried Maggie.

'Oh, we hope not, Mrs Fraser, we hope not. . . . We mustn't admit defeat, must we?'

Mustn't we? thought Maggie, admitting defeat.

So they decided to recommend to keep Dessie in care, but send Johnnie home.

Outside in the street, Maggie rubbed a tired hand over her eyes and admitted to herself that she wanted to hit someone – hard. But a hand came out and took her arm, and a kind, friendly voice said: 'You look whacked! Come on, I'll get you a coffee.'

Maggie looked up into the concerned face of Bill Hamilton and sighed. 'I don't know what you're doing

51

here, but thanks! Yes, I do need a coffee.' She walked along beside him in silence for a while, and then said in a helpless, saddened tone: 'I failed, Bill.'

'Nonsense!' said Bill, sturdily. 'You had a temporary set-back. It takes time to fight bureaucracy!' He steered her into a nearby café and sat her down at a table in the darkest corner he could find. 'Now,' he said, smiling, 'you can cry on my shoulder!'

Maggie smiled. 'Oh Bill! You don't know what you're asking! I might just do that!'

They sat quietly together, not talking much. But presently, Maggie began to feel curiously rested – and her natural optimism began to rise again.

'That's better,' said Bill. 'You look almost hopeful!' He watched the sad curve of Maggie's expressive mouth begin to turn upwards, and added gently: 'You'll win, you know, in the end.'

But Maggie, thinking of Dessie and Johnnie by the sea together, was not so sure.

A couple of days after the meeting, Maggie went down to see them. She brought Johnnie a box of colours and some paint brushes from the Painting Man, and she brought Dessie a bright red dress.

Then she said to Dessie, painfully: 'They're not going to let you go home.'

'Good,' said Dessie.

Maggie looked at her anxiously, hurt by the flippant young voice. 'Will you be all right – in the home?'

'Yes,' said Dessie, and her mouth went straight and stern. 'I'll be all right. I've been growing a shell – like them crabs. . . . I'll be OK' She paused, and looked across at Johnnie, already absorbed in his painting. 'What about him?'

Maggie followed her gaze with something like despair. 'He's going back.'

Dessie looked appalled. 'To Big Joe? They must be crazy.'

Maggie privately agreed. Aloud she said: 'He's been given a suspended sentence – they think that will keep him in order.'

'Why?'

'Because if he does it again, he goes to prison.'

'He'll do it again.' Dessie's voice was flat. 'You know he will.'

Maggie did not answer. What can I do? she thought. I am just a junior case worker. They won't believe me when I say that man is a killer. It's murder to let Johnnie go back . . . but I can't prevent it.

'I've managed to persuade them that Johnnie ought to go back into hospital to have those tests for his ears.'

'That's a good idea.'

'It would be, if Big Joe will let him.'

'Can he stop him?'

'If they want to operate, someone has to sign the paper.'

'What about that Julie woman?'

Maggie sighed. 'His mother . . . yes, I can try her. . . .' Then a glimmer of a smile touched her and she looked sideways at Dessie. 'In any case . . . I know the police sergeant – Sergeant Mackay – he'll kind of *lean* on Big Joe, I think . . .'

'Johnnie'll be all right in hospital. . . . They were good to him in there . . .'

'That's what I thought.'

They smiled at one another, and both looked across at Johnnie, still absorbed and oblivious. They felt companionable and conspiratorial – and about the same age.

'How long have we got?' asked Dessie abruptly.

'Another week.' Maggie looked at her sadly. 'It was all I could manage . . .'

Dessie's brief smile flashed out again. 'Thanks, anyway. We'd better make the most of it, hadn't we?'

Maggie felt herself wanting to weep at the stoicism and resignation in the young voice.

But Dessie ran down to the shore and carefully fetched back a handful of shells and pebbles for Johnnie to paint.

Beyond his first attempt to get out of bed and look for his brothers and sister when he was in the hospital, Johnnie had not asked to see them, or even asked how they were. This slightly puzzled Maggie, until she reflected that he was probably well aware that they were safer and better looked after now, away from their parents, than at any time in their lives. Johnnie trusted her. He therefore assumed that the kids would be all right, since she was in charge. It was a sobering thought.

But when she told him about them going home again, and about his own extra stay in hospital, he flatly refused to go.

Carefully, Maggie tried to explain about his ears and the doctors – about his mother and the course in housekeeping that should make her more efficient – about Big Joe and the threat of the suspended sentence. She did not know how much he took in, but he kept shaking his head violently, looking white and sick and determined. 'No,' he said. 'No! Not on their own . . .'

'Your mother will be there –'

Again the decisively shaken head. 'No!' he repeated. 'No!'

54

Maggie was nonplussed.

At last, in desperation, she called in Dessie to help. But Dessie, to her consternation, sided with Johnnie.

'It wouldn't work, see,' she said. 'Johnnie knows what it'll be like for them. Their ma was never any good. . . . She won't change now.' No more than mine will, or my vindictive aunt, she might have added. It was clear in her sardonic face. But she did not say it.

'Johnnie did a lot for them kids,' she explained. 'Got their tea and such. . . . Did all their washing, too.'

'All of it?' Maggie was astonished.

'His ma never done it. So he did.'

'How d'you know all this?'

Dessie smiled and tossed her wild hair out of her eyes. 'Sometimes even Johnnie talks!' But after a moment, seeing Maggie's anxious face, she said abruptly: 'All right. I'll ask him. But it won't do no good.'

She went away and found Johnnie, and used her customary way of making him listen to her. She took him by the shoulders and turned him to face her.

'Johnnie,' she said. 'This is important. The doctors can make your ears better. So's you can hear properly. Hear everything. Don't you want to?'

He looked at her attentively and then nodded without trying to speak.

'Well then,' said Dessie, 'why not stay in hospital?'

Johnnie's face screwed up with the effort of explanation. Then after a long pause, he said, slowly and clearly: 'Not – all – night.'

'Why not all night?'

Another long pause, and then he said, struggling to get it out: 'Big Joe . . .'

Dessie was the one to nod this time. 'Thought so. You're worried about the kids without you there. That it?'

Johnnie pronounced very carefully and deliberately one of his unexpected long words. 'Vul – vul – ner – able.'

Dessie looked mystified. 'What?'

Obediently, Johnnie repeated it. The word echoed and boomed in his head, and his voice came out harsh and strange. But he knew what it meant. There was a whole picture in his mind of how it would be in that house without him. Kevin and Treesa struggling to get their own tea, the baby crying and no-one to change him . . . the washing not done. . . . Big Joe coming home and shouting . . . his tea being cold, or not ready, and more shouts . . . perhaps worse than shouts. . . . And only little Kevin to stand up to him, because his mother would either go out and leave them all alone, or crouch in the corner, weeping . . .

He remembered how when he was younger, after a beating, he would often wet the bed at night. He would wake, ashamed and frightened, and creep downstairs to wash the sheet. Sometimes he got away with it. But if Big Joe found out, there was another beating. And another wet bed. Kevin was the same. When he heard his father shouting downstairs, the worst always happened. Johnnie washed his sheets, too. And Treesa's. And the baby's. Before long, he had accepted the role of family drudge. The more Big Joe shouted, the worse it got. And then Big Joe would jeer at him. 'You big baby! Just you clean up after yourself, see!' Johnnie had grown out of that humiliation now. He was too big. But he still remembered it. And he still covered up for the kids. . . . How could they possibly cope without him?

'No!' he said to Dessie. 'Not – all – night!'

Dessie saw that he was under stress again ('in a state,' she called it). She leant forward and patted his arm. 'OK, I'll tell them. Not to worry. Let's go out. ... .'

And she took him down to the seashore and raced with him on the sands.

But later, she reported back to Maggie and repeated the strange long word that Johnnie had used.

'Vulnerable? Did he really say that?'

'Yes. Twice. What does it mean?'

Maggie thought: My God! What does it mean? Vulnerable . . . all my children at risk – in care and out of care – Johnnie himself, with his odd, unexpected intelligence and his damaged ears. . . . Vulnerable? How can I answer that?

Aloud, she said: 'It means . . . they can be hurt . . .'

Dessie's answering look was a strange mixture of contempt and compassion.

'We can all be hurt, can't we?' she said.

Sister Ruth decided, shockingly, that she hated her job. She didn't dare tell Sister Augustine, her superior, who was tall, angular and decisive, and who ran the children's Convalescent Home with admirable efficiency. It wasn't that Sister Ruth minded the work, or the children – in fact, rather the reverse. She got too fond of the children. She love seeing them bloom in the calm and cheerful atmosphere of the home – and she hated having to see them go back to all the hazards and problems from which they had just begun to escape . . .

It seemed altogether wrong to her that you should give children hope, and then take it away again. Respite was for adults, who knew what they had to face, and understood what a small time of rest was for. . . . But children, Sister Ruth felt, should not have

57

to learn such philosophy so young. Time after time she watched them relax and soften and suddenly begin to laugh and play without any shadow over them – only to see them grow tense and pale again as the time to go home approached. . . . It ought not to have to happen. But she did not know how to prevent it . . .

Sister Ruth was small and round and smiling – usually. But she wasn't smiling now. She was almost cross. She realised, of course, that one mustn't be cross. In her calling, it was quite wrong. One's own emotions should be kept under firm control – always. But to see those two, Johnnie and Dessie, preparing with black courage to go back home, spending the whole of their last week in a kind of valedictory pilgrimage to all their favourite places, wandering hand-in-hand through the untidy garden, watching the younger children climbing in and out of the tree house, drifting away by themselves to the shore to look at the sea. . . . It was too much. It broke her in two to see such fortitude, such deliberate saving up of quiet peace and strength for a time when they would be needed . . .

Dessie even said to her in her cool, abrupt voice that was far too adult: 'This last week, we're just doing the rounds, see? Gotter remember it all, haven't we?' She gave Johnnie's hand a small, sharp tug and pointed towards the shore: 'Look, Johnnie! All them yachts – lots of little sails, see?'

Johnnie looked after her pointing finger and smiled and nodded. 'Like seagulls' wings,' he said, quite clearly.

Dessie turned her head and added flatly to Sister Ruth: 'See? He doesn't miss a thing! Got artist's eyes, Johnnie has. . . . But it's gotta last a long time, see?'

They went on down to the shore.

Sister Ruth found herself, like Maggie earlier, wanting to hit something – hard.

Bed-time was usually quite soon after supper for the children, but one night Sister Augustine decreed that there should be a party. It was the last evening for several of the children - including Johnnie and Dessie - and the staff wanted to make sure that no-one had time to be sad.

There was a lot of extra food, with crisps and sausage rolls and icecream – everyone's favourite fare. There were balloons and paper hats, and someone produced some packets of sparklers, and the record player was put on extra loud. The children ran about the darkened garden, watching the sparks light up the leaves, and laughing . . . laughing . . .

At last, everyone finally went off to bed, and Sister Ruth stood looking at the debris and felt worse than ever.

'I know exactly how you feel,' said Sister Augustine in a surprisingly gentle voice.

Sister Ruth looked up in astonishment, her round face pink with guilt. 'You – you do?'

'Of course.' Was there a faint fleck of laughter behind that schooled, quiet voice? Or was it sympathy?

Sister Ruth found that she was growing steadily more astounded. 'It's just that – it seems so *awful* . . . sending them back . . .'

'I know.'

'Couldn't we. . . ? Isn't there any way we could . . . prolong things? Or – or at least keep in touch. . . ?'

'With all of them?'

Sister Ruth went even pinker, and began to stammer even more. 'I – I know it's impractical . . . I know we –

we're supposed to be doing them some good down here
– b-but I – ' She clasped her hands together very tightly
and screwed her eyes up too in case the angry tears
should fall out. 'I d-don't think I can bear it!' she whispered. 'There must be s-something else we c-could
do – ?'

Sister Augustine looked at her sternly. 'You could go
out and train to be a social worker. . . . You would find
yourself up against the same problems. That nice young
woman, Maggie Fraser, feels just as inadequate and
useless as you.'

'Does she?'

'She cannot be in each of those children's homes
twenty-four hours of the day. . . . She cannot watch
every move they make . . . notice every absence . . .
recognise every sign of trouble. . . . We each of us can
only do what is within our own capacity, within our
own sphere of activity. . . . Certainly, we do a good job
here. But it is only one way of helping. There are many
others. None of them are perfect . . .'

'But – but it isn't *enough!*' cried Sister Ruth, no
longer even hiding the brightness in her round brown
eyes.

'No,' said Sister Augustine gravely. 'It is never
enough.'

Late that night Dessie woke to find bright moonlight
lying in a strip across her bed. She got up and went over
to the window to look out. Moonlight poured down on
to the sleeping garden, and on to the sea beyond. The
shadows were black and sharp, and the trees seemed
like silvered cardboard cut-outs against the night sky.

Johnnie must see this, she thought. Johnnie will want
to paint this. I've never seen moonlight on the sea

before . . . and nor has he.

Silently, she slid into her jeans and jersey, and went out of the girls' dormitory and down the passage to where the boys were sleeping. Johnnie's bed was near the door, she knew. Sister Ruth wasn't very strict about lights-out, and many evenings Dessie had sat perched on Johnnie's bed chattering to him while he drew pictures for her before settling down for the night. . . . Now, she could tell even before she touched him, that he was awake.

'Come on,' she whispered. 'Something to show you . . .'

Johnnie looked up into her face, glimmering at him in the dark. He seemed quite unsurprised at her arrival. Without any hesitation he got up, also slid into jeans and jersey, and followed her out.

They crept down the stairs and along the hall passage to the front door. But here Dessie realised the big bolts and the old-fashioned heavy key would make far too much noise. So she turned aside to the little boot-room near the conservatory. There was a small garden door here that might not make so much of a grating when it was unlocked . . .

Dessie was a born conspirator. Years of practice in avoiding trouble had made her a skilled and silent escaper. The key turned sweetly under her hand. The little door swung open without a sound . . . and they were out in the moonlit garden.

At first, Johnnie just stood still and stared. He looked at the black shadows on the path, and the clear white moonlight beyond, and the stencilled patterns of moving leaves on the white steps leading down to the sea. He looked up at the sky which was luminous and huge behind that high, sailing moon, and he watched a small, pale cloud scud across, dimming the stars as it went. Then he looked down again, beyond the garden, and saw the moonlight on the sea.

He drew a sharp breath and stood gazing, and gazing. 'Silver . . .' he said, in a voice of dream.

'Come on!' Dessie tugged at his hand, anxious to get him away out of sight of the rows of windows in the sleeping house.

Johnnie seemed to wake from a trance and turned dazzled eyes in her direction.

'It's all right,' said Dessie. 'We're going down there . . . it'll still be there. . . .' Swiftly, she pulled him after her and led him down the steps to the shore.

The sand looked white in the moonlight, and a broad path of silver lay on the sea. . . . When Johnnie stood at the water's edge, he saw that as each wave broke there was a small, brilliant gleam of silver on the ridge of its spreading curve. . . . He stood entranced, watching the line of silver as it came, each time, near to his feet in a sudden arching glint . . .

After a time, he knelt down and reached out his hands as if he wanted to let the lines of silver run through his fingers like strands of silk. But when his hands touched the water, the silver was gone. . . .

'You'll get your clothes wet . . .' said Dessie's practical voice beside him. 'Here . . . take them off. It won't be cold . . .'

Without thought, they flung their clothes on to the sand and went very quietly, hand-in-hand into the moonlit sea . . .

It was like swimming in silver. When they lifted their arms, the drops fell off them in silver sparks. . . . When they moved slowly through the water, the silver wake of the moon went with them. . . . When Johnnie took one hand out and dipped it in again, silver seemed to spread on him like molten metal . . . he could not stop looking at it. . . . Every ripple and eddy seemed to have its own shape and its own pattern, etched with silver against the darkened sea . . .

Silently, he set off to swim away along the path of the moon.

'Hey!' said Dessie. 'Come back! Not out there . . . you'll drown . . .'

Patiently, she hauled him back into his depth, and then left him to idle and dream and watch the silver move as the sea moved around him . . .

Sister Ruth had heard a noise in the house, and being a conscientious worker, even when off duty, had gone down to investigate. She heard the small garden door open and shut again, and followed on silent, slippered feet to see what was going on.

By the time she got into the moonlit garden, Dessie and Johnnie were down on the shore. For a moment she stood blinking in the brilliant light while strange half-forgotten aches and dreams stirred in her at the sight of all this unsullied beauty. Then, sighing, she padded silently across the path and down the white steps to the shore.

But there she stopped, and stood absolutely still in the shadows, her dark habit merging with the black rocks and the last few trees at the edge of the garden wall . . .

Beyond her, in the quiet sea, Dessie and Johnnie swam gently to and fro, awash with silver. They did not speak, or splash about like playful children. . . . They just moved softly through the water while the moonlight poured down on their heads and on the smooth surface of the night-dark ocean . . .

Sister Ruth drew a breath almost as sharp with wonder as Johnnie's. . . . And she did nothing more at all . . .

Presently, Dessie led Johnnie out of the sea and took him by the hand and made him run up and down on the sand to get dry. Then, laughing a little and scolding a little, she made him dress again. He moved like someone dazed and half-asleep – stumbling with enchantment. At last they stood side by side again at the water's edge, and Dessie took Johnnie by the shoulders and turned him round to face her.

'Listen!' she commanded. 'No-one can take it away! Do you hear me? It's yours . . . all this . . . for ever.' She waved a hand at the silver sea, and repeated it softly: 'All yours . . . understand?'

Johnnie looked into her face intently. It was blanched by moonlight and its shape seemed strangely sharp and clear. . . . But it was Dessie's face, and he knew it and trusted it . . .

He smiled, and stooping down, picked up a white pebble and put it into her hand. 'Mine . . .' he said obscurely, 'and . . . yours.'

Sister Ruth was back in the house before them. She glided ahead of them like a dark, silent ghost. She watched them come back up the steps, and waited till they had crossed the garden and slipped through the little door into the house. She stood quite still in the darkness while Dessie relocked the door and led Johnnie back upstairs to sleep . . .

Nothing, she decided, but nothing must interrupt that gentle idyll . . . no-one must dim that radiance. . . . No matter what anybody else might think, she knew it was right . . .

'I won't tell *anyone*,' she thought, screwing her round kind face into a frown of determination. 'Not even Sister Augustine . . . not unless she asks, – and she won't!'

When the house was quiet again, she moved softly through the shadows back to her own small room. But before she slept, she opened the window and looked out.

The moon still shone serenely down on the silver sea . . .

When Johnnie got back to his own house, he found the other children there before him. They looked well fed and well scrubbed, if a little subdued, and they greeted Johnnie cheerfully.

'Hallo,' said Kevin. 'You better?'

Johnnie nodded.

'We had a smashing time,' went on Kevin, not noticing Johnnie wince. 'Treesa's got a dog.'

'Dog?' Johnnie looked round wildly. He had always wanted a dog of his own . . . a real live furry, bouncy animal that would come when he called . . . that he could take for walks in the park . . . that would curl up on his bed at night, and love him without being asked to. . . . It was a long, lonely pipe-dream, for he knew no animal would be safe from Big Joe's rages . . . anymore than he or his Mom or the kids were ever really safe . . .

Now, Treesa proudly held out a bright yellow fluffy toy dog, and waited for Johnnie to admire it. Once again, he pushed back a useless hope, and smiled at his little sister.

'Yellow Dog Dingo,' he said distinctly.

'What?' Kevin looked mystified.

Treesa snatched the stiff little dog back again and ran off, half-expecting it to be taken away from her.

Julie, his mother, came in carrying the baby. She also looked surprisingly well fed and well scrubbed. Her

65

hair was brushed and hung smoothly, and she was wearing a new dress.

'Nice. . .' said Johnnie, and nodded at her with approval. The blue colour suited her, he thought.

She put one arm round his shoulders and hugged him. 'Better then? You look a different boy . . .'

A different boy. Yes, thought Johnnie. Yes, I am. His hearing was much better that day. . . . He did not stop to reflect that after a fortnight of peace and quiet and no emotional stress or sudden onslaughts of Big Joe's shouting, the bells in his head had subsided to a mere occasional buzzing, and the fog between him and other people had thinned to a gentle mist.

But all the same, he knew he was a different boy. Behind his eyes he could still see the moonlight on the sea . . . and Dessie's face turned to him in urgent emphasis as she said: 'No-one can take it away . . . understand?' He sighed. Yes, he understood. But now, here was his mother trying to be nice to him, and the kids doing their best to welcome him home . . .

He took the baby from his mother and settled him in his high chair.

'I got the tea,' his mother was saying brightly. 'Sit down, Johnnie. Baked beans all right?'

For a moment Johnnie shut his eyes. His throat closed tight. How could he tell her that he still saw that scalding saucepan of beans falling out of his hands – still saw the look on Big Joe's face as he came towards him . . .

He sat down, and smiled at his mother. It wasn't her fault, after all.

'Baked beans'll be lovely!' he said.

Big Joe, meanwhile, had an even bigger chip on his shoulder than usual. The Court was nagging him about his fine, which he had to pay off each week. The police sergeant was nagging him about his suspended sentence and not laying another finger on young Johnnie. The Social Services people were nagging him about his wife, and had been teaching her all sorts of things he didn't want her to know . . . he didn't want his house made orderly and neat as a new pin. He didn't want a house-proud nagging wife who told him to wipe his feet. He didn't want things changed at all . . . let alone inter-fered with by those busybody do-gooders from The Welfare. . . . Things were bad enough without them changing everything. . . .

As it was, of course, his young wife Julie was not the smashing good-time girl with blonde curls and a reck-less sense of party-fun that he'd first taken up with. . . . Now she was a whining, terror-stricken woman with lank hair and a look of perpetual fear on her face. He hated that look. It made him want to hit her, or at least shout at her even more than usual. And if he did, the look got worse.

And now they wanted to put Johnnie in hospital every day . . . something about his ears, and goodness knows he was stupid enough already without being deaf as well. . . . It would leave Julie and the kids without anyone to do the work. . . . It wasn't fair . . . and he wasn't going to stand for it.

But, according to the police sergeant, if he didn't stand for it, there would be hell to pay. . . . Privately, Big Joe thought there would be hell to pay anyway – one way or another.

At the hospital next day, all sorts of wonderful things began to happen to Johnnie. They began with a tuning fork which they struck and held to his ears, one by one.

When he smiled and nodded at the strange, vibrating sound, they smiled back and wrote things down on a chart.

They put earphones on his head and played him all kinds of noises – bells and whistles and high bleeps and low bleeps . . . and even voices, high and low. . . . And they watched his face to see his reactions, and noted them all down on the chart. . . . Then they played him some music.

The look on Johnnie's face was so full of incredulity and joy, and his smile got so radiant that the two doctors and their assistants blinked and looked at one another in triumph.

'High frequency,' said one.

'No doubt about him hearing that,' agreed the other.

Johnnie sat still, totally entranced. . . . He had reached a world of marvels and mysteries beyond his experience. He never wanted to come back.

For the first few days they just experimented with Johnnie's ears, finding out what he could hear and what he could not.

Johnnie cooperated, at first in a somewhat bewildered way, but gradually with growing confidence and even eagerness. He could hear things! He could even hear voices quite clearly with some of the electronic equipment he was given. And music . . . he could hear music whenever he asked for it, and that was more marvellous to him than any speaking voice.

The doctors also found out things – some of them deeply disturbing. For instance, on Mondays, Johnnie could never hear anything at first. He appeared to be in a state of shock or total withdrawal. . . . He would put the earphones on obediently . . . but no expression crossed his face, and it took a long time for them to raise even a flicker of awareness. . . . Also, if someone inadvertently raised his voice, or an unexpected person came into the room and shouted across the noise of the machinery to his colleagues, Johnnie froze. His mind ceased to function. His ears seemed totally unresponsive. . . . He appeared to be dull, lifeless and incurable . . .

But by Monday afternoon, things began to improve. . . . And by the end of the week, he was hearing many sounds and joyfully beginning to recognise them. Sometimes he actually laughed out loud.

'So it is partly an emotional block . . .' said one doctor to the other.

'Clearly. And weekend stress at home seems to put him back where he started . . .'

The Painting Man and Maggie were often invited to these initial exploratory sessions, and asked to contribute what they knew. . . . Even Dessie got brought into it, when they wanted Johnnie questioned. Only she seemed to know how to reach him, and how to ask what they wanted without frightening him into retreating blankness again.

'Have you any idea when all this started?' they asked Maggie.

'Not too precisely, I'm afraid. . . .' She pushed the hair out of her eyes and looked down at her notes, frowning a little at their inadequacy. 'Apparently, Julie Cass ran off with Big Joe, taking Johnnie with her, when he was six . . .'

'That means, presumably, that he was talking and hearing perfectly well till then?'

'Yes. That's probably how the school missed it. They do the first deafness screening at six. . . . He was perfectly normal then, and at a different school in a different town . . . and he was reading well. Dessie tells me he went on teaching himself to read from the blackboard lessons which he could see. And now he reads a great deal – often quite advanced books. In fact, anything he can get hold of.'

'So his vocabulary should be high. . . . But his pronunciation might be quite strange . . .'

'Very likely. . . . There must be a lot of words he has never heard spoken by anyone . . . and of course his own family background doesn't help at all. . . .'

'What about his own father? Is anything known about him?' That was Bill Hamilton, seeing another side to the story.

'Only that he was away a lot, and the girl got bored and lonely. . . . She won't talk about him much. I think she is genuinely fond of Johnnie, in her own way, and she's afraid the father might take him away . . .'

'Good thing if he did!' growled Bill.

'But would he?' the doctor asked.

Maggie shrugged helplessly. 'How should I know?'

'Most men want to watch their own sons grow up,' said Bill, staring at Johnnie's beautiful blond head.

Maggie nodded. 'Apparently, Julie met Big Joe in a café where she was working as a waitress. . . . I suspect he had a certain swaggering, butch sort of charm then . . . before the drink set in. . . . When he asked her, she just ran off with him. I suppose Johnnie's father came back on leave and found her gone – with no forwarding address . . . it must have been a shock.'

'Which of them is she married to?'

Maggie looked perplexed. 'I don't know for certain. . . . She draws the children's allowances under Joe Harman's name . . .'

'What about Johnnie?'

Maggie sighed. 'Cass . . . her maiden name . . . that's on his birth certificate. I checked.'

The doctor smiled at Maggie's anxious expression. 'You've certainly done your homework.'

70

She shook her head. 'Not enough,' she said. 'But I've tried . . .'

'Can't we trace the father?' It was Bill again, persisting.

'How? She won't tell us his surname . . . I don't know where to start looking.'

Dessie, who was sitting in the corner helping Johnnie to play 'bleep' games with a computer board and coloured lights for each different sound, looked up.

'He works on an oil rig. His name is Danny. Johnnie showed me his picture once. . . . And he drew a thing like an oil rig when I asked him what his father did.'

The doctor looked interested. 'An *oil-rig*? An engineer or something? That would account for the high intelligence . . .'

Maggie burst out in despair: 'But what can I do? I can't circulate every oil-rig with a questionnaire: Did any of your workers called Danny know a girl called Julie Cass?'

'It might be worth a try,' said Bill.

'But what good would it do? He'd have no legal claim over Johnnie. . . . Big Joe as his stepfather would have more rights. And in any case, I don't know whether someone away on an oil-rig would be any better at providing him with a good home?'

'*Anything* would be better,' said Dessie flatly.

All the adults turned and looked at her. Something in the rough anger of her voice touched a chord within them. They were all angry about Johnnie. All of them.

'Well,' said the doctor, 'something will have to be done soon. We've done nearly all the tests now. . . . Decisions will have to be taken . . .'

'What exactly is wrong with his ears?' asked Maggie, hoping she would understand the specialists' jargon.

But her doctor from the Social Services Committee

was there, and he smiled at her and said: 'Shall I try to explain?'

'Make it simple!' growled Bill, and everyone laughed.

'Well,' began the doctor, with a small wink at Bill, 'in the ear, bone acts as a conductor of sound. . . . So, on the conductive side, he has obviously had a good many cuffs on the ear, which have caused rupture of the tympanic membrane – that's the ear-drum. Also, from the x-rays we can see that he has suffered more than one minor fracture of the bones at the base of the skull. . . . These small fractures can lead to all sorts of trouble.' He turned to look at Maggie. 'You know what a lesion is?'

Maggie nodded.

'Well, he has what we call "traumatic lesions" in some of the small bones in the middle ear . . .'

'Can all this be put right?' asked Maggie anxiously.

The doctor smiled at her reassuringly. 'If not put right, at least made a lot better. . . . I'll come to that in a moment. You see, that's only one side of things. There's another kind of deafness called sensorineural – in the nerves – also often brought on by blows or ear infections caused by blows. And this type of deafness includes acute bell-ringing and noises in the head. And any extra or sudden loud noise or heavy vibration from an engine and so on can cause the boy acute suffering . . .'

Maggie sighed. 'Can you – ?'

This time, the doctor shook his head. 'We cannot cure it, no. But we can help it. I'll go into that in a minute . . .'

'Don't tell me there's even more?' said Bill, feeling somehow angry and outraged on Johnnie's behalf.

'I'm afraid so, yes. On top of all this, there is the

psychological side. Johnnie is obviously more deaf and unresponsive after a weekend at home. This suggests two things. Children often put up a wall against battering and scolding and *refuse* to hear, behaving like an autistic child.' He turned again to Maggie. 'You must know all about those kind of problems!'

Again, Maggie nodded.

'But it might not be *refusal*. Children may also *fail* to hear out of sheer fright or stress. I think this is clearly part of Johnnie's trouble. He can obviously hear better when his circumstances are calm and safe.' He glanced at Bill. 'Didn't you tell me he seemed to hear better in the Park when he was drawing with you?'

'Yes,' said Bill, swallowing a lump in his throat. 'He did.'

'Exactly. Loud noises and particularly shouting voices confuse him and cause him to retreat inside himself. I've seen it happen even here when someone comes into the room too suddenly. . . . But it is also clear that the boy has taught himself to lip-read quite well, and is very bright at catching on *when he wants to*. He can follow quite complicated conversations, and even join in if he tries. . . . On the other hand, he does not seem to have been taught any of the deaf-and-dumb sign language. Probably because he *can* speak when he puts his mind to it, most people never realised he was deaf or needed any help.'

Bill made an explosive kind of snort.

The doctor grinned at him. 'I agree. We've all been singularly stupid about the boy. There's one thing, though. . . . Thank God he *could* talk before all this happened to him. . . . It makes his recovery towards normal communication much easier.'

'Does it?' said Bill. 'Well, tell us what *can* be done.'

Bill is always the practical one, thought Maggie.

73

What a tower of strength he is. She turned to him with a sudden radiance in her smile. Bill blinked.

'In practical terms,' said the doctor, also blinking a little at Maggie's smile, 'we can operate to repair some of the damage on the conductive side. . . . And we can clear the Eustachian tubes if mucus has formed in them, and this will help to make his hearing a lot clearer. We can't cure the sensorineural side, but we can fit specially sensitive hearing aids nowadays. They are highly sophisticated devices, like miniature audio machines, and each one is built individually to suit each patient's special needs. . . . This might make an enormous difference to Johnnie's final adult life out in the world. Of course, he ought to go to a special school for the deaf for a while to learn how to use his new hearing aid, and various communication techniques and ways to learning. But he is obviously a clever boy, and thank God he has taught himself to read. . . . Education will not be a real problem for him.'

Once again he paused and looked from Maggie to Bill, and then to the other doctors who were listening to his careful explanation. 'But, above all,' he said, sighing, 'he needs a calm and restful environment, with no stresses and strains. . . . If he had this, it is very likely much of his nervous deafness would diminish of its own accord.'

It seemed that everyone echoed his sigh, and one of the other doctors added, in a crisp, angry voice: 'And if he has this kind of operation, he simply cannot go back to a home where he is knocked about. . . . It would probably kill him.'

They all stared at one another.

Finally, Maggie said in a heavy, tired voice: 'I'll see if I can get the mother's consent for the operation. That's enough for you, isn't it? Maybe he could go on a very long convalescence afterwards . . . while we think what to do.'

'And find his father,' added Bill.

Maggie looked at him affectionately. She had grown very fond of this square, quiet man with the eyes of a visionary and the hands of a master craftsman.

'I believe you'd like to adopt Johnnie for your own son,' she said, smiling.

'I would,' agreed Bill promptly. 'Tomorrow. If they'd let me . . .'

He was looki at her oddly, and Maggie saw something in his eyes that disturbed her. She looked away in confusion. 'I only wish you could,' she said.

When Johnnie got home from the hospital that evening, his mother was cooking tea, and the kids were squabbling happily on the rug by a real coal fire. The room looked tidier than usual, and quite welcoming. There was a clean cloth on the table, and four new blue mugs set one at each of the children's places.

'Sausages! said Kevin. 'Look, Johnnie! Bangers! Mom's cooking them now. The Welfare Lady give her a bag of stuff . . . and all them new mugs!'

Johnnie smiled.

His mother turned round from the stove and looked at him anxiously. 'You all right, then? What they do to you up there? Can you hear any better?'

Johnnie understood what she was asking. He knew she had a pathetic belief that the doctors could work miracles overnight. He did not know how to explain to her, though, the long process of experiments and tests that had to come first. . . . He knew why – but it was too hard to explain.

'Not yet,' he said, and sat down at the table.

When tea was over, he got up to put the younger ones to bed, but his mother stopped him, saying: 'No, you set there a bit. You must be tired after all them tests. . . . I'll see to the kids . . .'

She started up the stairs with the baby in her arms, and Treesa clinging to her skirts. Kevin lagged behind, looking longingly over his shoulder at Johnnie and the bright fire in the grate. . . . He didn't want to go to bed yet . . . he was seven . . . old enough to stay up late and watch telly . . .

But Johnnie wasn't watching telly. He was staring into the fire, watching the red-gold patterns in the glowing coals . . .

At that moment, Big Joe came in. He kicked the outer door shut with his foot, and stood swaying in the doorway. Johnnie could see at a glance that he was very drunk, and very dangerous. He had an open whisky bottle in his hand.

'Get upstairs, Kev,' said Johnnie, speaking quite distinctly, but trying to keep his voice quiet.

Kevin, after one scared glance, ran up the stairs and joined his mother. Julie was standing frozen at the top of the stairs, still holding the baby in her arms. Treesa had already hidden behind her skirts.

'All very cosy,' said Big Joe. 'Quite the ideal home. And who paid for the coal?'

'The Welfare, Joe,' Julie's voice was beginning to rise in terror.

'Welfare!' shouted Joe. 'I thought I told you not to let 'er in any more! I don't want her charity! I'll give you welfare!'

He started towards the stairs.

Johnnie felt a strange wave of black courage come over him. Julie was his Mom. The kids were his kids. His brothers and his sister. He was responsible for them. Big Joe was not going to bully them any longer.

'You're tea's in the oven,' he said, trying to speak

76

clearly. 'Bangers and mash . . . you like that. . . . Shall I get it for you?' He didn't know he could say so many words at once. But he could.

'Oh, so you can talk now, can you?' Big Joe sounded even more sarcastic. 'What've those doctors been doing to you, then? Pity they can't make you a bit brighter while they're about it . . . I don't need talk around here, see?' And a heavy hand came out and cuffed Johnnie on his ear.

'Joe!' said Julie, suddenly also finding courage. 'Stop it! Leave Johnnie alone!'

'Leave him alone, is it?' shouted Joe, now thoroughly roused. 'Defying me now, are you? Who's boss around here?'

He started up the stairs, waving the bottle. The children backed away. Julie, for some reason even she could not understand, stood her ground.

Big Joe advanced. 'All these fancy ideas!' he roared. 'I'll teach you!'

Johnnie saw his arm raised with the bottle in it, poised to smash down on his mother's face. He could not bear it.

Like lightning, he dashed up the stairs, dodged round Big Joe, and got between him and his mother. 'Don't!' he said. His voice boomed and rattled in his head. 'Don't!' And he put out his hands to push Joe away. The bottle came down on his own head. But it was a glancing blow that hit him sideways on and caught the point of his shoulder as it descended. Johnnie blinked and shook a sudden trickle of something warm and sticky out of his eyes . . .

He did not notice that Big Joe was already staggering, with one hand to his head, and a strange twisted expression on his suffused face. And he did not hear the even stranger gurgling noises that were coming

77

from his throat. . . . He simply put out one hand again, almost pleadingly – he couldn't lift his other arm for the moment – and tried to stop Big Joe from hitting his mother with the bottle.

But Big Joe spun round, off balance, took a wild step backwards, lurched into the banisters with a crash of broken timbers, and toppled headfirst through the rails to fall in a sprawling heap on the living-room floor . . . . The whisky bottle, which he was still clutching, shattered in his hands, and he fell forward on to its sharp, jagged edges . . .

Then he lay still.

Julie and the children stood absolutely motionless staring and staring. Johnnie stared too. . . . Then he turned and ran down the stairs, out of the house, and away down the dark streets, with the sound of splintering wood and glass echoing in his aching, damaged ears . . .

Once away from the house and his own blind panic, reason took over for a moment. They will need help, he thought. I must get help.

He saw a phone box on the street corner and ran up to it, panting. But it had been smashed, and the phone hung uselessly down on a tangle of broken wires. . . . No good, he thought. No good. What shall I do?

There was another phone box further on. He remembered it from his paper round. Near the paper shop. At the end of the next street. He ran on, breathless and frightened. He had never been able to use the phone. He could not hear what was happening at the other end. . . . But it must be like the headphones in the hospital. He could use those. . . . He must try.

999. That was what you dialled. He knew that. He would have to use both hands. One to dial, and one to hold the phone. . . . Experimentally, he tried to lift his

bruised arm. It hurt sharply where the bottle had hit the shoulder bone – but he could use it. He tried. 999. A voice said something into his ear.

'Help!' he said. 'Help!'

The voice gabbled again. 'Address,' it said. '*Address!*'

He heard that. 'Fourteen Boyne Road,' he said. 'Help! Ambulance!' And then his voice croaking with terror: 'Police!'

He couldn't do any more. He was shaking too much. He couldn't go back either. Not to that sprawling, awful figure – and the slowly darkening stain on the floor. He left the phone box and ran on through the dark. The Park, he thought. It will be quiet there. . . . I can hide in the Park.

Hide? He did not stop to think about that word. Or what it implied. Not yet. . . . He must get away, get away somewhere quiet, where he could think. . . . He ran on through the little dark streets of the town until he came to the Park. It would be shut, of course, after dark . . . but he knew a way to get in. . . . Round the end by the lake there was a twisted railing and a gap just big enough for a boy to get through. . . . He found the gap and wriggled past the rusty bent railing and slid down into the wet grass inside the Park.

He hadn't noticed it was raining. But his jersey was soaked already, and the cut on his head had matted his hair so that a mixture of rain and something stickier was running into his eyes. . . . Shelter, he thought, Where? I know, the bandstand . . . nobody uses it now . . . it will be dry under the bandstand roof . . . I can hide there.

Hide. There it was again. That word. It terrified him. He ran on across the grass until the tall dark shape of the bandstand loomed ahead of him.

Swiftly, without pausing to think, he climbed up the ornate ironwork, clambered over the side and dropped down on to the rotting wooden floor. There was an old tarpaulin lying in one corner, and the cover off an ancient bass drum. . . . He crawled underneath and pulled the tarpaulin over him. The drumhead cover he used as a pillow, folded under his head. Then he lay still, gasping, trying to get back his breath. His lungs hurt with running, and there was a piercing pain in his ears. The noises in them seemed worse than ever, booming and pounding . . . bells and whistles screamed in his head, and fireworks seemed to be exploding all round him . . .

'I must think,' he said, 'I must think!'

He held his head in his hands and rocked it to and fro to ease the pain. One hand got all sticky, and he explored the place where it hurt, feeling curious. A flap of skin seemed to be loose somewhere. . . . But it didn't hurt a lot. Only his head ached and ached, and his ears were on fire with inner sirens and clanging bells. . . . Think, he said. Think!

It was my fault. I must have pushed Big Joe. If he's dead, I must have killed him. . . . The police will come . . . they won't hurt the kids, though, or Mom . . . she didn't do anything. It's only me. . . . So I'd better keep on running . . . then they'll know it was me. . . . They won't bother Mom if I keep on running. . . . What would they do if I went back, though? Would they shut me up in prison, like they said they'd do to Big Joe? Probably they would . . . I couldn't live in a prison . . . no sky . . . no Park to run to . . . I couldn't. . . . What about Mom and the kids, though? They'll be all right, won't they? They'd be better off without me, anyway. Big Joe often used to say so . . . he shuddered even at thinking Big Joe's name. . . . Without Big Joe to bother them, they'll be all right . . . they won't miss me . . . the Welfare Lady will see that they're all right, won't she? Won't she?

He pondered anxiously.

I could write her a letter, he thought. I can write letters. I could tell her to look after them . . . but I can't go back . . . I can't. . . . No sky . . . I couldn't bear it . . .

He curled tighter into an aching ball of misery. His clothes were wet and cold. His head was beginning to throb fiercely now, and his ears, where Big Joe had hit them, were one long jangling agony . . . and his shoulder hurt whenever he moved it. . . . He was tired, and frightened, and alone . . .

But I can't go back, he said to himself. I can't.

Late in the night, something warm and damp appeared out of nowhere and curled up beside him. A wet tongue licked his nose.

'Go away!' growled Johnnie. 'Get-Lost! Go away!'

But the little dog wouldn't go away. It only curled up tighter and seemed to shiver at the ragged sound of Johnnie's voice.

'Oh Get-Lost,' said Johnnie, and suddenly put his arms round the little wet dog and hugged him close. 'I'm in bad trouble . . . real bad trouble. . . . And you're no help at all!'

But the little dog was some help. And all at once Johnnie found he was weeping. Uncontrollable tremors shook him all over, and he wept for his mother Julie and the kids, and even for Big Joe whom he never meant to hurt, and for himself because he didn't know where to go or what to do. . . . And the little dog whimpered in sympathy and tried to lick his tears away. In the end, worn out, he slept curled up with the dog in his arms . . .

In the morning, Johnnie remembered the paper shop. It owed him a week's wages, and it opened very early. Sometimes he did an early morning round, too, when they were short of boys. He couldn't do one now, though. People would be looking for him soon. He had to get away. If he could collect his money, at least he would be able to take a bus somewhere . . . or a train? He didn't know how much train fares were . . . probably a lot. . . . Maybe he could thumb a lift, then . . . all the older kids at school did . . . they used to boast about how far they'd got at the weekend . . .

Would anyone stop for him, though? People might be on the lookout . . . or they might ask where he was going.

Where was he going? He didn't know . . . then he remembered the conversation he had had with Dessie about his Dad. . . . He could hear her voice in his mind . . . he could always hear Dessie's voice in his mind when he wanted to. . . . 'When you're older, you can go and find him . . .'

He would look for his Dad. He could say: 'I'm going to see my Dad. . . .' It would be true, after all . . . they would believe that. . . . Up north, Dessie had said. North Sea Oil. . . . He still had her map with Scotland on it, and the North Sea, and the little man with a furry parka which he had drawn in the sea. . . . He would go North.

Cautiously, he crept out of the bandstand and stood looking around him. Get-Lost followed him, equally cautious and equally silent. The Park was very still in the early morning. Rain lay in sodden puddles on the path and hung in silver drops along the railings . . . the grass was silver with rain. There was no-one about. The gates were still shut.

For a moment he stood looking at it lovingly, as if

82

nothing bad had happened. It all looked so clean and fresh in the early morning. Untouched by anyone. The colours were brighter somehow – especially the trees all wet with rain. He loved things that grew . . . they seemed to him friendlier than people . . . they went on growing, quietly and steadily, drinking the rain. . . . They didn't bother you . . . but they were always there, and they seemed to welcome you when you came. . . . He put his arms round the trunk of a tall beech tree and hugged it for comfort. 'You are strong,' he thought. 'Stronger than me . . . you don't run away . . .'

I wish I could see Dessie, he thought. She would know what to do. . . . Or the Painting Man . . . he would know, too. . . . But Dessie would be best. Only I can't. I can't tell anyone. They would be in trouble too if I did. But I would like to see Dessie just once . . .

He squeezed through the railings again, and Get-Lost squeezed through, too. 'Goodbye, Park,' thought Johnnie sadly. He had loved the Park. He hated leaving it. Then he looked down at the dog. 'Go away, Get-Lost!' he said again. 'You can't come with me. I'm going away.'

The little dog gave him a questioning look and did not budge.

'Oh – go on! Go away!' said Johnnie again, and made a half-hearted swipe at the dog. It backed away and looked at him reproachfully out of large, soulful eyes. But Johnnie turned his back on it and set off for the paper shop. He couldn't, he simply couldn't stop to deal with stray dogs now.

He did not know what the time was, but by the look of the light it must be near opening hours for the paper shop. He arrived just as Mr Patel was putting up the papers ready for the round boys when they came. He had not opened the shop yet, but he saw Johnnie through the glass and came to unlock the door.

Johnnie did not know how he looked with his blond head dark with rain, and a thick even darker stain on one side. There were smudges of weariness under his eyes, and streaks of rain and tears on his face. His clothes were a sodden ruin, and he looked so white and lost that Mr Patel was appalled. He knew about Big Joe and the earlier court case. Everyone in the district knew. After all, it was Amrik Singh Patel, General Stores, whose papers they all bought, with the local news splashed across the front page. Johnnie was a good boy, and he never made mistakes on the paper round. Amrik had never had any complaints. Now, it seemed to him, the boy had obviously had another dose of Big Joe's heavy hand. He'd better see if he could help at all.

'Well, Johnnie. . . . Be coming inside . . . you are looking wet through . . .'

'Please,' said Johnnie, afraid to waste any time, 'Mr Patel – my money?'

Amrik Patel nodded and smiled. 'Yes, I am knowing. One week. I am just being opening the till this minute.'

His English was still a bit strange at times, though he had been running his little neighbourhood shop for several years.

'Would you be liking some breakfast, Johnnie? I am eating.'

Johnnie shook his head. He was hungry, but he knew he must not stay. . . . The town was waking up . . . they would start looking for him soon. He had to get away . . . now, at once. But when he shook his head his ears screamed and the wound in his scalp hurt sharply. . . . The room spun, and Mr Patel's concerned brown face seemed to dissolve in mist. . . .

He came round sitting in Mr Patel's chair in the back room. Amrik's sloe-eyed wife, Marjula, was leaning over him, bathing the cut on his head with warm water and a soft sponge.

'Be keeping still,' commanded Amrik. 'She will be finishing before you can say Robinson . . .'

'Jack Robinson,' said Johnnie distinctly.

Amrik Patel beamed at him. 'That's right. Jack Robinson. You will be being better all at once. . . . Now I am making some tea . . . and this sandwich you will be eating, isn't it?' He handed Johnnie a thick wedge of bread spread with peanut butter and a slice of cheese. 'Nothing is all so bad when you are eating, I am thinking . . .'

He looked doubtfully at Johnnie's white face and then his eyes fell on the sodden, rain-soaked jersey. 'My goodness gracious me, we must be having that off, yes, at once . . . sooner than Jack Robinson. . . . I will be lending you my spare one. . . .' He went nimbly across to the door and took his own dark brown jersey off the hook. 'Maybe it will be a little big,' he said, smiling, 'but it is being dry, you see . . .'

Johnnie submitted helplessly while the old wet jersey was stripped off and the new one pulled over his head. Marjula had deft, gentle fingers, but even so the roll-neck of the sweater hurt his injured scalp. When it was on, Amrik Patel surveyed him carefully. The shop-keeper was a small, dark man with very bright brown eyes and a quick, friendly smile. But when he was not smiling, his expression was watchful and sensitive, and he had a high, intellectual-looking forehead. He often told his friends he was a Thinking Man. And he was.

Looking up at him in a haze of weariness from the warm folds of the brown jersey that was not much too

85

large, Johnnie saw that he could trust him. At least, as far as he could trust anyone now. He began to search in his pockets for a scrap of paper . . . . But his jeans were soaked with rain, too, and the spare drawing paper folded up inside his back pocket was a sodden mess.

Marjula suddenly spoke urgently to Amrik, and went out of the room.

'She is saying those jeans will not do,' explained Amrik. 'She is fetching some spare ones. . . .' He looked at Johnnie's hands twisting the soggy piece of paper, and made an inspired guess. 'You are wanting to draw something?' (He knew about the Painting Man in the Park, and Johnnie's surprising gift for drawing. . . . After all, Bill Hamilton, the Painting Man, often came into his shop . . .)

Johnnie shook his head. 'Write . . .' he said. 'A letter . . .'

Amrik Patel nodded with instant understanding. 'OK. I am fetching you an envelope and a piece of paper. . . . Do you want a pen?'

Johnnie held up the stub of pencil he always kept at the bottom of his pocket.

Mr Patel clucked like a hen. 'No. no. Smudgy that will be. A pen is better. Be eating while I am getting.' His movements were all quick and light, too, like a small brown bird's, thought Johnnie. He disappeared into the shop and returned in a few moments with a pair of neatly ironed brown trousers, rather looser than Johnnie's own jeans, but not too baggy. Johnnie was quite big for his age and did not seem all that much smaller than the wiry little Indian . . .

'Be putting them on. Here is being a writing pad and a pen, and an envelope. . . . You can be keeping the rest of the pad to be drawing on. I will be in the shop.'

Johnnie was suddenly terrified. He got to his feet unsteadily. 'You won't . . . you won't. . . ?'

Amrik smiled. 'Be resting, Johnnie. No-one is coming. . . .' He thought Johnnie was probably only keeping out of Big Joe's way after another beating. If that was so, he would do everything he could to give the boy a bit of respite. It was all wrong to treat a good boy like Johnnie so badly . . . all he needed was a bit of ordinary human kindness. . . . It never occurred to Patel that Johnnie might be in really bad trouble. But if it had, he would still have tried to help.

Johnnie struggled into the clean, dry brown trousers. They hung a bit on his narrow hips, but the thoughtful Marjula had supplied an elastic belt. When he had pulled it tight, he felt better. Even so, he was still haunted by a dreadful sense of haste. He was staying too long . . . he was giving in to Mr Patel's kindness and his friendly smile. . . . He ought to get away . . . now. At once.

He took Mr Patel's pad in his hand and wrote on it in his careful, copperplate writing: 'Please look after Mom and the kids.' Then he drew a set of headphones, like the ones he had been using in hospital, and underneath he wrote: 'Thank you.' He hoped the Welfare Lady would understand. He picked up the envelope and began to address it. Mrs Maggie Fraser, the Welfare Lady. . . . Then he thought hard. He knew her name all right, and he knew where the Welfare Office was . . . he'd been there often. . . . But he didn't know it's proper address. And he hadn't got a stamp . . .

Amrik Patel came back and saw Johnnie holding the envelope in despondent fingers. Something about the boy's desperate sadness and indecision troubled him. 'Can I be helping?' he asked.

Johnnie was ashamed of being so muddled. He had

meant to be so quick and decisive. He should be away by now. Not sitting by Mr Patel's warm fire, eating peanut-butter sandwiches. 'The Welfare Lady . . .' he said slowly.

'Oh yes, Mrs Fraser. . . . Of course. She is wanting you to be writing to her when there is being trouble at home? Shall I be giving it to her?'

Johnnie stared at him. 'Give – ?'

'She is coming in every day for her paper. . . . I will be seeing she is getting your letter, Johnnie . . . do not fear . . .'

Johnnie was still staring at him. At last, he stuck down the flap of the envelope very firmly, and put it into Amrik Patel's slim brown hand. He did not say any more. He got up and went out into the shop. Amrik Patel followed him.

'Here,' said Patel. 'Be wearing my baseball cap . . . from America. . . . It will be keeping Marjula's plaster dry. . . .' Carefully, so as not to hurt his injured scalp, he placed the red and white cap on Johnnie's blond head. Johnnie accepted gravely.

'Thank you,' he said. He meant to say thank you for the clothes, for the sandwich and the warm fire, and for the strange feeling of trust that Mr Patel's clever brown eyes seemed to give him. But all he could manage was 'Thank you. . . .' His astonishing smile flashed out for a moment and he added softly: 'Goodbye.'

Maybe Amrik Patel understood. He watched the boy as he left the shop in his borrowed clothes. He saw him stop and look round anxiously, as if afraid of the outside world. . . . Patel was not surprised.

But suddenly he remembered something, and ran out of the shop after him.

'Johnnie! Wait!'

He saw the boy start violently, and look as if he

would run away. 'Your money!' he called. 'I am forgetting your money!'

Visibly, Johnnie relaxed. His tense shoulders sagged a little. He turned back, and once more the vivid, sorrowful smile flashed out.

'Here,' said Amrik, holding out two pound notes. 'Be having a little extra this time. . . . I am thinking you are a good boy . . .'

Johnnie took the money.

A good boy? he thought. And shuddered. Behind his eyes he could still see that sprawling figure on the floor.

'Thank you,' he said again, and turned away and walked very quietly and carefully down the street.

I must not run, he thought. People look at boys who run. I must walk. Until I get out of the town . . .

Amrik Patel looked after him and sighed. It was all wrong. All wrong. A good, steady boy like that. . . . Life was most unfair. . . .

Along the empty early morning streets, Johnnie still walked on. . . . Behind him, a small, wet mongrel dog padded along, keeping to the shadows . . .

On the outskirts of the town, he stopped to think. There was a big main road about a mile or so further on, he knew. But which way led to the North? It was still raining hard, or the sun might have told him. He was usually good at guessing time and direction from the sun. But there were only grey, heavily massing rainclouds to look at. And a big sign with a loop and a roundabout on it saying: Bedford M1. Northampton M1. Coventry M1. Luton M1. . . . It was very confusing . . . which was North? Northampton sounded right . . . but he didn't recognise the names of all the towns. . . . If only one had said Scotland . . . or even London. . . . He knew London was South . . . which way should he go?

There was a garage by the roadside. He decided to go in to the forecourt, and ask the way. As he turned, he caught sight of Get-Lost again and stopped to scold the dog and shoo it away. 'Go on home! Haven't you got a home? You can't come, you know . . . I'm going away . . . I told you! Go on. Go!' The dog cringed away and slunk off into the shadows. Satisfied, Johnnie went over to the garage and stood by the petrol pumps. Which way is north? He practised it in his mind. Presently, in his queer, growly voice, he said it aloud – not to anyone in particular, but to see how it sounded.

'Which way is north?'

'That way, son,' said a voice behind him. 'All the way to John o' Groats!'

Johnnie heard the voice, but not the words. He turned and saw a big, burly man in overalls pointing ahead with one powerful hand.

'That way?'

The man looked him up and down. If the strange quality of his voice puzzled him, he did not show it. 'Where are you trying to get to, son?'

'To see my Dad,' said Johnnie, looking up at the lorry driver with candid eyes. It was true, after all. He *was* going to see his Dad. If he could find him.

But the burly lorry driver was observing him with a doubtful gaze. He took in the boy's white face and hazy look of shock. He did not see the neat plaster on his forehead, though, because it was hidden under Mr Patel's cap. But even so, something bothered him about the boy.

'Is anything the matter, son?' he asked. 'You're a bit young to be wandering about on your own, aren't you?'

Johnnie drew himself up. 'I'm twelve,' he said. 'And I have to see my Dad – it's important.'

Still the lorry driver hesitated. 'Didn't your Mum ever tell you not to hitch lifts with strangers?'

Johnnie looked puzzled. 'Strangers?' he said, and suddenly smiled.

The man took a step back, as if something had hit him.

'Please . . .' said Johnnie, still looking up into his face. 'It's important . . .'

All at once, the man relented. Somehow, the boy's trusting gaze shook him. It was clearly something the kid had to do – and if he was really going to see his Dad, it must be all right.

'Does your Mum know you're going off on this jaunt?' he asked, making one last attempt to be cautious.

'Yes,' said Johnnie clearly. 'She knows.' That was true, too. Julie did know.

'OK,' said the man, at last answering Johnnie's smile with one of his own. 'Hop in.' And he pointed to a heavy lorry with an open back loaded with crates, that stood at the side of the forecourt.

'You are going *north*?' asked Johnnie, determined to make sure.

'North it is!' said the lorry driver, and swung himself up into the cab.

Johnnie climbed up beside him. 'Thanks!' he said.

Part II

The Search

Back at Fourteen Boyne Road, authority took over. Big Joe was taken away in an ambulance. The police came and asked a lot of questions. Maggie Fraser arrived and took charge of the frightened children. And, after consulting Sergeant Mackay, she took charge of Julie Cass as well. During all the questions, the children said nothing, and Julie insisted in a flat, toneless voice that Big Joe had just tripped and fallen. Nothing was said about Johnnie.

It was not until some of the chaos had died down and the children had been put to bed, that Maggie said sharply: 'Where is Johnnie?'

There was a silence. Then Julie said slowly: 'I don't know. . . .'

'*You don't know?* What do you mean?'

'He . . . didn't come home . . .'

Julie didn't know quite why she was lying, but in her muddled way she was trying to protect Johnnie. She could still see him standing in front of her with his hands outstretched to protect her, and Big Joe towering over him, with the bottle in his hand . . .

'*Didn't come home?*' All sorts of frightful possibilities were going through Maggie's mind. Big Joe, murderous and drunk, with a bottle in his hand, and this awful, irrational hatred of Johnnie. . . . Could the boy be lying injured somewhere . . . injured, or worse?

'Mrs Cass – Julie, please try to remember. . . . When did you see Johnnie last?'

'At – at breakfast time. . . . Before he went to the hospital . . .'

Maggie got up. 'All right. I have to go now. You try to get some sleep.'

'Sleep?' repeated Julie.

For a moment Maggie paused, seeing the exhausted, dazed look of shock on Julie's face. 'Listen,' she said kindly, 'make yourself a hot drink. Take those pills the police doctor gave you. . . . I'll come back presently to see how you are. But I have to go now – to see about Johnnie . . .'

'Johnnie's out,' said Julie, in a voice like a sleepwalker. 'Johnnie didn't come home . . .'

Maggie gave her one more sharp glance and almost ran from the room.

'He might be just skiving off . . .' said Sergeant Mackay. 'He's done it before, hasn't he? Keeping out of trouble, poor kid . . .'

'Yes.' Maggie looked even more disturbed. 'But he might be lying dead in a ditch . . .'

'In any case we'd better put out a call for him . . .' said the Sergeant. He looked thoughtfully at his desk and its piles of papers. 'Do you think . . . Julie Cass could be lying?'

Maggie looked at him in surprise. 'Very possibly. But what for?'

'Maybe the kid saw something . . . and ran off in a fright . . .'

'In any case we've got to find him!' Maggie sounded quite desperate. 'Apart from anything else, the boy's deaf. He's not safe wandering about the streets alone. . . . He can't hear the traffic coming . . .'

'Oh, my God,' said Sergeant Mackay. 'The poor kid . . .'

By the time the call went out for a fair-haired boy dressed in shabby blue jeans and a grey school jersey, Johnnie was wearing Mr Patel's dark brown clothes, with his red and white baseball cap hiding the vivid blond hair; and he was perched high up in the cab of a lorry speeding northwards up the M1.

In the morning, Maggie was too harassed to go to fetch her paper from Mr Patel's shop, so he could not give her Johnnie's note.

It was not until the evening, when the news of the disastrous happenings at No 14 Boyne Road had spread round the district, that Mr Patel thought of the letter. By then it was too late to reach Maggie Fraser at the Welfare Office. He would have to wait till morning. If she didn't come then, he would have to deliver it in person, and that would mean leaving his wife to mind the shop while he went across town to the Social Security offices.

Maggie had spent an exhausting day trying to sort out Julie Cass and her affairs, while at the same time trying to think what to do about Johnnie. In the end she spent a second night at Julie's house, partly to keep an eye on the children and Julie, but partly, she knew, in the hope that Johnnie might come home. But he didn't.

She went back to Sergeant Mackay to ask if there was any news of him yet.

'Not of the boy yet, no. . . .' The Sergeant looked up at her sympathetically. 'But something rather odd has come up about Big Joe.'

'Well, what about him? Maggie felt she didn't really care to know anything more about Big Joe. It was Johnnie she cared about.

'It seems it wasn't the fall from the banisters that killed him.'

'Not the fall? What do you mean?'

'He was not dead on arrival at the hospital. He was suffering from a massive cerebral haemorrhage, brought on by heavy drinking. . . . The alcohol level in his bloodstream was horrific. He was probably already dying when he fell, but he took some time doing it. . . . There was nothing the hospital could do . . . He died early the next morning.'

Maggie shut her eyes and let out a long, shaken sigh. 'Then all those questions, about how he fell. . . ?'

'Or was pushed . . .'

Maggie glanced at him sharply. *'Pushed?'*

The Sergeant's bright, observant eyes were full of tired wisdom, and – strangely enough – full of compassion for the follies of mankind. 'It's a possibility, you know . . . domestic rows can be very confused. It's often impossible to sort out who did what. . . . But in any case it's scarcely relevant now. The injuries he sustained from the fall were actually slight – presumably because he was already limp when he fell. . . . There wasn't even much of a bump on his head, and the broken bottle only caused superficial cuts. . . . He was on his way out by then anyway. Nothing could have saved him.'

'Does Julie Cass know this?'

'Not yet.'

'Can I tell her?'

The Sergeant hesitated. 'Yes,' he said at last. 'Yes, of course. It can't do any harm now.'

'I suppose there'll still have to be an inquest?'

'Oh yes. But I doubt if it'll get further than Natural Causes – not even Accidental Death, with the medical evidence . . .'

Maggie looked at him silently.

'Yes.' Sergeant Mackay was no fool. He could follow her line of thought very well. He nodded sadly. 'If the boy did see something . . . and ran off in a panic. . . . It was all unnecessary.'

'And we can't reach him to tell him so,' said Maggie, agonised.

'We will.' The Sergeant's voice was unexpectedly kind. 'We will, in time.'

Time? thought Maggie. How long can a twelve-year-old deaf boy survive on his own?

The next day she sent for Bill Hamilton, hoping that he might have some idea where the boy might be. . . . At least, she told herself that was the reason, but she had a sneaking feeling that she herself wanted the comfort of his sturdy common sense.

But when Johnnie's Painting Man stood before her, she could tell at a glance that he was as distressed as she was. It was while he was standing there, starting to say: 'I'm so dreadfully sorry about all this . . .' that a human bombshell exploded into the room.

'Where is he?' it demanded, from behind a tangle of wild hair. 'What have you done with him?'

'Dessie!' said Maggie, half-smiling at the girl's furious face. 'Calm down! We haven't done anything with him. . . . We don't know where he is.'

Dessie stared at them. 'I told you!' she said accusingly.

'I told you Big Joe would do it again. I told you it wasn't safe. You knew Johnnie never ought to have gone back there. You knew! How could you let him? You *knew* something awful would happen!'

Maggie sighed. Yes, she knew. . . . And she had let it happen . . .

'And now he's missing, is he? What are you going to do about it?'

'Dessie, what *can* I do?'

'You could look for him for a start.'

'The police are already looking, Dessie.'

'The police! D'you want him picked up by the fuzz? He'd be terrified!' She looked at them contemptuously. 'Don't you see? We've got to find him first!'

They looked at her, shaken by her passionate insistence. Then Maggie said in the tired voice of one who had been lying awake all night asking herself the same questions over and over again: 'Yes, but *where,* Dessie? Where d'you think he might go?'

'The Park?' Dessie looked up at the Painting Man, still belligerent and accusing. 'You oughter know. . . . You used to meet him in the Park.'

Bill Hamilton nodded unhappily. 'Yes, I did. But he wasn't there today – or yesterday. I looked all over the Park for him. . . . Everywhere!' His square, sensitive hands were clenched together in distress. Dessie saw them, and some of her anger cooled a little. He obviously minded, too.

While she was drawing breath for another tirade, there was a timid knock on the door.

'Come in,' said Maggie wearily. Who else could possibly be dealt with now?

The dark, intelligent face of Mr Patel came round the door. 'I am sorry,' he said humbly, 'to be disturbing you, but I am having a letter for you.'

198

'For me?'

'From Johnnie . . .'

'*What?*' The three of them turned on him so fast, that poor Mr Patel backed away in alarm.

'It is being all right,' he said hastily, 'I have brought it. . . . You did not be coming in for your paper yesterday – '

'*Yesterday?*' said Maggie.

'*Yesterday?*' repeated Dessie, sharply.

'He left the letter *yesterday?*' asked Bill Hamilton.

Mr Patel handed the letter over and stood watching them while they read it. Maggie read the note in silence, and in silence passed it to Dessie and Bill Hamilton. In fact, she could not speak for a moment. Nor could she hide the tears in her eyes. '*Please look after Mom and the kids.* . . .' Johnnie's words were so direct and so simple – but they implied so much.

'Why didn't he sign it?' asked Bill, remembering how he had told Johnnie always to sign his work at that first, magical meeting.

Dessie looked at the picture of the earphones with a critical eye. 'He did, in a way, see? That's his hospital tests. . . . He's thanking you for those. . . . Looks like he was running away and didn't want to put his name to it . . .'

'Why not?' Bill asked.

Dessie's own face went pale and set as she worked out the implications. 'Because. . . .' She looked up at Maggie, and suddenly shut her mouth firmly and said nothing at all.

'Maybe,' said Mr Patel politely, 'I should be telling you what has been happening?'

'Yes,' agreed Maggie. 'You should.'

When he had finished recounting it, he added, wringing his hands in a curiously old-fashioned gesture of distress: 'Truly, I did not be knowing Johnnie would be running away. . . . I would have tried to prevent him. . . . I thought he was only hiding from Big Joe, perhaps. . . . I did not want to be making things harder for him – only to help . . .'

'Mr Patel,' said Maggie, sounding angry and warm-hearted all at once: 'You are the only one who *did* help! We are his friends, and we did nothing – *nothing*. He had neighbours, too, you know . . . they have told me since how they often used to hear Big Joe shouting. . . . But they never helped . . . they never reported it . . . they never took Johnnie in, or offered him any protection. . . . They were afraid, they said, of interfering! You are the one, Mr Patel, who took him in and fed and clothed him. And you come here and try to *apologise!*'

Mr Patel looked bewildered. 'I am not apologising, only I am being sorry!'

'We are all sorry,' said Maggie bitterly. 'All of us – now it is too late.'

'It's not too late!' cried Dessie. 'He's gone off some-where, that's all. We'll find him . . .'

'Can you think of anywhere he might go?' asked Bill Hamilton.

Dessie sank deep into remembrance of Johnnie . . . the sea? The nuns at the Convalescent Home? No, John-nie in trouble would try not to involve anyone else . . . that was what the unsigned note meant. . . . He was in deep trouble . . . or he thought he was . . . and that was why he hadn't come to her . . . or to Maggie . . . or to the Painting Man. . . . The Painting Man . . . a man's advice would help most. . . . '*Do you remember your Dad, Johnnie?*' She could hear her own voice, speaking slowly and clearly for Johnnie's ears. '*When you're older you can go and find him . . .*'

'North Sea Oil,' she said suddenly, aloud.

The others stared at her in astonishment.

'What, Dessie?' Maggie laid a hand on her arm, restraining an urgent desire to shake information out of her.

'His Dad . . . Johnnie's own Dad. . . . He had a photo of him, remember. . . ? A man in a tin hat and a sort of parka with a furry hood. . . . And Johnnie drew a thing like an oil rig. Remember, I told you? He knew he worked on something like that. He'd seen it on the telly . . . we guessed it must be North Sea Oil, because of the furry hood. . . .' She looked round at them with a kind of exasperated despair between tears and laughter. 'The silly kid . . . he's gone after his Dad, and he hasn't a clue where to find him. . . !'

The noise and the vibration in the cab hurt his ears terribly and seemed to make the throb in his head get steadily worse. Fortunately, it was too noisy to talk, so he didn't have to answer any questions. In any case, the lorry driver had the radio on as well, and bursts of loud pop music swelled in and out of his tortured ears in between the roar of the engine and the continuous shaking hum of the truck's wheels on the road.

He had had very little sleep all night, and presently, even with the pain in his head getting worse, he dozed off and slid down sideways in the cab. The truck driver glanced at him kindly enough, flung an old coat over him, and went on driving.

Johnnie began to dream . . . but his dreams were terrifying. . . . He could still see his own hands outstretched, and as if in slow motion, the huge, swaying black silhouette of Big Joe, stumbling backwards, twisting and falling, slowly, slowly, arms flailing, limbs spread out in untidy disarray. . . . He woke with a lurch of fear and the words: 'Don't! Don't!' shouting in his mind. . . . Had he shouted aloud?

But the man beside him was still driving, still occasionally singing to his radio, and not looking at Johnnie at all.

By now the noise was such agony that Johnnie realised he could not travel in big trucks any more. . . . When they stopped – he supposed they would stop sometime – he would have to get down and leave. . . . He would have to walk – or find something smaller and quieter. . . . Involuntarily, he put his hands over his ears and groaned.

The lorry driver glanced at him with sympathy. 'Noisy, isn't she? Never mind . . . we'll be stopping soon. . . . Could do with a cuppa, I shouldn't wonder?'

Johnnie could not hear the words, but nodded and smiled.

He had scarcely noticed the wide, rain-soaked countryside hurtling by as he sat perched high up in the cab. But now the lorry began to slow down, and the comforting arms of the trees came into focus, reaching out over a fence towards the hard shoulder . . . they looked green and cool, and shone with rain. . . . He longed to bury his head in their wet leaves . . .

The lorry pulled off the slow lane on to the hard shoulder behind a line of other parked trucks and slowly came to a halt. At last, at last, the roaring, grinding engine was switched off. . . . A blessed quiet descended on Johnnie's ears . . . he closed his eyes . . .

'All right, son?' The voice was kindly, but not particularly insistent. It wasn't asking awkward questions.

Johnnie opened his eyes and attempted a pale smile.

'That's better – you got a name, son?'

'Johnnie.' He wasn't hearing very well, after all that noise, but he had got very clever at watching people's faces. . . . He understood very well, so long as he could

102

see their mouths. He did not know what lip-reading was, but he was using it as a means of understanding all the time.

'Hi, Johnnie. Welcome to the club! Mine's Bob . . . Bedford Bob, they call me. . . . That's my home base, see? Like some tea?' He handed Johnnie a plastic cup and poured some dark brown liquid into it from his thermos. He filled a second cup for himself and then got out a packet of sandwiches.

After munching in silence for a few minutes, he glanced again at the white face beside him and peeled off one rather squashed cheese sandwich from the pile and offered it to him.

Johnnie swallowed and shook his head. He could not eat. His head throbbed like fire, his shoulder had stiffened and had a dull, persistent ache deep in the bone, and he was sick and dizzy. . . . And shocked, though he did not know it. . . . Whenever the picture of that room floated into his mind, his stomach seemed to churn in a lurch of terror. And grief. . . . He had meant to help . . . he had tried to save his mother from hurt . . . and the kids from more fright and violence. . . . But it had all gone wrong, and he had done something terrible . . . and he had left them – his Mom and the kids – helpless and frightened, with all that to face on their own. . . . He ought not to have gone . . . but what else could he do?

He found Bob, the lorry driver, leaning over him, looking worried. 'Not going to pass out, are you? Better get out in the air a minute . . .'

He climbed down from the cab and went round to help Johnnie out. . . . The ground seemed to heave under Johnnie's feet for a moment, but it righted itself as the air revived him.

'Sorry . . .' he muttered, and tried again to smile in

the direction of Bob's anxious face. Then he stumbled over to the grass verge and was sick into the bushes. When he came back, feeling somewhat hazy, Bob had gone off to talk to one of the other drivers. Now he returned, hunching his shoulders against the rain.

'Better? Climb in then . . . we'll be stopping later on at my favourite café for a proper meal. . . . Think you can last that long?' There was a glint of friendly humour in his eyes which, Johnnie noticed, were brown and set in a mesh of lines that had grown round them from long hours of concentration on the road and screwing them up against the sun . . .

Johnnie climbed back in. Perhaps at the next stopping place he could manage to find a smaller, quieter lorry. . . . In the meantime, to take his mind off things, he got out Mr Patel's pad and a stub of pencil and began to draw . . .

After another long, grinding spell of noise and dizzying vistas of wet road and swiftly receding countryside, Bob turned his truck into a layby beside a long, low transport café with a number of trucks outside it. Here he stopped, and once again a wonderful silence fell on Johnnie's ears.

'You coming in for a meal?' Bob's voice was quite concerned. Something about the boy's white face disturbed him.

Johnnie shook his head. 'No thanks.'

'Come on, I'll treat you.' Perhaps the kid was broke and didn't like to say so. He knew about pick-ups trying it on, but this one was different. 'It's a good place,' he said. 'Known Ma for years . . .'

'No,' said Johnnie, and smiled at him. 'Better . . . out here . . . in the air.'

It had stopped raining. A watery sun was trying to come out. Even among all the lorries and the petrol and diesel fumes, and the smell of hot tyres on tarmac, Johnnie could still detect the scent of rainwashed grass. There was a rough, uncultivated area over in the corner of the car park, with a long grassy slope and a few stunted trees. . . . He waved his hand vaguely towards it. 'I'll . . . go over there . . .'

Bob saw that he meant it, shrugged his shoulders, and went off to the café on his own.

Johnnie wandered over to the grassy bank and sat down. His head felt very tall, and there seemed to be a continuous jangling bell inside it. He sat staring at the back of Bob's lorry, and beyond it to the green countryside. . . . But as he gazed, half dreaming, into the middle distance, a sudden flash of black and white caught his eye. A small, furry object appeared from behind one of Bob's crates, leapt to the ground and streaked across the car park. . . . With unerring certainty it came straight towards Johnnie, tail waving a wild welcome, and hurled itself straight into his arms . . .

'Get-Lost!' said Johnnie in horror. 'What have you done? You're a stowaway! How can I travel with a dog? What am I going to do with you?'

He tried to sound angry . . . but he wasn't angry . . . his voice came out all wrong. . . . He seemed to be crooning to the scared little dog, and his arms tightened round it instead of pushing it away. The small alert head kept thrusting upwards, the brown eyes alight with devotion, and a wet pink tongue kept trying to lick his nose. . . . In truth, Johnnie was the only human being who had ever been kind to Get-Lost, and he wasn't going to let him go now.

Johnnie sat there, holding the rough, furry body in his arms, and looked at the sun on the leaves. . . . I love green, he thought vaguely . . . it's so cool . . . even the wind is green. . . . What shall I do with Get-Lost? He

105

can't find his way home from here . . . even if he's got a home, which I doubt . . . I suppose I must look after him. . . . He's my dog now. The words, as he thought them, made him feel somehow warm and comforted . . . he had always wanted a dog. . . . He said them aloud to Get-Lost. 'You're my dog now! You'd better be good!' Get-Lost's tail thumped even harder . . .

Bob, the lorry driver, had his usual breakfast and two large strong cups of tea. It was still only 10.30 in the morning, and he had driven nearly 200 miles. . . . But he was used to it, and he wasn't particularly tired. He called out a few cheerful remarks to his mates at the other tables, and they called back, exchanging jokes and the mild gossip of the road. . . . They also chatted up Millie, the one and only waitress who was plump and smiling, and old Ma behind the counter, who always made a good strong cup of tea. . . . But Bob was only half listening to the general back chat. He was thinking about the boy. It's not my concern, he thought . . . but somehow it was, it was. The kid looked so white . . . and anyway, what was a boy of that age doing, hitching alone all the way up the A1? Going to see his Dad, he said . . . but it was a funny way of going on. . . . In any case, Scotch Corner was coming up, and Bob would be turning off left to cross over to Glasgow. . . . Where did the kid want to go? North, he had said . . . but North was a big place. . . . He'd have to get him to talk somehow . . . talk, and take a decision . . .

'Ma,' he said, getting up from his table to go and lean on the counter. 'Do us a bacon sandwich, will you? Got a kid with me . . .'

But when he got outside with the sandwich in his hand, there was no boy waiting in the car park. Inside the cab there was a drawing propped up against the wheel . . . a very good drawing indeed of Bob's intent face, the fine lines round his eyes as he screwed them up in concentration on the road, and his jutting nose and springy, faintly curling hair. . . . Beneath it were four words: 'Thanks for the lift.' It was a clever likeness, and Bob was absurdly pleased. He wanted to tell Johnnie so.

But the boy had gone.

Johnnie didn't know where the road was going to, but he reasoned that Bob would certainly go back on to the northbound side of the A1, so he and Get-Lost crossed the big road, somewhat perilously, and went off down a small side road going eastwards. It was a nice road, he decided – not wide and grey and desolate like the motorway at the beginning, or the A1. It had trees all along it and they made dappled shadows under his feet. Beside him, little Get-Lost made another shadow almost under his feet, and whether he moved fast or slow, the little dog never left his side.

'You know,' he said, talking to it quite easily in his growly voice: 'You're a menace, that's what. . . . How am I going to feed you? I can't even feed myself. . . .' He thought about Mr Patel's money in his pocket. How long would two pounds last? He would have to be very careful. . . . Of course he could probably find odd jobs to do for people here and there . . . cleaning cars, or weeding gardens, or something. . . . He'd done it before . . . but a dog had to be fed. . . . So did he, come to that, or he'd never get far enough on the road to find his Dad . . .

He resolved to stop at the next place he came to that had a shop, and buy something to eat . . . he could always share it with the dog. . . . Probably, Get-Lost hadn't had much to eat in the old days in the Park, either . . . he wouldn't be fussy . . .

Something strange seemed to be happening to Johnnie as he walked along. He had never been alone in the country before. . . . The Park was the nearest he had ever come to this wide, empty, green world . . . and he loved it. . . . The beautiful shapes of the trees leaning over the road, the thick clumps of woodland in the valleys, the sloping curves of the fields, and something that looked like moorland and then range after range of hills beyond . . . all these dazzled him with their newness. Their uncluttered, unspoilt loveliness seemed to wash over him and heal him of all kinds of hurts . . .

Kevin would say it's smashing! he thought, and smiled. Smashing was just exactly what it wasn't. It looked as if nothing had ever smashed it – or ever could – though he remembered with a shudder the bulldozers closing on the bit of green grass and the empty houses at the end of his road. . . . They gobbled up green, like greedy, hungry monsters . . . could they gobble up these lovely quiet fields? He supposed they could – if the towns got near enough.

Towns? He wondered where he was. He remembered the last sign on the A1 before they stopped at the layby. It had said Scotch Corner . . . with Middlesbrough and Teeside on one side, and Penrith and Carlisle on the other. . . . And Newcastle had come in somewhere, but he couldn't remember exactly which side. He didn't really know any of those places . . . he ought to use some of his money to buy a map. . . . But then, even with a map, he wasn't sure where he was going – or even where he was. . . . He was looking at the edge of the Cleveland Hills, with the dark line of the North York Moors behind them, but he didn't know it.

Somehow, because of the new green world around him, and the little dog at his side, he didn't seem to care much where he was going. It was enough to be walking along this leafy road, entirely on his own, with no-one to shout at him, and his very own loving little dog padding along at his heels. . . . The thought of Kevin had raised a host of anxieties in his mind . . . but even these seemed less desperate up here. . . . Were they all right? Ought he to have gone? Would Mom look after them all right without him? But then there was the Welfare Lady. . . . She was very kind, and very firm with Mom . . . she cared about the kids. . . . She would see that they were OK. . . . They'd be better off without him, sure they would . . . they'd often said so before. . . . At least, Big Joe had . . .

He shuddered suddenly, and Get-Lost looked up at him, leapt straight off the ground on all four legs and tried to lick his nose.

'You nutcase!' said Johnnie, laughing. 'Crazy dog! You nearly knocked me over . . . get down!'

Get-Lost appeared to be laughing, too. But having achieved his object, he got down and walked sedately to heel. The green world enclosed them peacefully, and gradually Johnnie forgot his worries and just walked and looked around him with delight.

There was so much to see . . . so much that he hadn't known existed. . . . It was late spring, and there were flowers in the hedgerows. . . . He didn't know all their names, but he recognised bluebells and violets . . . and those pink ones he was sure he had seen in some book . . . campion, was it? Rose campion. . . . And then there were the birds . . . flashing in and out of the trees, coming down on to the road in front of him, starting up with a whirr of wings that even his ears could hear as he walked by. . . . He knew blackbirds and thrushes – he had met those in the Park, and robins, and even a jay once or twice. . . . But here there were black and white ones with delicate crests on their heads, who gave out a strange, piercing, lonely cry that echoed over the hills and even penetrated his damaged ears, it was so high

109

and clear and pure. . . . And once a green woodpecker with a red head shot past him into the thicket of leaves behind the hedge. . . . He knew that one from his bird book, but he'd never seen it alive before . . . and there were fat pheasants walking about in the fields . . . he knew those when he saw them. People ate pheasants . . . but when he saw them strutting in their bright spring plumage, he thought they were much too beautiful to eat . . .

The thought of eating made him worry about the dog again. . . . Dogs had to eat. They had to drink, too. He hadn't got any sort of water bottle or dish with him . . . how was he to get the dog a drink? Maybe there would be a stream somewhere at the bottom of the fields . . . surely in all this greenness there must be water somewhere?

He climbed over the next gate and stood looking out over the young green grass towards the hills. . . . They stood high on the horizon, layer upon layer of them, growing higher and higher, each ridge a different fading shade of amethyst and blue, till the farthest ones were almost a mere darkening of the sky. Cloud shadows moved across them, and reminded him sharply of the lake at home . . . the lake in the Park, and the Painting Man, and Dessie . . . and Mom and the kids waiting for him to come home . . .

Tears filled his eyes.

It would be so easy to go home and say: 'I'm sorry . . .' and let them all do what they liked to him . . . but it wouldn't help Mom and the kids if they put him in prison. . . . Better to stay away, and find his Dad . . . he would know what to do . . . he would be sure to put things right, somehow. . . . He'd only got to find him and tell him how bad things were, and he'd come home and get everything sorted out. . . . And when it was all straight again, he'd laugh and throw Kevin up in the air like he used to do with Johnnie . . . and sing 'Your Danny's home again . . .' like he used to. . . . Everything would be all right then. . . .

He blinked, and looked down at Get-Lost, who was patiently sitting on the grass, looking up at him with his tongue hanging out.

'Yes, you're thirsty, aren't you?' said Johnnie. 'Come on then, we'll go and find some water . . .'

They crossed the first field cautiously. Johnnie had no experience of the countryside, or farmers. Would they mind him walking about on their fields? He looked down at the land and wondered what it was growing. This seemed to be ordinary grass. It wasn't in rows, like wheat or barley. And it wasn't long enough yet to be called hay. . . . So he couldn't be doing any harm, could he? What about sheep, though? He could see a lot of them on the hillside. But they were far away. . . . Would Get-Lost try to chase sheep? He didn't think so . . . he was not that kind of little dog. But even so, he might. . . . He seemed to remember that Get-Lost – along with several others – had always chased cats. . . . And he hadn't got a lead or a piece of string . . . so he'd better be careful . . .

By the time he had crossed the second field, he could see the land dropping down to a small, deep valley before the first of the hills began to rise beyond it . . . surely there must be a stream somewhere there? He climbed over another gate set in a stone wall, and Get-Lost scrambled through after him. The grass was shorter here, more like springy hill turf, and starred with small yellow flowers. He looked down the slope, and sure enough there was a line of willows at the bottom, and a glint of water running between them.

'Come on!' he said, and began to run. The little dog ran joyously after him down the slope, and together they reached the swift-flowing stream sliding along beneath the queer, stunted arms of the pollarded willows. The water looked cool and clear between steep mossy banks overhung with clumps of fern. There was a thicket of brambles and nettles between the field and the stream, but they paid no attention to it, and crashed straight through to the water's edge.

'Look, Get-Lost. Water! Have a drink,' said Johnnie – his voice croaking with excitement.

The little dog needed no second invitation. With one questioning look in Johnnie's direction, he plunged in feet first, and put his bristly muzzle into the water. The stream was running fast, and the little dog tried to follow the moving water with his pink tongue – going further down-stream with every mouthful. This made Johnnie laugh.

'No!' he said. 'Stand still! It'll still be there if you stand still!' And he stooped and cupped his hands and drank the cold hill water before it could spill out of his fingers.

Get-Lost looked at him, head on one side, and then went back to chasing his drink down stream. . . . He got enormously wet, and he enjoyed himself hugely.

Johnnie found that he felt dizzy when he stooped forward, and his head began to hurt again. So he gave up trying to drink any more and sat down on the bank. His shoulder was aching, too, and so were his feet . . . in fact, he ached all over, when he came to think of it. . . . On a sudden impulse he took off his ancient track-shoes and put his tired feet in the water. It was cold and tingly, but it made them feel better. After a while he took them out of the water and lay back against some ferns on the stony bank and drowsed.

Get-Lost had finished playing with the water . . . but there were some very exciting smells out here in the country, and he was busy investigating some of them. . . . He didn't go very far away though, and even the most thrilling smell couldn't prevent him casting a wary eye in Johnnie's direction now and then. . . . At last, even he was tired, and he came and curled up at Johnnie's feet.

It was very quiet by the water – very peaceful. But even so, Johnnie was not asleep. He was thinking vaguely about oil rigs, and wondering how far away they were and how to get there . . . and were there more than one? He was still pondering about this when he suddenly felt Get-Lost stiffen beside him and begin a soft growl deep down in his throat. He could feel it vibrating in the dog's neck – even the hairs were quivering slightly. At the same moment he became aware that someone was watching him – and he sat up and looked around him at the water and the banks of the stream. . . . On the farther bank, staring straight at him, was an old, tattered man with a bushy grey beard, holding a blackened kettle in his hand.

'Nice little dog you got there,' said the old man, grinning at him through gappy, uneven teeth as blackened as his kettle. 'Been rabbiting, has 'e?'

Johnnie gazed at him, trying to follow his words. Rabbiting? Get-Lost? He wouldn't know a rabbit if he saw one.

'No,' said Johnnie. 'Drinking. He fell in . . .'

The old man eyed the dog's bedraggled fur and grinned even wider. 'Gotta bitta fire up yonder,' he said. ''E could dry off, like. . . . Fancy a cuppa?'

Cuppa? Johnnie heard that. He nodded vigorously. A cup of tea . . . out of the black kettle? A real, hot cup of tea?

'Yes please!' he said, and smiled.

The old man blinked. 'On yer own, are yer?'

'Yes.' On my own. That was true, at least. He was truly, totally on his own.

'Come on, then. S'not far.'

He followed the old man through a tangle of alders and willow branches into a small clearing just above the bank of the stream. Here there was a smoky fire burning, and on it an old black pot was simmering, and out of it came the most heavenly smell.

113

Get-Lost's nose twitched. He went near to investigate, but when he felt the heat of the fire, he backed off and sat down, gazing yearningly at the bubbling pot. Johnnie couldn't help gazing at it, too. All at once, he was ravenously hungry. But he was much too shy to say so.

The old man's eyes beneath their shaggy brows were piercing and observant. He did not miss the longing in either the boy's or the dog's anxious glance. 'Hungry, are you, boy?' he asked, and then, when Johnnie did not answer, he put on his gap-tooth grin and added: 'Plenty for all . . . gotta good rabbit today. . . . Rabbits is back now, you know . . . time was, you couldn't getta rabbit . . . when that mixy was on . . . killed 'em all, it did. White eyes . . . something cruel . . . turrble it was. . . . But now, they're back, see? Life's a lot easier now. . . .' He was talking more-or-less to himself, and as he talked, he was untying several tin plates which were dangling from the string round his waist which seemed to serve as a belt to hold his ragged coat together as well as a kind of hold-all harness for all his rattling equipment.

Johnnie gazed at the seamed, dark brown face that looked as if it had been smoked over many fires and withstood all the weather in the world – and decided that he liked the old man and could probably trust him.

'Tin-Can-Charlie, they call me,' he said, catching Johnnie's summing-up look. 'Last of the travelling tinkers, that's me. . . . Well, one of the last, anyways . . .'

'Travelling?' asked Johnnie, and looked down at the old man's feet. They were encased in broken boots tied up with string, but they looked workmanlike, and as if they were used to any amount of walking. 'Always?'

The old man chuckled. 'Most always . . .'

'Where to?'

'From here to there. . . . Leastways, I stops now and

114

then, d'you see? But not for long, boy – no, not for long. . . . Tin-Can-Charlie never stops for long. . . .' He glanced shrewdly at Johnnie and added with sudden directness: 'You travelling, boy?'

Johnnie nodded.

'Where to?' The questions were reversed, and there was a twinkle in his eye.

'North,' said Johnnie, saying it firmly to make himself believe in it.

'Where from, then?'

Johnnie paused and thought a while. 'South,' he said.

Tin-Can-Charlie laughed. 'You're a real man of the roads, son. Never tell anyone nothing you don't want 'em to know!'

He began to ladle out the bubbling stew on to two tin plates. Then he fumbled in one of his many pockets and brought out some slices of bread wrapped in newspaper. After handing Johnnie his share, he also passed over a tin spoon and said briskly: 'Eat, boy . . . never know when the next meal's coming. . . .' He cocked an eye at Get-Lost who was still sitting patiently just beyond the fire. Then he got out another plate and ladled some more stew on to it, threw in a piece of bread and poured a little cold water out of the kettle on to it to cool it.

'Here, dog . . . s'pose you're as good as us, any day. What's 'is name, boy?'

Johnnie smiled. 'I call him Get-lost.'

Tin-Can-Charlie's grin got wider. 'Yours, is he?'

'He is now,' said Johnnie.

Tin-Can-Charlie nodded. 'Adopted, is 'e? That's the best kinda dog to have. Here, Get-Lost, try a bitta rabbit stew . . . just the thing for dogs . . .'

'And boys,' said Johnnie, munching. He was surprised when Charlie went off into a cackle of laughter. But he was unsurprised by the fact that he could hear, and even join in a conversation. . . . And even make a kind of joke . . .

While they were eating the stew, Charlie had set the kettle over the fire, and presently a plume of steam came from its spout. Charlie unwrapped another screw of paper and produced some real tea in a battered packet.

'None of yer tea-bags for me,' he grumbled happily. 'This is the real stuff . . . stewed over the fire, black as tar, that's how I like it. . . .' He stirred some tea into the kettle and left it simmering while he got out two tin mugs, a can of condensed milk, some sugar and another spoon. 'Here, boy – put some heart into you, that will. . . .' He handed Johnnie a mug full of blackish brew, and began to sip his own.

Then he said in a casual kind of voice: 'How far north then, boy? North's a big place.'

Johnnie sighed. He wondered whether to tell Charlie about his Dad. . . . It surely couldn't do much harm . . . and maybe, since he was a much-travelled man, he would know what to do . . .

'Going to see my Dad,' he began.

Charlie nodded. 'That makes sense, that does. Boys oughter see their Dads. Stands to reason. Where?'

Johnnie looked at him. Then, slowly, he drew out the precious photograph. It was in a blue plastic case now, which Dessie had given him when they came back from the sea. . . . It was just as well she had, he thought, because the rain would have ruined it otherwise. . . . A sudden longing for Dessie almost overcame him. But he pushed it firmly down inside him, and held out the photo to Charlie.

'Oil-rig,' he said, and stopped. He couldn't think of a way to explain any more.

'Oil-rig, is it? Ekofisk, then . . . that's the nearest.'
'Is it?'

'Teesside. . . . The pipe line comes in there. . . .' He looked at the photo, and then at the boy beside him. 'Been gone long, has he?'

Long? Far too long . . . so long that Johnnie could only just remember him. . . . Just remember his voice calling him 'Oh Johnnie boy' and his wide, friendly smile . . .

'Too long,' said Johnnie.

Charlie was frowning at the photo. 'Trouble is,' he said, half to himself, 'they don't talk right up there. . . . Can't understand 'em – not a blurry word. . . .' He glanced at Johnnie. 'No good asking the locals,' he said. 'You'd never get a straight answer . . .'

Johnnie couldn't follow all this. He sat looking at him patiently, trying to hear what Charlie wanted him to do.

'You want the port,' said Charlie. 'Seamen come from most everywhere – London, even. . . . I been up there – on Teeside . . . come up on a trawler with a mate of mine . . .'

'Trawler?' said Johnnie. 'A boat?'

'A boat, boy . . . yes, a boat. . . . There's ways and ways of travelling, y'know. . . .' He grinned encouragingly at Johnnie. 'Not a bad place, the port. . . . They'll tell you where to go. . . . Engineer, is he?'

Johnnie nodded. He understood that word, at least. 'Yes,' he said, and then speaking clearly: 'an engineer . . .'

'They come in and out, you know.' Charlie was pouring some more black tea out of the kettle into his own mug. 'You'd have to ask. . . .' He glanced up again at Johnnie, and something about the boy's white face troubled him. 'Got anywheres to sleep tonight?'

Johnnie shook his head. But it hurt when he did that and he put his hand up to it before he remembered Mr Patel's baseball cap covering the plaster. Charlie was watching him. The bright, knowing eyes didn't miss a thing.

117

'What you done to your head, boy?' He reached out a hand, and before Johnnie could protest, he had lifted the cap off and was looking at the plaster on his head. Blood had seeped through it in a brown stain and made a sticky mess of the bright blond hair . . .

Charlie began to whistle through his teeth. He always did that when he was worried. . . . Now he leaned forward and twitched another small pan of water on to the fire and said, quite gently: 'Better bathe it, hadn't we? Can't leave it like that, eh? Hold still, I won't hurt you . . . gotta few herbs here . . . might help, see?'

Johnnie submitted. Get-Lost growled once, and then seemed to decide that Charlie wasn't threatening Johnnie after all. He sat beside Johnnie, watchful and tense, his eyes following every movement of Charlies' hands.

But Charlie was deft and surprisingly gentle. The old plaster was soaked off. The wound was cleaned again, the blood washed off the matted hair, and a fresh, pungent smell of herbs came up from the warm water in the pan and seemed to clear the fog in Johnnie's head . . .

'Nasty,' said Charlie, half to himself. 'Should be stitched by rights. . . .' He searched in his pockets again and produced a bright red tin of elastoplast. 'Keep 'em for blisters,' he said, grinning. 'Useful. Hold still now. . . .' He fixed the plaster and looked at Johnnie severely. 'Now, see here, boy. . . . If that head's botherin' you termorrer, you get it to a doctor, see?'

Johnnie nodded. It was easier to agree than to argue.

'And ternight you stay alonger me, see? I've gotta snug place in a barn . . . room fer two, I reckon. . . . Two and a little bit of a dog. . . .' He tweaked Get-Lost's ragged ears. 'Wasn't hurting him, dog, was I? No harm in old Tin-Can-Charlie . . .'

He saw that Johnnie was suddenly very tired and very disappointed . . . very near to tears, he thought. 'Can't

118

do it all in one day, boy,' he said, interpreting his look of stress correctly. 'Go further after a rest, see? The world's a big place, boy. . . . You can't cross it all at once, see?'

Johnnie nodded, swallowing tears and an extraordinary lump of despair that kept rising in his throat.

'Termorrer,' said Tin-Can-Charlie. 'We'll see what comes, eh? Now I reckon it's time you hit the hay!' He went off into another cackle of laughter at this remark, seeing it was all too apt. But he put a kind arm round Johnnie's shoulders and steered him across the clearing and past a bramble hedge to a small lean-to shed with a few bales of hay strewn on the floor.

'There you are, boy – see? Hit the hay!' He laughed again at his own laboured joke, and Johnnie smiled vaguely in his direction.

But weariness was coming over Johnnie in curious waves of exhaustion, and he sank down on to the floor and curled up on the first pile of hay his tired body could reach. . . . Get-Lost curled up too, protectively, at his feet.

Charlie, after a half-rueful glance, rummaged about till he found a piece of old blanket which he laid over him. 'Termorrer, boy,' he said kindly. 'It'll all seem easier termorrer. . . .'

'Yes.' Johnnie's voice was slow and already slurred with sleep, and it ended on a long, fading sigh: 'To-morrow – '

When Maggie tried to tackle Julie Cass about Johnnie's father, she met with a stony silence. The girl's mouth set in a sullen straight line and she refused to speak at all.

'Don't you understand?' said Maggie, desperately trying to get through to her. 'Johnnie may be trying to reach him. . . . We've got to know where he is . . .'

'I don't know where he is.'

Maggie sighed. 'Well, his name, then? You must at least know his *name?*'

Silence.

'And where he worked? Johnnie thought it was an oil rig. Was it?'

Silence.

'*Which* oil rig. D'you know that?'

Silence.

Maggie shook her head in despair. 'You realise – Johnnie may be in danger, wandering about the country on his own . . .'

'Johnnie can look after himself.'

'*Please,* Julie, *please* – try to think . . .'

But it was no use. Julie Cass was as unmoving as stone.

When Maggie reported this interview to Bill Hamilton and Dessie – who now seemed to be part of the Find Johnnie Team – Dessie tossed back her tangle of hair and said firmly: 'I'll talk to her.'

'But, Dessie, she won't talk to anyone.'

'She'll talk to me!' said Dessie, and marched off down the road, instantly making for Johnnie's house.

Maggie and Bill looked at each other.

'She will, too,' said Bill, trying to sound cheerful. 'Dessie will find a way if anyone can.' He suddenly put out a blunt-fingered hand and touched Maggie's hair. 'Don't look like that . . . we'll find him . . . I know we will . . .'

'It's my fault . . . I ought never to have let him go back – '

'It's not your fault. You were over-ruled, that's all. . . . God knows you tried to make it clear to them. . . . What else could you do?'

'I – I could have gone round there more often . . . I

120

could have kept him with me. Anything – *anything* rather than this!'

Bill's hand stayed on her hair, steadying and soothing. 'It's all right . . . you mustn't take it so hard . . . he'll come back.'

'But where *is* he? How on earth can he manage on his own? He only had two pounds in the world. . . . What will happen to him?'

'He's a very brave and resourceful boy,' said Bill. 'He'll survive. I'm sure of it.'

Dessie, meanwhile, had marched up the path and rung the bell at Julie's house, marched past her into the living-room, and now stood facing her – a picture of righteous indignation.

'How could you?' she shouted. 'What kind of a mother are you? First you let him get half-killed by Big Joe – and then you ask to have him back again when you know it'll all happen again – and then you let him run away – and now you won't even tell us where he might get to! You're not fit to be a mother! You won't lift a finger to help him! *What's the name of his father?*'

Julie backed away from Dessie's anger. But she was half-fascinated by the girl's raging loyalty. She looked magnificent somehow, standing there in her short school skirt with her wild hair flying and her eyes sparking with fury. . . . She wished, with a sudden twinge of self-pity, that she had a friend like that . . .

'After the inquest,' she said suddenly.

'What?'

'You heard.'

The anger died in Dessie's eyes. She stopped to consider what this meant. 'Big Joe died of natural causes. The doctors said so. Maggie told me.'

'Yeah.' Julie's voice was dry. 'But what kinda questions are they going to ask? Tell me that.'

Dessie was silent. Then she said: 'When's the inquest, then?'

Julie shrugged. 'A day or two, they said. No-one tells me anything.'

Dessie was looking at her hard. 'And you'll tell me then?'

'Depends. Doesn't it?'

The two pairs of eyes met. Dessie's seemed as old and wise and full of experience as Julie's. Perhaps older.

She nodded briefly. 'OK. I'll come back.' She turned to go. And then swung round, suddenly furious again. 'And when Johnnie does come back, I hope they take him away from you for ever, see! He might have some hope then!' She went out and slammed the front door.

Behind her, Julie Cass sighed and rubbed a hand over her eyes. She had done her best in her own way to protect Johnnie. But maybe the girl was right. Maybe she wasn't fit to be a mother.

Inside, the baby, Benjy, was whimpering, and she heard Kevin's voice trying to soothe him. She went back into the living-room and stood staring at the three children. . . . Treesa was sucking her thumb as usual and looking with huge eyes at her mother from behind the sofa . . . Kevin had the baby in his arms and was trying to rock him as he had seen Johnnie do many times in the past. . . . He was only seven, and it was hard for him to be head of the family all of a sudden . . .

'When's Johnnie coming back, Mom?' he asked, jigging the baby to and fro as he spoke. His eyes, like Treesa's were wary and too big . . .

Julie shut her own eyes and sighed again. It was too much. It was all too much. She couldn't bear it . . .

122

'Oh, stop going on about it, Kev,' she said. 'Johnnie'll be home again soon.'

In the morning, old Tin-Can-Charlie got up very early. He left the boy sleeping, but the little dog was alert and sat up with one ear cocked forward enquiringly.

'You stay there,' whispered Charlie. 'Keep guard, see? Don't want you where I'm going . . .'

He went out into the dewy morning and made his way silently down the banks of the stream towards a distant cluster of farmhouse buildings.

When he came back, there was a billican of fresh milk swinging from one hand and two brown eggs held carefully in his cap by the other hand.

Johnnie opened his eyes to a dazzle of sunlight streaming in through the open end of the shed. Get-Lost was scratching about in the hay over in the corner as if he suspected rats, but he hadn't left Johnnie to go out into the morning countryside, although all sorts of smells assailed his questing nose.

But when Johnnie got up and went outside, he went too – joyously. The old tinker was a little way off near the stream, crouched over his fire. He waved a spoon at Johnnie and beckoned him over.

'See, boy, an egg to your breakfast today! I bin makin' enquiries down yonder. Farmer's a friend of mine . . . lets me be, up here, never bothers me. . . . Been `coming here for years, on and off. . . .' He handed Johnnie a mug of tea and skilfully slid a fried egg out of his blackened pan on to a piece of bread and passed it over.

'The thing is,' the old man went on talking, but slower now and more insistently, making sure Johnnie

123

was paying attention: 'the milk lorry comes through early . . . picks up from all the farms hereabouts and drives on through right down to the depot near the docks – see?'

Johnnie was looking at him intently. He had followed most of it . . . but a curious thing had happened to his eyes this morning. . . . His head hurt rather more than yesterday, and he kept seeing double. It made lip-reading rather difficult.

'To – the docks?' He had got the essential point.

'That's it, boy . . . take you all the way. . . . Farmer'll ask for you.'

'What about Get-Lost?'

Tin-Can-Charlie grinned. 'I dessay he'll be allowed . . . if you keep a-holt on him.'

Johnnie looked round for the dog, and saw him chasing shadows not far away. He was leaping and pouncing as the leaves made dark, moving freckles on the sunlit grass. . . . Johnnie had never seen the dog really play before. He was like a carefree puppy . . . also, something strange had happend to his appearance. The long frolic in the stream yesterday must have washed off layers and layers of city grime. For the little dog was now quite fluffy and distinctly black and white instead of an all-over bristly grey. He looked a different dog.

Johnnie remembered that Get-Lost would be hungry, too, and began to break off a piece of his own eggy bread. But the old man stopped him and said: 'Don't waste it on him, boy . . . I got him something of his own . . .' and he tossed down a large lump of meat with a bone at one end. 'Enders, the farmer calls it . . .' he said, chuckling. 'Meanin' it's the bit 'e can't sell and no-one at home will eat! Little dog'll like it, though . . .'

Get-Lost clearly did. He hadn't seen such a breakfast in years – if ever. In fact, breakfast didn't come into his way of life very often . . . or dinner, come to that. But life with Johnnie was entirely different. He had someone of his own, now, and with a special feeling of safety and affection there seemed also to be the added bonus of food and shelter. . . . He had everything in the world he needed, and he blossomed. He was indeed a different dog.

The boy, though, thought Charlie, looked downright ill this morning. There were heavy circles under his eyes, and his face was much too white . . . and he seemed to be a bit clumsy with his movements. . . . Though right now he didn't look clumsy. He was drawing something on a pad, and his hand moved swiftly and surely on the paper.

'Boy,' he said, 'you see that doctor today.'

Johnnie looked up and smiled.

'You hear me? Get to a doctor, see?'

Johnnie nodded. 'OK,' he said in a tranquil voice. He always felt calm and happy when he was drawing.

'Gotta go now,' said Charlie. 'Lorry'll be along soon. . . .' He pondered for a moment, fleetingly wondering if he ought to go with the boy. . . . But a lifetime of independence and solitariness made him decide against it. . . . Anyway, he was such an old scarecrow, he told himself, it wouldn't help the boy much, travelling with him . . . put people off, more like.

He got up from the grass and waited for Johnnie to join him. As an afterthought he disentangled a battered tin dish and a spare water bottle from his rattling collection. . . . He could easily spare them, and they might come in handy for the boy during his travels, especially if he was sleeping rough . . .

'Coming, boy?' he said.

The boy seemed to shake cobwebs out of his eyes and stood up, holding out his drawing for Charlie to take. 'For you,' he said, smiling.

125

The old man gazed at it with awe. It was him all right. . . . There was the tattered old coat tied up with string, and the awful broken boots, and his old motheaten cap . . . and all his pots and pans slung round his waist. . . . But the face, now – was that really him? The eyes looked very keen and piercing underneath all that bush of eyebrow and hair . . . and the chin – bearded but quite strong, somehow. There was a kind of – kind of friendliness about the face in the drawing that he rather liked. . . . The mouth, now – it was almost smiling, but not quite. . . . Not giving anything away too easy, like . . . and there was a hint of a little dog down there in the grass for him to be smiling at, if he wanted to. . . . He looked quite kindly really, and rather sort of wise with that bushy beard . . . not the sodden old wreck he thought he was, at all . . .

'Is that me?' he said, in a voice of wonder. He was somehow immensely proud of what the boy had seen in his face . . . what this amazingly observant kid had managed to put down on the sheet of paper . . .

'It's you,' said Johnnie, and put his pad and pencil away in his pocket. Then he turned back and added, shyly: 'It's a thank-you.'

The old tinker's eyes were a deal less piercing than usual. They appeared to be misting over, and he hastily brushed a smoky hand across them. 'Best get along,' he said, in a gruff, brusque kind of way. 'Mustn't miss the lorry. . . .' Then he added, almost as shyly as Johnnie: 'I'll keep this – careful like. . . . I got a good inside pocket for special things. . . .' He began to stow it away in one of the deep recesses of his tattered coat. 'Come on!' he said, more to himself than to Johnnie. 'Getta move on, then!'

Johnnie called Get-Lost over to him, and together the three of them walked downhill to the farm over the sun-dappled grass.

126

The lorry put him down in the yard of the big milk depot, just across the road from the docks. Johnnie stood gazing at a tangle of cranes, boats, containers, warehouses, heaped up crates and packages, and men moving about on little motorised trolleys, shouting instruction at one another . . .

He didn't like it much – especially the shouting. His instinct was to turn and run. But he mustn't. He'd got to find someone to ask about oil-rigs . . .

The lorry driver had given him a piece of string for Get-Lost. But he realised now that the little dog hadn't got a collar. . . . He would have to buy one, he supposed. It wasn't safe for a little dog here in all this shouting chaos. . . . It wasn't very safe for him either, but he didn't think of that.

He still kept seeing double from time to time, and he shook his head, trying to clear his vision and make himself take some kind of decision.

'Can I help you, son?'

It was a man in a tin-hat, carrying a sheaf of papers on a clip-board. He looked official, but not particularly forbidding.

Johnnie got out his photograph and showed it to him. 'Oil-rig,' he said, very carefully, and added as an afterthought: 'Engineer.' He pointed to Danny's smiling face in the middle of the group.

The man in the white tin-hat nodded. 'Your Dad, is he?'

'Yes.'

He tipped his tin-hat back and scratched his head thoughfully. 'If you wanted the rigs out at Ekofisk, you'd have to fly out from Aberdeen. . . . But if you wanted the refineries . . .'

'Refineries?' It was a new word to Johnnie. . . . He had just got used to oil-rigs. What was this new place?

127

The man saw his bewilderment. Since the boy was looking for his Dad here, it seemed to him obvious that the man must work at the refineries. He tried to explain. 'The pipe-line comes in over at Seal Sands . . . that's where the refineries are . . .'

'Where – is – that?' asked Johnnie, croaking a little.

'It's out the other end – ' The man broke off and said, sounding suddenly close and anxious: 'You all right, son?'

The ground was heaving oddly under Johnnie's feet, but he looked up into the man's face and smiled.

'Yes . . . which way?'

The smile had its usual shattering effect. The man looked as if it had hit him on the jaw. . . . He turned away from Johnnie for a moment and called over his shoulder: 'Jim? You taking the tanker back?'

'Yeah,' answered a voice from inside a warehouse door.

'Got room for a little 'un?'

'Yeah.'

'And a dog?' asked Johnnie, anxiously.

'And a dog?' repeated the man, smiling.

'Yeah,' replied the laconic voice.

A petrol tanker emerged, backing out. . . . But Johnnie did not hear it coming. He was bending over Get-Lost, trying to pick him up out of the way . . .

'Look out!' shouted the man in the tin-hat, and rushed forward to bang on the driver's cab with his fist.

Vaguely, Johnnie saw two little dogs, two men running, and a whole lot of trucks, lorries, cranes and ships' masts all weaving about before his eyes. . . . Then the ground gave an extra large heave and the sky came down to meet the earth, and he fell . . .

There was a squealing of brakes and a confusion of voices . . . a lot of people seemed to be shouting. . . .

Dimly, he heard Get-Lost barking – yelping in terror. The dog! he thought. Have I killed him as well? *As well?* The question seemed to grow in his mind.

But a voice was saying over and over again: 'Are you all right? Are you all right, son? Are you hurt?'

He opened his eyes and saw an anxious face bending over him. Two anxious faces, one with a tin-hat and one without . . .

'That's better. . . . Don't move yet. How d'you feel?' It was the man he had been talking to before. . . . Beside him, the tanker driver was bending down too, looking very worried. . . . The worried face became several worried faces, all looking down at him.

'Fell in a heap . . .' said a voice. 'Swear I didn't touch him. . . . I was backing out. . . . But I stopped . . .'

'The dog . . .' said Johnnie, faintly. 'Please . . . my dog . . .'

But there was no need to worry. A warm, wet tongue licked his face and a furry head came close, butting into his shoulder. He tried to sit up.

'Hold still,' said the tin-hat man. 'No hurry . . . take your time . . .'

Johnnie sat up. He saw the tanker pulled up close behind him, and several other trucks and cars (there really had been several!) all pulled up, with anxious drivers standing about beside them.

'I'm all right,' he said groggily. His voice sounded very loud and strange.

'Ambulance is coming,' said the voice of the tin-hat man.

'Better make sure,' added the tanker driver.

Johnnie looked at the last man who spoke. He was youngish, brown-faced and wearing oil-company over-alls. . . . He seemed much too concerned and distres-sed. Johnnie felt guilty about all the fuss. 'Not – not –

129

your – fault – ' he said, distinctly. Then, in sudden terror, he added: 'My dog? . . . ambulance? . . . I don't need . . .' and passed out again on the hard ground.

He came round on a bed with curtains round it. A man in a white coat was bending over him, looking at his head, and a nurse was standing at the other side.

'Ah,' said the doctor. (Johnnie knew doctors by now.) 'Come round, have you? When did you do this?'

Johnnie looked round wildly. 'My – my dog? Where's my dog?'

'It's OK,' said the doctor kindly, 'He's outside, tied up in the car park. The man who came with you saw to him.'

'Man?' said Johnnie, puzzled.

'Never mind . . . we'll sort that out later. . . . Suppose you tell me about this . . . you didn't do it today, did you?'

'No.' Johnnie tried to shake his head, but it hurt rather, so he stopped. 'Fell . . .' he said, trying to sound distinct. 'Fell – down – on – a – '

'On a broken bottle? Yes. . . .' His voice was dry. 'It's quite a bump you've got there, you know. Are you sure you *fell?*'

Johnnie looked at him. It was too difficult to explain, or to lie. He simply closed his eyes.

'Why didn't you get it seen to sooner?'

Johnnie sighed. 'Not – bad – enough – ' he muttered.

The doctor looked at the nurse and sighed as well. 'You got a name?' he asked pleasantly.

Johnnie opened his eyes and agreed that he had a name.

'Johnnie, then. . . . You'll have to give them all your particulars later. . . . I'll explain what's happening, shall I? You've had an x-ray, and we're waiting for the result. . . . Meanwhile, I'm going to put a stitch in that flap of skin. Stop it from waggling about and hurting you, see? Then we'll have a look at your x-ray. . . . You know what an x-ray is?'

Johnnie nodded. Since they began on his ears, he'd had plenty of those . . .

'And then, if there's no harm done, we'll let you go home – been seeing double, have you?'

Johnnie tried to nod, but the nurse was holding his head still. How did the doctor know about seeing double?

'Shut your eyes, Johnnie. . . . Now, stretch out your hand . . . and try to put your finger on your nose . . .'

Johnnie did not shut his eyes at once. He had to wait till the doctor had finished speaking. How else would he know what to do? He had got used to listening hard to the doctor's demands, to following their instructions carefully and trying very hard to do what was required of him. He had been given some quite complicated tests to do with sound equipment, instrument panels with coloured lights, and earphones and lettered knobs to press. This request seemed easy.

But all the same, try as he might, his finger wavered about all over the place and could not find his nose.

He opened his eyes, defeated, and saw the doctor nod, smiling at him.

'It's all right, Johnnie . . . you tried . . . don't worry . . .'

In a little while, they had finished with him, and he was told to go and sit on a bench and wait for his x-ray results. Meanwhile, they said, someone would come to take down all his particulars.

While he was waiting, he thought he heard Get-Lost barking. Could it be? So far away? Or were his ears playing tricks? He got up and went outside to look for him.

131

Nobody stopped him or asked where he was going. The little dog was sitting forlornly beside the hospital casualty entrance, tied to some railings, and every time anyone came out or in he barked hopefully, asking them where they had taken his master.

'I'm here,' said Johnnie, interpreting those barks. 'It's OK. It's me . . .' and he bent down to comfort the little dog and stop his frantic barking. Then he saw that he was tied up with a real dog's lead and a real dog's collar was round his neck. 'Where did you get those?' he asked. 'Don't you look smart!'

Get-Lost agreed, slurping happily.

Then the words of the doctor suddenly went into Johnnie's foggy mind. 'They'll come to take your particulars . . .'

'Come on, Get-Lost,' he said, 'We're getting out of here – ' and he untied the dog's lead and walked away with him out of the hospital car park. There was green grass opposite, across the big road. It looked like a large, shady Park. It reminded Johnnie of his sanctuary at home. Instinctively, he made for it, and Get-Lost padded beside him. He like Parks too.

Behind him, the worried young tanker driver came back from his cup of tea out of the machine and went to ask in Casualty how the boy was getting on. The reception clerk was just getting the form out for Johnnie to have filled in.

'He's over there,' she said. 'Waiting for his x-ray results.'

'Over where?' asked the tanker driver, seeing no-one.

'Well, he was there a minute ago,' said the clerk, not very concerned.

The tanker driver went swiftly to the entrance where he had left the dog. That had gone too.

The doctor was called, and he came in waving an x-ray

plate and looking as harassed as Casualty doctors usually looked. 'Gone?' he said. 'Who let him go?'

'Is that his x-ray? Is anything wrong?' asked the worried young man.

'No – o' said the doctor slowly. 'No skull fracture. . . . But the boy has mild concussion . . . he should be resting at home, not roaming the streets . . .'

'Maybe I could catch him up – ' said the young man, feeling responsible, though he was not. 'He can't have got far – '

'Here, wait a moment – ' began the doctor.

The reception clerk added plaintively: 'We don't even have his full name . . .'

But the young man was already bounding down the Casualty Department ramp into the car park. . . . His tanker was pulled up not far away, for he had followed the ambulance to the hospital, wanting to make sure the kid was all right before he reported back at the depot. . . . But now he thought his heavy vehicle would be a hindrance rather than a help, so he rushed to the outer edge of the car park and stood looking up and down the road. No-one was in sight who looked remotely like a small boy with a dog. . . . But just across the road in the Park he thought he caught a glimpse of someone like him disappearing down a leafy path.

He crossed the road and started off after him. He didn't know why he felt responsible. . . . As the boy had said, it wasn't his fault . . . the kid had just passed out with concussion at his feet – or at his tanker's back wheels. He hadn't touched him – or the little dog. He was lucky, really. . . . But even so, he felt that he ought to do something. The kid was obviously sick and needing help. As the doctor said, he oughtn't to be wandering about on his own . . . he couldn't let him go off without a word . . .

All this crossed his mind as he walked rapidly after the fleeting shadow he had seen. Now, suddenly, he saw the boy and the dog ahead of him, walking slowly, as if not quite sure where to go. . . . He decided the best thing to do was to cut across the path ahead of him and wait for him to arrive. He didn't want to frighten the kid, so he took a few large strides across the grass and round a flower bed and came out on the path ahead of Johnnie. He stood there, smiling, hoping he didn't look too alarming.

'I thought you might like a lift somewhere?' he said, as Johnnie came up to him.

Johnnie looked alarmed. 'Not – back to the hospital?'

'No, no. . . .' It was clear he couldn't make him go back in there. The doctors must have scared him somehow. 'They said you were OK. Just needed a rest. . . . That's why I thought . . . maybe you shouldn't walk too far. . . .' He hesitated, watching the doubt and distrust fade from the boy's astonishing blue eyes. 'Where do you want to go?'

He saw the boy frown, achingly, as if trying to remember. 'The . . . refinery?'

'Yes,' the young man nodded encouragingly. 'That's where I'm going anyway . . . I was going to give you a lift there, remember?'

Johnnie agreed. He looked down at Get-Lost. 'And – the – dog?' He thought he remembered that the young man had agreed about Get-Lost before.'

'Yes, he can come too . . . He's safe enough now!'

Johnnie remembered the new collar and lead, and he remembered his manners. He touched the brown leather collar with appreciative fingers. 'Did you – ?'

The young man smiled. 'Oh no. That was the ambulance men. They keep one or two for emergencies. . . . When accidents happen, there's often a dog left running loose.'

134

Johnnie understood that. His brief, brilliant smile flashed out. 'Thank you – for – taking care – of – him. . . .' It was a long sentence for him, and his voice sounded gruff and odd again.

Jim, the young tanker driver, gazed at the boy for a moment in astonishment. Then he said, quite briskly: 'Well – we'd better be moving, then . . .'

Together, they retraced their steps to the main road. But here Johnnie refused to go back into the hospital car park. He and Get-Lost waited at the side of the road till the tanker came round through the exit gate and paused to pick them up. Dizzily, Johnnie climbed in, and Get-Lost climbed in after him and perched on his knee.

'How did you hurt your head?' asked Jim, changing gear at the traffic lights.

'Fell down . . .'

'You ought to go home and rest, you know. Does your mother know you're out?'

Johnnie nodded. 'Yes.' That was true. Julie did know he was out.

'Why do you want the refinery?

'See my Dad,' said Johnnie. He hoped that was true – oh, he hoped it was.

This time Jim nodded, seeming satisfied. If the kid was going to meet his father, everything would be all right. He could set him down in the main car park beside the central block and go on to the tanker depot round the side. He was hours late already. He would have to do some explaining. . . . But an accident was something one had to deal with. . . . Thank God he hadn't actually run over the kid. . . . Fortunately, the foreman at the depot was human – so long as the deliveries were done in the end . . .

He slowed the tanker and drew up in the main car park. There was a fleet of jeeps parked there, and a whole lot of sleek-looking cars. Money, he thought! Oil means money!

'This do?'

'Smashing,' said Johnnie – and suddenly laughed. It was a strange, hoarse kind of laugh, and it rather startled Jim. He turned to Johnnie and laid a hand on his arm.

'You know, I don't even know your name?'

'Johnnie.'

'Then listen, Johnnie . . . I know I didn't have anything to do with you falling down. . . . But you take care, now, see? Don't go rushing about. . . .' He reached into his pocket and brought out one of the Company customer cards. 'See here, my name's Jim Adams. . . . You can always get me here at the oil depot . . . the phone number's on this card, see? If ever you need any help, Johnnie, I'll be around . . .'

Johnnie smiled.

'And tell your Dad, the hospital says you're to rest!'

'Yes,' agreed Johnnie. 'Thanks for the lift – and – and everything!' The smile came again, briefly, leaving the pale face curiously grave and sad. The boy and the dog got out of the cab and stood on the car-park forecourt. When the tanker pulled away, Johnnie waved and the little dog gave one final bark of farewell.

I believe I'm haunted, thought Jim. I shall never forget that kid's face. I wonder what was up with him? Wish I could have done something about it. . . . He drove on, and soon work engulfed his doubting mind.

Johnnie and Get-Lost stood looking around them. The huge storage tanks of the refinery towered above them on the skyline, and one very tall chimney spewed out a thin stream of flame. Below the circular tanks was a motley collection of buildings, machinery, pipelines, gantries, storage warehouses and garages, and a long, central office building with an imposing entrance. In front of this entrance, to one side, stood a large notice board with two big maps on it. Johnnie decided to go over and investigate.

He stood on the tarmac, a tiny figure below those towering storage tanks, and looked up at the two maps side by side on the long display board. One map was of this particular refinery, showing the different departments, the tanks and where each road went. But the other was a map of the British Isles with the oil rigs, pipelines and refineries marked on it in large red letters, each of them with a Company sign beside it and a small flame representing the oil that came out of the North Sea . . .

Johnnie looked at it, appalled. For there were dozens – no, probably hundreds – of oil-rigs, and the North Sea was simply huge. It stretched all the way round the top half of the map. . . . Why, near Ekofisk, which Tin-Can-Charlie had mentioned, there seemed to be at least fourteen rigs . . . and there were some more up beyond Scotland in the farthest part of the North Sea. And some further east, half way to Norway. . . . The whole thing was vast . . .

Painfully, Johnnie remembered how he and Dessie had drawn a little man dancing in the sea, wearing a furry parka . . . and how he had thought in those far-off days that North was a smallish place somewhere near Scotland, with only one oil rig in it where everyone worked, and he would easily find his Dad once he got there . . .

But this – this enormous expanse of water, and all those rigs and refineries and pipelines . . . how would he ever begin to look for a man called Danny who was always laughing?

'What's the matter, son? World too big?'

Johnnie turned and found himself looking into a pair of friendly, intelligent grey eyes which were staring at him intently, almost with a faint hint of recognition in them.

He swallowed tears and said slowly: 'Yes . . . too big.' How did this man guess what was troubling him? Then he brought out his photo and held it out, adding despairingly: 'My Dad . . .'

The man looked at it attentively, and then turned it over and read the names on the back. Something seemed to change in his face as he read them, and he glanced swiftly at the boy before him. Then he called over his shoulder to a group of men coming across the car park towards him: 'Hey, fellas – come and have a look. Isn't that Danny Ross? Wasn't that his team on the pipeline installations?'

Another man leaned over and looked at it. 'That's right. Tom Blackie and Nick Price. . . . They went to West Ekofisk, I think. Didn't they, Reg?' He turned to a third man behind him. An excited babble of conversation broke out among them.

The first man said gently, looking at the blond head and tired, luminous smile: 'So you're Danny's son, are you? And you're looking for him, eh? Don't you know where he is?'

Johnnie shook his head sadly.

'What made you think he'd be here, son? This is a refinery. He works on the rigs.'

It was almost impossible to explain. Miserably, Johnnie tried; 'They said . . . down at the port . . . try the refinery . . .'

'I see.' He looked at Johnnie searchingly, puzzled by the whole set-up. 'What's your name, son?'

'Johnnie.'

'Johnnie Ross . . .' he mused. 'D'you live here, Johnnie?'

It was Johnnie's turn to look puzzled. 'No.' Then, thinking it out: 'I came north . . . to find him . . .'

All at once, with the realisation of the vastness of his search and the new knowledge that his photo was actually of a real, live man who did exist and was called Danny Ross, Johnnie's eyes filled with tears and he did not know how to hide them.

Frank, the oil-rig engineer from Aberdeen, was used to Company engineers working for long stretches away from home. . . . It did not seem all that odd to him that Danny Ross's son should come looking for him. . . . Only, it *was* odd that he didn't have an address or know where to look. 'Come to think of it,' he went on talking half to himself, 'he did talk about his wife and son . . . and how he couldn't get home often enough. But that was – 'he shot another glance at Johnnie, 'some years ago. . . .' He suddenly noticed Johnnie's tears and his tired, confused smile.

'Tell you what,' he said, 'would you like a ride out to the airport? We're all going to take the charter flight back to Aberdeen . . .'

'Aberdeen?' Johnnie sounded totally bewildered.

'Look,' said the man patiently: 'We'll have time to talk in the jeep . . . and it can bring you back wherever you want to go afterwards. . . . We'll keep the plane waiting if we hang about, and I would like to help if I can . . .'

Johnnie couldn't follow all this. He was becoming increasingly muddled and exhausted. But he smiled dimly at the man, and tried gamely to keep up.

The man blinked. 'Listen,' he said, 'my name is Frank. And this is Reg. We used to work with your Dad long ago . . . you struck lucky, kid. . . . Now come on, climb in with me and tell Uncle Frank all about it.'

Before Johnnie could say anything, the little party

swept him along with them into a nearby jeep and started off with a crunch of tyres through the main gate. Johnnie found himself next to the man called Frank, with Get-Lost between them.

'Nice little fellow, that,' said Frank encouragingly. 'Now, tell me all about it. . . . Let's start at the beginning. You're Johnnie.'

'Johnnie – Ross,' he said, trying it out with shy pride.

Uncle Frank nodded. 'And you've come up to find your Dad. . . . Where from, Johnnie?'

'South,' said Johnnie, and tried in vain to sound convincing.

'Just south – nothing else?'

'I – wanted to see him . . . about s-something s-special . . .' Johnnie always stammered when he was very tired.

'Something special, eh? So how did you get here?'

'Hitched . . .'

Uncle Frank looked impressed. 'By yourself?'

Johnnie shook his head. 'Me and Get-Lost.'

The little dog had been curled up very small between them, but hearing his name, he thumped an eager tail and sat up straight.

Frank looked down and laughed. 'Well, bless my soul! A boy and a dog hitching together, all the way from the south to Teesside! How about that!' Then a thought struck him. 'Does your mother know?'

'Yes,' said Johnnie. 'She knows . . .'

After he had explained as much as he could about his journey up to Teesside and his search, there was a lot of discussion among the engineers which he could not follow. He was very weary by now, and his head felt tall again. But he tried not to let himself doze, in case he missed anything important. The jeep was running busily along a main road by now, and things flashed by too fast

140

for him to see what they were, or where he was going. But he did catch a glimpse of a sign with an aeroplane on it and the words: 'Teesside Airport'.

At length, Frank turned back to Johnnie and spoke gently to him again. 'We came down here as a team to do some work on the pipeline, and now we're going back to headquarters in Aberdeen. That's where all the records are, and where we get told where we're going next. Understand?'

By turning his head to look intently at Frank as he spoke, Johnnie had got most of this. He nodded, silently.

'Good. Now, do you want to stay here in Teesside, or do you want to go on looking for your Dad?'

Johnnie looked at him in amazement. 'Go on, of course,' he said, distinctly.

Frank smiled at him. 'Don't sound so indignant! I was only trying to find out what you wanted! Now, see here, Johnnie boy, we think you should come to Aberdeen with us on the plane, and maybe I can find out where Danny Ross is from the records at Company Headquarters when we get there? How d'you like that idea?'

Johnnie's answering smile was even more dazzling than usual. 'Fly? In a plane?'

'Why not? I expect we can fit you in . . . you're only a little 'un!'

'What about him?' asked Johnnie, glancing anxiously at Get-Lost.

Frank grinned. 'If you think you can keep him quiet – the pilot's a friend of mine – he's not fussy!'

Johnnie was straining to catch his words. 'Keep him quiet' seemed to be the essential ones. 'Yes,' he said firmly. 'I can.'

The jeep turned into the approach road to the airport, skirted the terminal buildings and came to a halt by a group of other jeeps near to one end of the runway. A small plane was waiting for them out on the tarmac, and the engineers all piled out of the jeep and began walking towards it, still talking.

Johnnie had a chance at last to look at them more closely. Frank was a sturdy, sunburned man, with thick iron-grey hair and very bright sea-blue eyes that saw a long way off. . . . He walked with his feet very wide apart, rolling a little, like a sailor, and he seemed to exude confidence and strength. So did the other engineers – they all seemed the kind of men who would be good in emergencies – but Frank did most of all. . . . Johnnie felt very safe all of a sudden . . .

The other engineers all had very sunburned faces, and now Johnnie noticed that several of them had the most crazy hats on: one had a cowboy stetson, and another had a Mexican sombrero; one had a jutting chin and smoked a fat cigar under a peaked golfer's cap; and another had a weatherbeaten face and chewed gum all the time. . . . It hadn't really occurred to Johnnie that people came down to the oil refineries and pipelines from all parts of the world, in order to see the installations . . . but now he suddenly realised that besides Frank and Reg who had actually been working on something there, these others were visiting Americans or Mexicans, or that very fair blue-eyed one might have come over from Sweden. . . . From other oil-rigs, he thought dreamily, and one of them is probably the one where my Dad is . . . only they don't know it. . . . He felt very tired, but almost content at last . . . after all, Danny had a name. He was Danny Ross, and he was real. . . . And he, Johnnie, would find him somehow . . .

He stumbled a little with weariness, and Reg turned to him and took him by the arm. 'Hold up, son! Frank's just asking if we can take you with us . . . I expect he can wangle it. Frank's good at wangling!' He laughed comfortably, and Johnnie tried to join in, though he didn't hear the joke.

Presently, Frank came back, smiling. 'That's all right, then . . . but you've got to give the little dog a sedative pill, in case he gets too excited. . . . Can you manage that?'

Johnnie understood that. He produced Tin-Can-Charlie's tin dish and said: 'If I could get some water . . .'

'I'll get some,' volunteered Reg, and disappeared into a nearby hut.

'I daresay a biscuit might help it to go down as well,' said Frank, finding a packet of stale ones in his pocket.

Get-Lost indicated in no uncertain terms that biscuits were just what dogs liked. Reg returned with the water, and Johnnie held Get-Lost's mouth open and pushed the pill down his throat. Get-Lost gulped indignantly, and then accepted a biscuit with alacrity. After this, he had a noisy, slurpy drink, and Johnnie took him purposefully round the nearest tree.

The engineers watched him, smiling among themselves.

'He's very like Danny,' said Frank, in a bemused voice.

'Isn't he, though,' agreed Reg.

They all climbed aboard the little plane, and Frank showed Johnnie how to fasten his seat belt.

'Ever flown before?'

Johnnie shook his head.

'Don't be frightened at take-off – or landing, come to that! Matt's a good pilot, and it's perfectly safe! Once you're up, you'll enjoy it. . . . You can look out of the window from that seat. . . .' He settled down beside

143

Johnnie, once more spreading calm and confidence around him. He turned to Johnnie again seriously before the engine of the plane got too loud and added: 'When we get to Aberdeen we'll find out where Danny is working, and we can probably get a message to him. Don't worry!'

'No,' said Johnnie vaguely. And then, suddenly alert again, he looked into Frank's face and asked shyly: 'Why?'

'Why what?'

Johnnie waved his hand at the plane and Reg and the other engineers, and tried to include a ride in a jeep and biscuits for Get-Lost and Frank's concern and kindness in the overall sweep. 'All – this?'

Frank smiled at him. 'I knew your Dad, remember . . . you're rather like him!'

'Am I?' Johnnie was very pleased. His father had a good sort of laughing face and fair hair that blew in the wind . . . Johnnie didn't know that his own pale face was far more beautiful and far more disturbing than the one in the photo – or that his blond head was somehow far more distinctive even than his father's . . .

The other passengers were all on now, and settling themselves cheerily. One of the cowboy hats got on, and the Mexican sombrero, and they seemed to be busy slapping friends on the back. There was a lot of laughter and back-chat. Johnnie couldn't follow their quick remarks, but when one of them smiled at him and gave him a thumbs-up sign, he smiled back.

The noise of take-off was rather awful, especially for Johnnie's ears, but it seemed to get better once the plane was in the air. The vibrations disappeared, and they seemed to be floating almost without movement above the land. . . . He looked down, and already the airport looked tiny and he could see the sea, and the shape of

144

the coast all the way up north towards Scotland. . . . He could see little fields and hills and miniature cars and lorries going along thin ribbons of roads . . . and even ships making white wakes in the sea . . .

The flight fascinated Johnnie. There was so much to see, and the world looked so different from above. . . . But even so, he had got out his pad and pencil, and his hand was not idle. . . . He sat on, half-listening to the men talking and half-dreaming, and all the time his hand was setting down Frank's kind, steady smile, and the Mexican sombrero and the cowboy hat, and little Get-Lost's furry shape curled up in a tight ball of alarm beside him . . . and the strange, light view of clouds outside the window . . .

At last the plane came down and landed him on another strip of flat grey tarmac. He thought he and the plane and all the passengers would shake to pieces as they taxied in, but they didn't. Frank climbed down and led the way to a cluster of terminal buildings. Little Get-Lost, who had been both terrified and half-asleep all through the flight, now felt a lot better, but Johnnie still had to carry him. Dyce Airport was cold and windblown but at least it was land!

Frank settled Johnnie and the little dog in a kind of waiting room, and brought him a cup of hot, sweet tea and a sandwich from the machine. The other engineers all dispersed, calling out goodbye to each other and to Johnnie – all except for Reg, who said he would wait with Johnnie while Frank made some enquiries.

Reg was a quiet man who didn't talk much. He let Johnnie be, eating his sandwich and drinking his tea, and lit a cigarette and sat peacefully beside him.

Presently Frank returned, his blue eyes looking slightly troubled as they rested on the tired boy before him.

'I've got through to Personnel at Headquarters,' he said.

Johnnie looked up at him, his eyes alight with hope. He did not quite catch those two long words, but he understood what Frank was telling him.

'Danny's not on Ekofisk now, son . . . though he was for several years. . . . They think he's gone north to the Shetlands.'

Johnnie gazed at him, straining to catch the sense. 'North to. . . ? Is that a long way?'

Frank nodded. 'A very long way . . . almost as far as you've come. . . . But your Dad's name is definitely on the register of engineers at Sullom Voe . . .'

This was too difficult for Johnnie. 'At . . . S – ?'

'Sullom Voe. . . . That's as far as I can get down here.' His eyes flicked to Reg for a moment, signalling unknown things.

'Can't we ring through to Sullom Voe to make sure?' asked Reg, right on cue.

Frank agreed. 'That's just what I'm going to do now. . . . It'll mean hanging on a bit longer. . . .' He hesitated, and then added to Reg in a quiet undertone: 'Were you going on leave now?'

'I was. Why?'

'How would you feel about an extra spell of duty up at Sullom Voe?'

Reg shrugged. 'Suits me – if you can wangle it. . . . And if Danny really is up there?'

Frank laid a kindly hand on Johnnie's arm. 'Be patient, Johnnie. I'll see what else I can find out.' He strode off again, leaving the two of them to while away a few more empty minutes. Reg bought Johnnie another cup of tea, and a packet of biscuits for Get-Lost.

At last Frank came back, and this time there was a distinct spark of mischief in his eyes. 'All right. We're going up to Sullom Voe on another job. How does that appeal to you?'

Reg grinned. 'World's best wangler, you are.'

Frank grinned back. 'Job wanted doing. I volunteered. The bloke I spoke to up there says Danny is definitely around somewhere.'

'Well, that's good news, isn't it, Johnnie?'

The boy nodded, by now speechless with hope and weariness mixed.

'So,' went on Frank, still with a hint of mischief about him, 'as the charter plane's going on up there anyway, I thought we'd take some spares along. After all,' he smiled at Johnnie with enormous kindness, 'we can't let Johnnie go all that way on his own, can we?'

'Sure can't,' agreed Reg laconically. But he was smiling, too.

Johnnie had struggled to keep up with all this. Now he said anxiously: 'Where – are – we – going?'

'To Sullom Voe. That's another pipe-line and another refinery. . . . Right up in the Shetland Islands. . . . You're certainly going to see the world, Johnnie. Come along, it's time we went.'

Without waiting to see if Johnnie or Reg were following, Frank strode off again, back the way he had come, until he came to the charter plane which was still waiting on the run-way. The three of them climbed back in, with Get-Lost showing some reluctance.

'It's all right,' said Johnnie. 'Noise won't hurt . . .'

But it did, of course. It hurt his ears and his injured head terribly this time at take-off. . . . But as the plane climbed over the sea, the sound diminished again, and the vast expanse of blue-grey North Sea was so beautiful that Johnnie forgot about pain altogether. . . . Get-Lost had burrowed his way inside

147

Johnnie's brown jersey, and that was warm and extremely comforting. . . . Like a sensible dog, he went to sleep.

The sudden changes of colour, the shadows and strange patterns of currents in the sea below him enthralled Johnnie. He had never realised the sea was so big – so varied and ever-changing. He remembered the south coast sea he had been to with Dessie . . . blue and sparkling by day, and silver and full of magic by night . . . it had not looked quite like this . . . not cold and grey and choppy and huge. . . . But it had been deep and pure when he swam in it . . . deep and green like glass under the waves by day . . . and almost black at night . . .

Sharply and very clearly, he wanted Dessie beside him. He could feel her hand in his, strong and confident, pulling him to safety . . . he could hear her voice on that last night saying urgently, forcing him to hear her: 'No-one can take it away! It's all yours . . . for ever – see?'

I wish I could talk to Dessie now, he thought. . . . She'd never believe all this! I would like to see her again . . . soon . . . but my Dad will put things right. . . . He found his eyes blurring as he gazed down at the sea. . . . He was actually nodding off, half-asleep . . . how could he waste this marvellous adventure of flying over the sea by falling asleep! He sat up with a jerk and had another look. . . . It was still there, grey and limitless . . . with wrinkles in it that were waves, and tiny flecks of foam. . . . The plane droned on . . .

At last it came down on yet another strip of tarmac, on the airport at Sullom Voe. And again Johnnie's ears hurt like fire as the plane landed and the vibrations shook him. . . . But this time it was close to the sea, and a strong wind was blowing which smelt of salt and seaweed and an indefinable tang that was mixed with snow and herbs and sunshine, and to the experienced traveller, Frank, was simply the smell of the North.

To Johnnie it was strange and exciting, but he didn't know how to describe it. . . . Smells meant a lot to him, and so did colours. . . . Since one sense was blurred to him, the others took over and were extra strong and extra sensitive.

'Is this north?' he asked Frank, sniffing the sharp, cold air.

'It sure is,' said Frank, smiling. 'Very north. . . . Up there, beyond the Shetlands, is nothing but sea and ice to the North Pole . . .'

'Come on,' said one of the ten-gallon-hats. 'Chopper's waiting.'

Frank saw that Johnnie was shivering a little in the sharp wind, so he took off his own fur-lined jacket and draped it round Johnnie's shoulders. Not to be outdone, the American engineer came up to them and dropped his ten-gallon hat over Johnnie's head. It nearly swamped him, and everyone laughed.

He was too bemused and tired by now to wonder what was happening next. The party all moved across the tarmac to where a helicopter stood waiting. After a small amount of parley between Frank and the pilot, Johnnie and Get-Lost were allowed to get on with the rest of the party. Get-Lost was still rather dopey from his tranquilliser pill, so he did not make much protest, but even so the pilot told Johnnie to hold him very tight, especially on take-off and landing. Everyone was settling themselves down cheerfully on the cross-benches, laughing and chatting among themselves. Another of the cowboy hats got on, greeting friends noisily as he came. . . . The safety regulations were explained with great care, even though most of these men were apparently always travelling about like this. . . . They all had to try on their life-jackets, and the pilot said a lot of things that Johnnie couldn't hear. But he got the general idea. If they ditched in the sea, the chopper would float till a tug came and towed them in. . . . If they broke up, there were the life rafts. . . . But if anyone fell in the sea, it was terribly cold, especially out where the oil rigs were, and they would probably die in minutes. . . . No-one lived long in the North Sea up here . . .

Johnnie wondered what Get-Lost would do. He could swim, but how long could a dog last in cold North Sea water? He shivered.

Frank's voice said, comfortingly close to his ear: 'Not out to the rigs this trip . . . no need to worry. . . . We're going across the Mainland up to Sullom Voe. All the same, everyone's got to know the drill . . . OK?'

Johnnie smiled and nodded. He trusted Frank. If he said things were OK, they must be. Little Get-Lost burrowed deep inside Johnnie's borrowed jacket and trembled. . . . Would this journey in the sky never end?

When the chopper blades began to turn and they took off, the noise was rather awful, and the shuddering vibrations were terrible, but it seemed to get better once they were airborne. The shaking vibrations disappeared, and they seemed to be hovering (still noisily) over the little stony fields and crofts, almost like a large and clumsy dragonfly . . .

Johnnie looked down and saw sea on three sides, and a long stretch of land ahead, with low, peat-dark hills and tiny flocks of sheep, and never a single tree in sight. . . . There were little silver bays and inlets, even inland lochs and thin silver ribbons of streams, and on some of the beaches there were boats drawn up, and in some of the bays there were boats out fishing. . . . There were very few houses, though – Frank told him they were called crofts, the old ones – and the people who worked on the land were still poor and had to work very hard to make a living . . .

The chopper passed over a number of small villages and one or two towns, and even quite a large one that seemed to be a fishing boat port. . . . But Johnnie was getting very tired now, and his dazed mind failed to take in everything he saw . . .

Reg was sitting close to him, the other side of Frank, and he now leaned forward and held out a thermos cup of coffee. 'One of the blokes back there sent it up to you,' he said, grinning. 'Thought you looked peaky!'

Gratefully, Johnnie gulped down the hot coffee. It was very sweet, and it made him feel better at once.

'Won't be long now,' said Frank, and gave his arm a gentle squeeze.

They came down at last to the helicopter pad on the edge of the big oil terminal. Johnnie had already seen the huge storage tanks on the skyline, and the tall chimneys with their small plumes of flame. . . . But now he saw the beauty of Sullom Voe, with its deep water inlet looking dark against the sun, and its wide, curving shape with the bare, peat-covered headland behind. . . . On one side, all was peace and empty, quiet shores. . . . On the other . . .

He found himself looking at the two lives of Sullom Voe, and what the oil had done to these lonely islands. On the one hand there were soft-coloured hills rising above the long, slender stretch of still water – on the other there was the pipeline coming ashore, the vast oil storage tanks, and jetties, wharves, cranes, and buildings, and big ships and little ships, supply ships and support ships and tankers, all sailing in and out of the narrow straits to and from the port. . . . This side of the Voe seemed black and forbidding, harsh in the clear light and full of all the wrong shapes for the steep sides of

151

the Voe, and the ancient stony fields and little crofts and small, pale beaches of The Mainland. . . . He looked at it all, and shivered a little in the wind.

'It brings them work, and money . . .' said Frank, interpreting the look on his face.

Johnnie nodded. His Dad was part of this busy, restless scene of round, black silhouettes and raw new buildings. . . . Maybe he had even helped to bring the pipe-line to this shore . . . he ought to be proud of it, really. . . . But somewhere deep behind his eyes he could still see the unbroken line of hills beyond Tin-Can-Charlie's smoky fire . . . and the way the grass seemed to wash against the treetrunks in a green tide down near the stream at the bottom of the valley. . . . And he remembered his vision of the bulldozers gobbling up the green like hungry monsters. They'd done it up here, all right. . . . Except that the land wasn't green . . . it was brown with peat and scoured with sea winds, bare and stony and strong . . .

He felt very confused. He was in the midst of all the work his Dad loved . . . he was even near to finding his Dad at last. . . . And all he could do was feel a kind of sadness because the little cottages looked so small beside the giant oil containers . . . small, like toys – like doll's houses which a large, careless foot could easily tread on and break . . .

'Come on,' said Frank, 'you're tired, son. . . . Best get out of the wind while I ask some more questions . . .'

Once again the kindly Reg took charge, while Frank went off. There was another waiting room, and another plastic beaker full of tea from the machine.

'It's been a long day for you, Johnnie,' said Reg, looking at the dark shadows under the boy's eyes. 'Have a rest till Frank gets back . . .'

Johnnie sat back on his hard chair and closed his eyes. . . . Would they really find his Dad? Was he here, in this grey welter of oil buildings? Or was he somewhere far away on a rig, miles out at sea?

When Frank found the man he had spoken to on the phone from Aberdeen, he said without preamble. 'Where's Danny Ross, then?'

The other engineer looked a bit vague and replied cheerfully enough: 'Oh, he's around somewhere . . . saw him a couple of days ago . . . I'll ask . . .'

But before he could move, another voice spoke from across the room. 'Did you say Danny Ross? He's been sent down to Milford Haven, didn't you know?'

'When?' said Frank, finding himself suddenly exasperated. The second man came out from behind the desk he had been sitting at and said pleasantly enough: 'Oh – about a week ago. . . . Wanted to find his wife and child down south, or something. Got a special posting. Took his crew with him and all.'

Frank swore softly. All this way! he thought. All this way, and now Danny Ross is the other end of the country! The poor kid!

When he got back to the two of them, he stood looking down at the boy with pity. He looked so weary, and so frail, sitting there. . . . And the news he had to tell was not what the kid wanted to hear. He glanced at Reg, whose enquiring eyebrows had shot skywards at his approach. Faintly, he shook his head.

Johnnie opened his eyes, feeling a shadow in front of him. He saw Frank's face, and his own expression became one big question.

'He's not up here after all, Johnnie. . . . Seems the man I spoke to was wrong. Your Dad got sent down to Milford Haven about a week ago.'

Johnnie was straining desperately to follow Frank's

quick, decisive speech. A week ago? A *week* ago? *Where?* 'Mil – ?'

'Milford Haven . . . in South Wales. . . . Seems he was looking for you, son.'

Johnnie gazed at him, astonished. 'Looking for me?' He heard that, very clearly.

Frank nodded emphatically. 'Wanted to get down south, he said . . . to find his wife and kid. . . . So he got himself posted to Milford Haven. . . . The trouble is – ' He glanced at Reg again, uncertainly, and then back to Johnnie, 'we're on a job up here, now. . . . We can't leave again till its done. . . .' He paused, thinking it out. 'We could keep you with us, of course, and take you back to Aberdeen . . .'

'How far is it?'

'Milford Haven? A long way, son. . . . As far as you've come, and more. . . .' Frank's calm, friendly face was sober at the thought of all those miles, and the small gallant boy beside him. All those long miles – a hopeless wild-goose chase, all for nothing. . . . He felt very guilty, somehow.

'Do – choppers go there?'

Frank shook his head. 'Not from here. . . . You might get another plane from Sudburgh tomorrow . . . it's mostly ships that go to Milford Haven. . . .' He had spoken without thought, but now the significance of his words suddenly hit him.

Johnnie had turned to look at the busy quayside. There were two long tankers tied up out at the ends of the jetties, and a support ship with its forward super-structure looking almost top-heavy was nosing its way into its berth. . . . And there was another big tanker going away from them, gently chugging its way out of Sullom Voe to the open sea beyond . . .

Looking for me? thought Johnnie. My Dad, looking

for me? It made him feel very tall. He ought to hurry up and find him, then . . . not keep him waiting. . . . He ought to get down to this place Mil – something . . . wherever it was . . .

'Could I . . . go on a ship?'

Frank looked at him. 'Alone? I think you really ought to stay with us . . .'

'But if my Dad's gone to M – ?'

'Milford Haven . . . yes.' He was still looking at Johnnie, in a doubtful, summing-up sort of way.

'Do ships go there . . . every day?' His voice was growly, but he got it out clearly enough.

'All the time . . .'

'Is one going *now*?'

Frank sighed. The boy was really very determined in a quiet sort of way. . . . He couldn't help admiring him, even if all this travelling about wasn't very good for him, and highly irregular.

'Oh come on, let's give the kid a break,' said Reg, smiling a little at Frank's anxious face.

'All right,' Frank made up his mind. 'Let's go down to the quay and ask . . .'

Little Get-Lost was a bit confused. First they were on land, in a country of lovely rabbity smells. . . . Then they were in the air in something that shook and made a lot of noise and felt very unsafe indeed. And then they were down again on land, and then up again in the air. . . . And now, at last, they were safe on land again, but with no time at all to explore, and everything smelling of oil and paint and tar, and an occasional whiff of sea which he couldn't recognise at all . . .

Johnnie by now was getting extraordinarily exhausted and light-headed. Except that his head felt heavy, not light. It had been a long, strange day, and the air trips had made his head hurt more than ever. He stumbled a little as he went down to the edge of the jetty, and Frank stopped kindly and waited for him.

'There's one thing about it,' he said, smiling a little, 'if I can get you on a tanker, you can sleep for three days if you like. . . !' His smile was kind, and Johnnie, remembering that his own Dad was looking for him somewhere down south, stood up straighter and smiled back.

After a certain amount of chat and cheerful argument, Johnnie and Get-Lost were allowed on board a large, flat-decked tanker with iron railings and a streamlined bridge section and after accommodation at the stern . . .

'It's a Company tanker,' said Frank, 'and you're Company Personnel, see?' He grinned at Johnnie and gave Get-Lost a friendly pat on the head. 'And he's a Company Dog,' he added, his grin getting wider. 'I've told the Captain who you are,' he went on. 'And when you get to Milford Haven, someone'll take you to the Company Offices. . . . They'll know where your Dad is. . . . Do you think you'll be OK on your own?'

Where your Dad is . . . that came over clearly to Johnnie's tired ears. . . . He nodded and smiled. 'Yes . . . thanks . . .'

He wanted to tell Frank how marvellous the flight was . . . those patterns on the sea, and the shape of the land below him . . . the ride in the jeep, the cups of tea, and all Frank's careful questions and telephone calls. . . . He always seemed to be trying to thank people for all sorts of things he couldn't put into words. He felt helpless somehow in the face of Frank's kindness – and Reg's, come to that. . . . All he could do was smile and murmur: 'Thanks!' again. But Frank seemed to understand for he smiled back and patted him on the shoulder. Then, feeling the thin shoulder under his hand, he added quietly: 'Keep the jacket. It may be cold on deck!'

156

'I drew this . . .' said Johnnie, and held out his drawing which he had done on the plane. He had drawn Frank's head, his profile calm and alert, and beside him the wide window of the plane, and below it a tilted, distant landscape of fields and hills, a wandering coastline and a wide, darkening sea . . .

'Why – that's beautiful!' exclaimed Frank, pleased. 'You even got in the cowboy's stetson!' And sure enough there was a hint of it behind Frank's head, and a roundish, cheerful face with a big wide mouth carrying a fat cigar. . . . There was Reg there, too, and one ear of a cowering, frightened little dog . . .

'Don't miss much, do you?' he said, laughing. 'Be good now. Keep out of the way. Don't fall overboard. And get some sleep. OK?'

'OK,' said Johnnie. 'I'll tell my Dad . . .'

'Tell him what?'

But Johnnie couldn't think how to say it. He just gestured graphically at the big tanker and Sullom Voe, and the sea and the sky, which was beautiful and clear as a thrush's egg . . . and murmured 'Everything . . .'

Frank understood. He gave the boy a brief hug, and clambered back on to the quayside and waved a casual hand. The patient Reg, who was waiting for him, also raised a hand to Johnnie in farewell.

'Goodbye!' he called. 'Good luck!'

Johnnie waved back. But he did not call out. He had said all the thanks and goodbyes that he could.

Frank turned away towards the quayside buildings, and Reg fell into step beside him.

'I wouldn't mind a boy like that myself!' said Frank.

Reg grunted. 'A boy who'd do all that to find his father is really something,' he agreed.

'Look at this!' Frank held out the drawing. 'The kid's a real artist!'

Reg looked at it with interest. 'My God, that's you!' He sounded as surprised and delighted as Frank had been. He chuckled. 'And that's me, isn't it? And Roly . . . and those two guys from the States. . . . Well, look at that!'

They examined the drawing again, and laughed together. Then Reg said, curiously: 'How come the kid doesn't know his Dad's address or anything?'

Frank sighed. 'I didn't like to ask, in case I upset him. . . . They're separated, I suppose. . . . A lot of oil-rig marriages go on the rocks! I think I did hear something . . . but I thought it was Danny looking for his wife and kid, not the other way round. . . . Perhaps I got it wrong. . . .' He sounded faintly puzzled. 'I'm sure he said she walked out on him . . .'

'Maybe she did. . . . But you were obviously right about Danny looking for them. . . . I suppose it's only now when the boy's old enough to do things on his own that he's managed to come looking . . .'

'Maybe . . . there's something odd about it, though . . .'

'I s'pose his mother does know about it?'

Frank looked troubled. 'He said so . . . somehow I don't think the kid's a liar . . .'

'No,' Reg was thoughtful. 'He didn't say much. . . .'

Frank laughed. 'Definitely a boy of few words. . . .' He thought of that strange, growly voice with its odd, slightly monotonous tone, and pondered. Was there something wrong there? But the boy was so intelligent and so appreciative. . . . 'Maybe he was just shy . . .' he said.

Reg nodded. 'Plenty of spunk, anyway. . . . I hope Danny Ross is down there when he gets there.'

'So do I,' said Frank.

He and Reg strolled on. They might as well get a lift in

one of the Company landrovers down to Brae, and
spend a comfortable night at the hotel. . . . He thought
of Johnnie and the dog, spending their first night at
sea . . . they'd be well looked after, though. The skipper was a good sort of bloke who didn't mind an odd pas-
senger or two. . . . And the crew were a good bunch,
too . . . the boy would be in safe hands . . .

By the time Frank had had a couple of drinks in the
hotel bar, he felt better about the whole thing . . . the
kid would find his Dad all right down at Milford
Haven. . . . Everything would work out. . . . But it
might be a good idea to ring the depot at Milford Haven
when he got back. . . . After all, it was his fault the kid
came all the way up here in the first place. . . . But in the
meantime, maybe he'd have another drink.

'Come on!' said Reg. 'Stop worrying! He'll be all
right.'

'Of course he will!' agreed Frank, and raised his glass
to a distant Johnnie on a darkening sea. 'Safe journey,
Johnnie!' he murmured. 'And a happy ending!' The
boy's smile haunted him . . .

'There's a spare bunk in here, boyo,' said a burly seaman
in a dark blue jersey, opening a small cabin door below
decks in the tanker's after accommodation. 'You doss
down here, see, you and the little tyke. . . . No-one'll
bother you down here. . . . And if you want to go up
top, keep to the after deck, mind. . . . The main decks
are often under water on a tanker, see? You wouldn't be
safe on the cat-walks on your own, let alone with a dog!
Wouldn't be allowed, see? You get some sleep,
boyo . . . you look as if you could do with it!' His smile
was friendly, thought Johnnie, and his eyes crinkled up
with a mixture of good humour and mischief when he

spoke . . .

Thankfully, Johnnie sank on to the neat small bunk, and Get-Lost curled up beside him without more ado. Weariness had at last caught up with both of them, and Johnnie could barely summon up a tired, transparent smile in answer to the seaman's kindness before he sank into oblivion . . .

The seaman, who was already beginning to take a personal interest in this mysterious Company Boy who had been wished on to him, had a look to see that he was comfortable, and then tiptoed heavily away.

Johnnie was so far down into sleep that he didn't even notice when the tanker actually got under way. It was still standing quietly at the jetty when he first dozed off, but some time later he stirred long enough to hear the engines thrumming quietly in the settling dusk. . . . There was no real night at this time of year up at Sullom Voe . . . only a lessening of light after sunset, and then a slowly increasing glow towards sunrise . . .

Some time about two in the morning, Johnnie woke to see a sky aflame with dawn, and he crept out of his bunk and up on to the after deck to have a look. The long, low tanker was slipping quietly through the waters of Sullom Voe, making a smooth v-shaped wake behind, and a small white frill of surf at her prow. . . . Across the Voe, the dark outline of The Mainland coast reached down to a gentle sea already stained with the faint rose of dawn. . . . Above it, the sky seemed immense and pure, washed with every shade from palest gold to deepest crimson, with flamingo wings of cloud above the low, bare hills . . .

The boy was enchanted. He stayed there a long time, huddled in Frank's furry jacket, with Get-Lost curled against him for warmth and comfort. . . . But when the sun had finally climbed up over the dark eastern side of

Yell Sound, behind the hills and the oil tanks, Johnnie felt sleep wash over him in an irresistable tide, and he slid down on to the deck, happy to sleep out under those wide skies. . . . He sank deeper into sleep with every breath, until the ache had gone out of his head, and the tiredness out of all his limbs. . . . He lay spread out and quiet, with the dog curled up beside him, and one hand stretched out to grasp reassuringly at a furry black and white ear . . .

The burly seaman, stepping lightly along the deck as sailors do, found the boy there and carried him back to his bunk. . . . The dog followed anxiously, not very happy about this new kind of moving world he was on, and leapt up beside the boy at once, determined to stay close. . . . But Johnnie was fathoms deep by now, sleeping the sleep of exhaustion, and he did not stir.

'You stay there now,' said the seaman to the dog, 'and look after him, see? He's safer down here . . .'

Get-Lost winked a brown eye at him and promptly went to sleep, too. Satisfied, the seaman went off on his original errand, wondering what it was that had brought the boy up on deck . . .

The voyage from Sullom Voe to Milford Haven was a godsend to Johnnie. To begin with, he could rest all day and do nothing but gaze at the sea, which he loved. . . . And then, it was blessedly quiet, except when they passed another ship and let the deep voice of their siren salute her . . . and even that noise didn't hurt like the plane or the helicopter take-off. . . . This noise was low and rich-sounding and somehow exciting . . . it spoke to Johnnie of busy ports and foreign seas, and big ships taking the tide, and great voyages of exploration, and coral reefs and palm trees and far, far horizons, and distant, fading shores. . . . When the voice of his ship, the tanker *Marie Lou* out of Sullom Voe beating round the grey Scottish coast-line down towards Wales and Milford Haven, let out that deep, vibrating sound – all Johnnie's dreams and adventure stories and half-forgotten books that had once thrilled him seemed rolled into one . . .

He was Drake, sailing forth to conquer the world – he was Captain Hornblower, – he was Sir Walter Raleigh and Nelson, and at the same time he was a boy called Johnnie, alone with his dog, setting out on a big adventure . . .

The sea enthralled him. He could never have enough of watching it, every curve, every cresting wave, and every swirling eddy was different from the last. The colours merged and melted and changed as he watched them – blues and greens and purples, great heavy chunks of dark water gliding steadily past him, sometimes almost black as he looked down, and sometimes so pale and clear that he almost thought he could see the bottom . . .

The weather was calm and clear, but even so there was a choppy wind when they came out into the open sea, and a certain amount of swell built up. . . . He didn't mind. . . . The ship felt like a horse under him, moving gently over the small hills and valleys of water, as if engaged in a gentle, ambling canter. Now and then, perhaps, it might have to lift a little higher, as if to waft quietly over a small fence . . . but Johnnie could feel its strong, balancing steadiness under his feet on the deck, and he unconsciously swayed to it, like a rider encouraging his fine, spirited race horse. . . . Only of course, it wasn't a race horse, or a finely-balanced yacht sailing close to the wind . . . it was a heavily loaded, slow-moving tanker, wallowing sluggishly in the busy shipping lanes between one oil port and the next . . . .

Johnnie didn't care . . . to him it was a yacht – a three-masted schooner – a great liner – a Greek trireme – a Viking raider – a tall tea clipper crowded with sail. . . . It was everything he wanted, and he was, for a little while, entirely free and happy . . .

Get-Lost wasn't so sure. There was no grass and no trees on this moving contraption, and the floor didn't keep still very well. . . . But he was a philosophical little dog. If his master was content to live on a kind of floating skating board, it was all right with him. Only, when he dared to look over the rails, there seemed to be an awfully big pond out there . . . much bigger than the lake in the Park. . . . It didn't look safe at all . . . so he kept very close to Johnnie, and did not pull on his lead or try to go off on his own and investigate. . . . Now and again, Johnnie remembered he might be scared, and put out a hand to reassure him. That was enough for him.

Meals seemed to come round pretty often, by Johnnie's reckoning, and he was taken down to sit with the small crew and eat whatever they were eating. It was mostly very good, and when he shyly brought out Tin-Can-Charlie's dish for Get-Lost, they cheerfully filled it with scraps. In fact, the little dog became rather like the ship's mascot, and they all made a fuss of him.

At night, though it was never very dark, the crew gathered in a little group to play cards, sometimes below decks and sometimes up on top, and someone usually strummed a guitar. Once or twice they all joined in when the strummer reached a familiar pop song chorus. . . . And once the burly seaman who looked after Johnnie sang a sad song in a lilting Welsh tenor. . . . Johnnie couldn't always hear the guitar's notes, unless he bent his head close to the vibrating sound box – but the pure Welsh tenor voice crept into his ears and sang there all by itself . . .

Johnnie drew nearer. 'What's the song called?'

The burly man turned to him and smiled. ' "The Ash Grove". . . . It's an old Welsh song – ' He grinned at the circle of faces round him. 'Too good for these boyos!'

'Are you a singer?'

The man laughed. 'Good grief, boyo, no! I'm a plain ordinary seaman. . . . Welsh as a leek and working on a Scottish-built tanker owned by an American company with oilports all over the world. . . . How's that for hands-across-the-sea?'

Johnnie couldn't catch all that. ' – American?'

'Surely . . . an American oil company, is it? And you're a Company Boyo, so I'm told . . .'

A Company Boyo? Was he? Johnnie stood tall. His father, Danny Ross, was a Company Engineer . . . so that made him a Company Boyo, he supposed . . .

'Going to see your Da, is it?' said the Welshman, smiling at him.

Johnnie nodded.

'It's a powerful way to come, for a little 'un,' he glanced over the side at the darkening sea. 'Not that you're that little, mind!' He grinned. 'Expecting you, is he?'

For a moment, Johnnie hesitated. Then he remembered Frank saying: '. . . he was looking for you, son . . .'

'Yes,' he said. 'He is.' And smiled, with radiant certainty.

The Welshman blinked. 'Well – there now! Company Boyo Johnnie, and his Company Dog. What d'you call him?'

'Get-Lost.'

He went off into a shout of laughter. 'Hey, fellas, what d'you think the little tyke's called? Get-Lost! How d'you like that!'

164

There was a general warm buzz of laughter. But John-nie did't mind. It sounded friendly enough. Even so, he put out a hand and rubbed at the dog's ears, just in case he was offended.

'Mine's Jack really,' said the Welshman, offering Johnnie a piece of rather sticky chocolate. 'But they call me Tonsils Taffy – because I will keep singing, see?' He laughed again, and Johnnie understood that he was clearly saying: Never mind us laughing. My nickname is as silly as your dog's . . .

'Tonsils Taffy,' he said slowly, trying it out. 'Could you . . . sing another song?'

'Could he sing another!' exclaimed one of the crew, and the others all groaned loudly. 'He's always singing another!'

But the guitar-player began to strum again and put his head close to Tonsils Taffy's for consultation.

Then Tonsils Taffy stood up and turned his face towards Johnnie and sang 'David of the White Rock'. And somehow the song seemed to be about Tonsils Taffy and all singers, and all strummers of guitars on lonely tanker decks at night under the stars, and all small boys and their dogs who might be listening, enthralled, while in the midst of a most perilous and frightening adventure . . .

'Sing, brave harp, sing . . .' sang Taffy, and the guitar strummed like mad, just as good as any harp, 'Thy brave heart beats . . . in the songs that we sing!' sang Taffy, lifting up his strong, beautiful voice to the stars. 'Through all the ages that echo shall ring . . .'

Yes, thought Johnnie, hearing it with total clarity. . . . That echo shall ring . . . I shall always hear it. . . . He looked up into the face of Tonsils Taffy, glimmering at him in the half-dark. It looked strange and remote, like all the faces of the Welsh bards through all

165

the long ages of spellbinding Welsh song. . . . He would never forget it – or the song that it sang . . .

'Thank you,' he said.

The journey to Milford Haven took two nights and two days. Johnnie watched the coastline of Scotland receding, and small islands coming into sight ahead and then disappearing into the mists astern, and the changing, deepening colours of the water as they headed out into the real Atlantic Ocean. He watched the seabirds flying up and settling in white drifts on the cliffs as they passed, and how some of them followed the ship and sat happily on the sea, riding the waves. . . . He marvelled at all the new things he saw. . . . He had no idea the world was so big, or the wide Atlantic so powerful and so full of rich light and shade . . .

The quiet sea had done wonders for his head and his damaged ears. . . . He felt tranquil and clear-headed, and the bump where the bottle had hit him had gone down and no longer hurt him. . . . The noises in his ears had subsided a lot, too, and he found himself almost following the conversations round the table at meal times. . . . He even managed to catch the jokes sometimes and laugh with the crew . . .

There were one or two extra engineers going down to Milford Haven, too, but they slept in the spare engineers' cabins and ate with the Captain and his two officers, so Johnnie didn't see much of them. Though if he met them strolling about the deck, they always smiled at him and his dog, and occasionally called out: 'All right, son?'

Yes, Johnnie would say. Yes! I'm all right! I've got somewhere warm to sleep, and plenty to eat, and no-one's shouting at me . . . and I'm going to find my

Dad. . . . I'm all right . . .

He watched the sea change colour again as they went close to the Mull of Kintyre, with the coast of Ireland a faint line (so someone said) on the seaward horizon. . . . And down they went into the North Channel and the Irish Sea, with the seabirds crying ever louder as they came down the coast of Wales, and the deep blue-green water of the Atlantic faded into the silvery greys and clouded amethysts of the coastal waters near the end of their journey.

Presently, he saw the gentle Welsh headlands closing in as they nosed into Milford Haven Sound, and the wide grey sea disappeared behind the line of hills astern. . . . Before him was a smooth, silver expanse of water, with several long wooden jetties running right out into the bay from either shore. At the furthest of these lay a long super-tanker, tied alongside the T-shaped jetty, discharging her oil into the pipe-line which ran ashore to the refinery on the hill beyond. Johnnie noticed then that there were tall chimneys and oil storage tanks set in clusters on several of the surrounding headlands, and one or two of the slender chimneys had small tongues of bright flame coming out of the top. Strangely enough, though, they didn't look very out of place, or even very ugly, placed carefully in the dip of the headlands – even the tall dark chimneys were not very big or obtrusive, seen from a distance . . .

Beyond the jetties, Johnnie saw a number of smaller boats and trawlers making their way in and out of Milford Haven harbour, which was crowded with small ships and cranes, especially in the inner dock where the fishing fleet tied up and the busy fish market still flourished. . . . Even further on, he could just see Pembroke Dock which was full of quite big shipping and a lot of small boats chugging busily in and out. . . . But out here, approaching the nearest jetty, it was calm and quiet, and there was a little curved horseshoe bay with a lot of small boats pulled up on the shore, and a yacht club with a boatyard in front of it . . . he could even see a few old men sunning themselves on benches in front of the clubhouse . . . .

The jetty they were approaching ran out from a low, reddish cliff, with one or two big houses on it, and Johnnie could just glimpse yet another collection of oil refinery buildings, storage tanks and tall chimneys, away over the other side of the headland.

Johnnie watched the smaller ships and trawlers and the little motor boats bustling in and out of the harbour beyond . . . and he watched his own big tanker move gently across the quiet water towards the jetty, marvelling at the skill which brought the huge long ship into its berth alongside the jetty with no fuss at all – only a gentle bump and a clanging of bells and throwing of ropes, and a rattle of windlass and cable as she was tied up.

The vast grey cylinders of the oil storage tanks at the refinery on the headland stood crouched against the sky-line, and there seemed to be an awful lot of pipes and tubes and cable running along the narrow length of the jetty from the tanker to the land. It was like Sullom Voe, only the Sound was wider and bigger and busier . . . and the other side didn't look so quiet and empty and strange as The Mainland in the Shetlands . . .

They had to wait a long time for security clearance – at least that was what Tonsils Taffy told him. . . . Oil was a precious cargo, he said, and a dangerous one. No little boats could come near, no visitors, no jeeps along the jetty until the cargo was safely discharged into the pipeline. No-one could smoke, no naked lights of any kind could be allowed near the ship. . . . But if anyone was not wanted in the off-loading process, they were allowed to walk off the ship and along the jetty to the shore . . .

'See then, Company Boyo, seems I'm the one to take you to the Company Offices. . . . Will you come along with me, then?'

Johnnie followed Tonsils Taffy over the gang-plank on to the T-shaped jetty. At the last moment, Get-Lost got panicky when he saw the gaps between the wooden jetty and the water beneath, so Johnnie picked him up in his arms. It was a long, echoing walk along the thin path of the jetty from the deep sea tanker berth to dry land . . .

They went through a blank-looking security gate at the end of the jetty, and once they reached solid earth, Get-Lost looked apologetic about his fright and allowed himself to be put down on all four feet. He trotted along behind them politely, not pulling on his lead, though the smells were most distracting.

There were a couple of small green jeeps pulled up by the security gate, and two or three of the people from the tanker got into one and roared away down the road. Tonsils Taffy stopped to consult one of the drivers.

'You wait here, see, boyo. . . . The Captain, he said he'd talk to head office for you . . . he's got to report in anyway when the oil is discharged, see? So maybe he'll take you up to the offices himself . . .'

He left Johnnie standing in the private road beside the security gate while he checked with the driver about further instructions. Then he came back, smiling. 'Orders is, I take you down to Mr Harris's house . . . that's the big house just here, see? Mr Harris is the Personnel Officer – and he'll come down to see you, isn't it? Aren't you the lucky boyo?' He laid a friendly arm around Johnnie's shoulders and led him down a short sandy path curving round the cliff-top to where a big, raw, new red-brick house stood squarely in its own sparse grounds on the inner edge of the headland above the little horse-shoe bay.

There was a porch and a verandah on the seaward side of the house, and here Tonsils Taffy paused and waved an expressive hand at the expensive patio tables and chairs placed strategically in the sun to overlook the bay and the calm, silver sea.

'Make yourself comfortable, he says, boyo . . . it may be a bit of a wait for you. . . . Will you be all right now?'

Johnnie nodded. He was busy trying to get out his latest drawing without crumpling it. He held it out to Tonsils Taffy shyly, without speaking. He had learnt by now that this was the only satisfactory way to say thank you – and people seemed to like it. . . . He could always draw them something that would please them. But this one – this one – he had put his heart into . . .

There was the small circle of men, lounging in comfortable, lazy attitudes on the deck . . . with the abandoned hands of cards left lying in the middle. . . . And there was the guitar player, his head bent over his instrument, and his fingers curled caressingly over the strings. . . . The light gleamed a little on one edge of the guitar and one side of his face . . . he looked intent and happy. . . . And there, standing with his head thrown back, proudly singing, was Tonsils Taffy, balancing lightly on his toes to the movement of the ship, and his bush of wild Welsh hair streaming back from a forehead as noble as any Welsh bard's, and a strange, ecstatic look on his face as he sang about David of the White Rock to one enchanted boy . . .

'Di-ew, is that me, boyo? Tonsils Taffy? You've made me look like a grand Welsh tenor at an Eisteddfod! Look at that, will you! Why, boyo, you're an artist!'

He was extraordinarily touched by the drawing . . . there seemed somehow to be a strange power about it. . . . He could feel the song – the whole broad sweep of it as he sang – and the sudden surge of certainty and glory in his own voice when he knew he was singing well. . . . There was knowledge in that drawing – and love. He could see now the blanched, still face of the boy looking up at him when he had finished singing . . . and he could hear the small, pulsing silence all round him before the spell was broken. . . . There was, when he came to look at it, a darkish mass in front that might be a boy or a dog, looking up at him. . . . But all the light and all the glory was centred on his singing, uplifted, ecstatic face.

'Boyo,' he said in a shaken voice, 'there's music in this drawing, look you. . . . It's magic!'

Johnnie heard that. He smiled. 'Yes,' he agreed, remembering the sound of that beautiful clear Welsh voice singing to the stars, '. . . magic!'

He waited a long time, alone on the verandah. He began to wonder if they had forgotten all about him. Below him, in the little horse-shoe bay, he could hear the voices of children shouting now and then, and an occasional loud barking from a dog . . . and once or twice he heard the sharp call of a tug out in the Sound. . . . But for the most part it was quiet, and the house behind him, for all its red brick opulence seemed empty and cold . . .

But at last a car drew up in the drive, and a man got out and came towards him. It wasn't the Captain of the *Marie Lou,* but a tallish, grave man in a city suit. He looked at Johnnie very kindly, but there was something about the troubled expression in his eyes that made Johnnie go cold. He was used to looking at faces to get some kind of clue about what was going on. This one spoke clearly to him. Something was wrong.

171

'Didn't anyone look after you?' exclaimed the man, sounding worried already. 'I thought my wife was at home . . .'

Johnnie looked at him attentively. He did not speak. There did not seem to be anything to answer yet.

'So you are Johnnie Ross?'

He nodded.

The man sat down in one of the patio chairs beside him. 'I'm sorry to sound doubtful, Johnnie. But what I have to tell you is a serious matter. I must be sure I am talking to the right boy. Danny Ross's son?'

Johnnie drew out the photo and handed it to him. The man looked at it for a long time, and from it to Johnnie's face, and then slowly turned it over and read the message on the back.

'Where is your mother now, Johnnie?' He spoke quietly.

'She's – at home. With the kids.'

'Kids? She has other children? Are they Danny's, too?'

Johnnie shook his head. 'No. Big Joe's.'

The man was silent for a moment. He was looking down at a sheaf of papers in his hand. 'It says here,' he explained carefully, 'that he married Julie Cass, your mother, in 1970 – is that right?'

Johnnie nodded again, but less certainly. He didn't know what was required of him. But he supposed that was true.

'How old are you?'

'Twelve,' he said.

Brad Harris, the Personnel Officer, smiled at him encouragingly. So Danny married her a year after the boy was born, he thought. That figures. And in spite of that, she runs off with someone else and has several other children. . . . Danny said she was feckless . . .

172

feckless and faithless. . . . But the boy doesn't look like that. . . . Aloud he said: 'Does your mother know you've come to look for your Dad?'

Johnnie hesitated. 'I – yes, she does.'

'Why do you think she has been so long about telling him where she was?'

The boy looked puzzled. 'I – I don't know.' That was true, too. He had never understood why Julie would not talk about his father, would not tell him where he was, or even who he was. . . . It was a mystery . . .

'You see, Johnnie, he was looking for you. He tried everywhere he could think of to find you. He even got himself transferred down here so that he could be nearer to the Midlands, where he thought you were. . . . He even went to the police about it . . .'

'The police – ?' Johnnie's heart thudded.

'To try to trace you.' The man smiled at him with much compassion. Johnnie was afraid of that smile. 'He wanted to see you, Johnnie. He wanted to get to know his boy. . . . He was proud of having a son like you . . .'

Wanted? thought Johnnie. *Was* looking for you? What does he mean?

'Is your mother on the telephone?' asked Brad Harris suddenly.

Johnnie shook his head.

'I think I really ought to write to her first . . .' went on the man, sounding even more worried and indecisive. 'Perhaps – perhaps you should go back home now, Johnnie, and – wait to hear from us . . .'

Johnnie looked at him. He had come hundreds of miles by land and sea and air to see his Dad, and this man wanted him to go home? He said slowly: 'He is my Dad. . . . I've come – to – see – him. . . .' Then he stood up and tried to look very tall. 'I am a Company Boy,' he said.

Brad Harris stared. He was terribly shaken by the

173

boy's sudden dignity. Also, he knew Danny Ross, and the likeness was unmistakeable.

'If – it – is – bad – news,' said Johnnie, suddenly understanding the man's awkwardness and the kindness in his smile.

The man put an arm round his shoulders and drew him down again beside him on the smart patio chair. 'Listen, Johnnie – '

They always say 'Listen!' thought Johnnie, struggling to catch every word. What do they think I'm doing?

Harris went on carefully and gently, trying to explain something totally awful and impossible. 'I am what's known as the Company Personnel Officer. My name is Brad Harris. . . . I knew your father well – and I liked him a lot. . . . It was my doing that he got transferred down here. He asked so particularly to come back down south to find you. . . .' He sounded as if he was blaming himself for something. Even Johnnie's ears picked up the note of grief and self-accusation behind it. . . .

Brad took a deep breath. He was a kind man, and this was very difficult and all wrong. He ought to be talking to the wife, not to a pale, beautiful twelve-year-old boy already strung with a dignity and endurance beyond his years.

'In our profession, Johnnie – the oil rigs and pipeline installations – there are a lot of very dangerous jobs. . . . The sea is dangerous, the winds are dangerous, and all the work on the rigs and the underwater pipelines are dangerous. Even the oil itself is dangerous. You must have noticed all the safety precautions on the tanker, didn't you?'

Johnnie nodded.

'Your father worked with a team – this team – the one you have on your photograph. . . . They came down with him to Milford Haven and went to work on the explorations off the coast. . . . In his team, two of them worked "in the wet" and one on top. Danny was the top man. They had a boat, and what they call a submersible. . . . But a few days ago, while working, there was an explosion under water. . . . One of them, Tom Blackie, got into trouble. Something fell on him. His air line got jammed and he couldn't get it free. . . . Nick Price tried to help him, and got snarled up too. So Danny went down in the submersible to find them . . . he got an airline to Tom Blackie and got him to the surface, where the rescue team were waiting. . . . Then he went down again for Nick. By then, Nick was in bad shape and his air line was broken. So Danny had to get out of the submersible himself to free Nick and get a new line to him. . . . In the end, he gave Nick his own airline. . . . We got Nick up safely . . . but Danny. . . .'

He looked at the boy beside him in despair. How did you tell a boy that his father was lying dead, unrecoverable, under half a ton of rock at the bottom of the sea?

'I – I'm afraid – Danny didn't make it.'

The boy was quite silent, staring at him.

'He was quite a hero, Johnnie. . . . Do you understand? He saved two men – his own mates. . . . But – the explosion caused a rockslide, you see . . .'

Johnnie said at last, in a strange, detached voice that sounded like ashes: 'Danny – Ross – is – dead?'

Brad Harris swallowed anxiously. 'I'm sorry, Johnnie. Yes, he is.'

He wondered what he ought to do next. . . . Somehow he'd got to get hold of the mother . . . and keep the boy safe until she arrived. . . . There wasn't much you could do about grief. . . . But you could see to the practical things . . . there would be papers to sign, and money to hand over, and a funeral to arrange, he supposed. But there was something else that he ought to do

175

for the boy that was beyond all that. . . . Somehow he ought to be able to break through that stony silence . . . but he didn't know how . . .

'Will you tell me your mother's address, Johnnie? We can send her a message, you know. . . . She'll be able to come and fetch you home . . .'

Home? thought Johnnie. I can't go home. . . . I came to ask my father what to do . . . and now I shall never know the answer. . . . I came to find a man called Danny who was always laughing and who used to toss me up in the air and sing to me. . . . He was a Company man – a brave man, they said, a hero. But I wanted to talk to a real live man with a laughing face and bright gold hair who they said looked like me. . . . They said he was proud having a son like me . . . and I was proud of having a father like him. . . . And now I shall never know him . . . I shall never know what he was really like, and whether he really wanted me for his son.

'When – ?' he asked slowly.

'Three days ago,' said Brad Harris, feeling helpless and inadequate before this dry-eyed, quiet boy.

I was only three days too late, thought Johnnie. . . . All that way, all those miles, and I could have come straight here if I'd known . . .

'Your mother –' repeated Brad, afraid of that careful calm. 'If you could – ?'

Johnnie closed his eyes. His throat felt too tight and he couldn't swallow. The earth seemed to heave and sway round him. Danny Ross is dead, it sang to him, and his ears heard it all too clearly. Danny Ross is dead . . .

'Hold on – ' said Brad Harris's voice, alarmed now. 'I'll get you some tea. . . . It's all right, don't worry. We'll look after you –'

Dimly, Johnnie heard him go. The silence he left behind him seemed huge. It roared in his ears. Danny

Ross is dead, Danny Ross is dead, said the silence. . . .
Slowly, he remembered where he was and what he must
do. . . . He couldn't bring more trouble on his mother
now . . .

Brad Harris was a kind man, and he hurried into the
house and put the kettle on. . . . He came back,
anxiously and swiftly, balancing a cup of tea in one hand.
But when he got there, the boy was gone.

PART III
The Summerhouse

The inquest took place on a cold, raw spring morning three days after Dessie's stormy visit to Julie Cass. The day was grey, the court was grey, and Julie Cass was grey with fright.

But it was mostly a formality. Julie stood up in the shabby courtroom and said yes and no in a sullen voice when required to do so. She recounted in a flat tone how Big Joe had come in, weaving on his feet. How he had shouted at her and come up the stairs after her. . . . And just before he reached her with the bottle in his hand raised ready to strike, he had seemed to trip and fall sideways, crash through the banisters and tip himself headlong down on to the floor below . . .

The doctor explained about the cerebral haemorrhage. The police explained about being called to the house, along with the ambulance. . . . They didn't explain who had called them, and nobody thought to ask. . . . Sergeant Mackay looked searchingly at Julie, but did not ask a single question about Johnnie. Not then. The verdict, as he expected, was death from natural causes . . . not even accidental death . . . the doctor's evidence was too precise. . . . Sympathy was expressed for Julie and her children, left fatherless . . .

179

Questions were asked, however, outside the courtroom, about the children and whether they were back in care or not. Maggie was obliged to explain that they were still with their mother, Julie, now that the period of risk was past. . . . And in any case, they all wanted to stay where Johnnie. . . . Too late, she realised what she had said. Ah! The bright young local reporter pounced. The eldest boy – Johnnie – the one who had got so badly beaten up before. Was it true then that he had gone missing?

Then, of course, the news was out. Locally first, and then nationally. Sergeant Mackay decided that a general police call was not enough, and he had better talk to the media. He wanted, like everyone else, to get the boy safely home . . . best to get the public alerted as well, they might be a great help. . . . He told them how badly Johnnie had been beaten up before. . . . He said the boy might have seen something of the final violent episode and run away in terror. . . . He was a good boy who had been used to looking after his own brothers and sister. . . . He would not run off without cause . . . or without *thinking* he had cause. . . . And he was deaf as well, and probably confused. . . . He was very much a child at risk, who needed help. . . . If anyone saw him, would they please report it to the nearest police station. And if Johnnie himself was able to watch the telly or to read a paper or listen to a radio, he wanted to say to him: 'Come on home, Johnnie. Everything is all right now, and your family need you.'

He repeated this final remark several times. Johnnie's picture – albeit a rather blurred one – was flashed across the screens and splashed on the front pages of the next day's newspapers with the words: *'Have you seen this boy?'* shouting at everyone who saw it . . .

Maggie was interviewed too, and she repeated

Sergeant Mackay's words: '*Come on home, Johnnie, it's all right . . .*' Bill Hamilton was also asked to give his impressions of Johnnie. He was, he said, an extremely gifted and intelligent boy whose whole future was overshadowed by constant ill-treatment resulting in serious partial deafness. . . . He needed medical care, surgical intervention, and a lot of help and special education . . . and he was getting none of it while he was on the run. . . . He had never been led to believe that anyone would help or understand him. Please God, someone would now . . . please God, someone would find him and persuade him to come home before some further tragedy befell him . . .

'Do you think,' said the far-too-knowing interviewer, 'that something *has* already happened to him? That he never actually ran away at all?'

There was a long, anguished silence. Then Bill Hamilton replied in a low, firm voice: 'We believe not. . . . There is no point in assuming the worst . . . to us, he is just a lonely, frightened boy who has run away.'

Dessie, watching this interview on telly, nodded her approval, and then went storming round to see Bill Hamilton and said: 'Get me on that box! I want to talk to Johnnie. He might listen to me!'

It was not difficult to arrange. By now the story was becoming news and the search was nationwide. It seemed impossible that one twelve-year-old boy could vanish so completely. Dessie, hair as wild as ever, appeared on the screen, looking directly into the cameras.

'Johnnie,' she said slowly, 'if you can hear me, come home! Me and Maggie and the Painting Man are all here. We'll look after you. Nothing to run for, Johnnie. D'you hear me? *Nothing to run for!* This is Dessie speaking to you. Please come home!'

181

The television crew were touched by her insistence and sincerity. So were the viewers.

But Johnnie didn't come home.

Meanwhile, Dessie had also tackled Julie. Sergeant Mackay had encouraged this, knowing Dessie might do better than he would at getting some facts out of the girl. He still didn't see what Julie was afraid of, but Dessie would find out.

She did, and some very strange facts emerged.

Yes, the boy's father was called Danny. Danny *who?* Danny Ross. Yes, he was an oil-rig engineer, working on pipeline installations. The last time she saw him he was working on Ekofisk, or was it West Ekofisk? She couldn't remember. Yes, (sullenly) he had married her . . . after the boy, Johnnie was born. . . . The house they had lived in was his. He paid her a good allowance . . . he was quite generous. He came home on leave when he could, but she was alone with the boy a lot and couldn't go out, so she got bored. . . . So when Big Joe came along and asked her to go with him, she just went. . . . Yes, she kept it quiet and didn't leave any address, in case Danny Ross wanted his son back . . .

'But,' protested Sergeant Mackay, when Dessie reported this to him, 'I thought Maggie Fraser told me Julie was married to Big Joe?'

Maggie, who was also there listening to Dessie's revelations, met the girl's eyes in a look of mutual despair. 'Yes,' she agreed. 'That's what she told me . . . but we never actually saw a registry office entry, did we? Or any marriage lines . . .'

'Well, let's hope it wasn't bigamy as well as everything else!' He sighed in disbelief. 'So there was no legal tie? Then why did she stay with him?'

Maggie shrugged. 'Why *do* women stay? She seemed to be hypnotised by Big Joe. . . . And then there were the children . . .'

Sergeant Mackay was thinking it out. 'No forwarding address . . . a new name in a new town . . . I suppose no-one ever caught up with her. . . . And Johnnie?'

'Registered in her name – Cass – before the marriage to Ross. . . . He never knew his father's name at all –'

Dessie said suddenly: 'Johnnie told me Big Joe used to call him No-name Johnnie and tell him he didn't belong to anyone – that's why he wanted to find his Dad.'

'Yes,' said Sergeant Mackay sadly: 'I see.'

He did see. They all saw. They all, in their several ways, saw a picture in their mind of a small, lost boy wandering through an uncaring world alone, looking for a father who would own him and protect him . . .

'I could wring her neck!' said Dessie, through her teeth.

'Dammit,' exploded Sergeant Mackay, 'he's *got* to be found! He must be somewhere!'

The first person to respond to the publicity and report in was Bedford Bob, the long-distance lorry driver. He had gone up north, delivered his load, picked up another, and was on his way back when he heard it on the cab radio. He stopped at the next town and went into the police station.

'I don't know if it was him,' he said. 'But he said he was going to see his Dad . . . and he did this drawing. . . . You can borrow it now, but I want it back!'

Tin-Can-Charlie never listened to radios or watched telly, and he never bought a paper. He sat over his smoky fire and thought about the boy, and occasionally took out his precious drawing and looked at it, shaking his head in renewed surprise and pleasure. A day or two later, he decided it was time to move on, so he packed up his gear and slipped along the leafy sunlit lanes . . .

The farmer and the milky-lorry driver didn't connect 'a young friend of Charlie's and his dog' with a missing run-away from down south. . . . But the man at the dock remembered Johnnie and the way he had asked about his Dad, and how he had fainted suddenly on the dockyard floor. . . . He thought he had better ask the tanker driver what happened to him when he took him on to the refinery . . . though there had been nothing said on the news about a dog. . . . Was it the same boy? Or just a local lad going up to see his father? He wasn't sure. He decided to wait till Jim, the tanker driver, got back from his next trip . . .

The doctor at the Teesside Hospital was mostly too busy to watch telly or listen to anything except his own bleeper. But the story did eventually reach him. He wondered vaguely where a run-away boy round Bedford way might get to. . . . It didn't occur to him that the kid brought into casualty with a cut on his head had come from anywhere in particular, beyond the streets of Middlesbrough. . . . There were lots of boys that got hurt in brawls . . . and quite a few who were wary of giving names and addresses. . . . Besides, the story hadn't said anything about a dog. . . . He remembered the dog, particularly, because the kid made such a fuss about it. . . . The boy was obviously local. . . . All the same, he did wonder . . . but another rush of work came along, and he forgot. . . . It was several days later that a nurse found the baseball cap lying in a corner, and threw it in the disposal bin . . .

It just happened that Jim Adams had been sent southwards on a delivery by his firm, and he didn't hear about the Johnnie story till he got back. By this time, it was three days after the story broke – almost a week since the time he had set a small boy and a dog down by the refinery main gate. . . . But he remembered Johnnie very clearly, and all the frightening business about his fainting almost under the wheels of his tanker, and the trip to the hospital. . . . Deaf? Battered? At risk? Yes, that would explain the strange gruff voice, the concussion, the brilliant, sorrowful, cloudy smile. . . . At risk? In need of help? He picked up his phone and called the police . . .

Frank and Reg had completed their job at Sullom Voe in three days, and flown back to Aberdeen that evening. They both wondered how young Johnnie was getting on at sea, but there was no way they could reach him to find out. . . . But next day, all hell broke loose.

The police rang Ekofisk to find out where Danny Ross was. The oil-rig put them back on to Aberdeen. The office staff at Aberdeen put them on to Sullom Voe, who promptly returned them to Aberdeen where Frank and Reg had just arrived the night before. . . . By this time, the television and radio stories about Johnnie had reached the main offices – they had even reached the oil-rigs and Sullom Voe . . .

Frank, horrified at the story of Johnnie's battering and deafness and his obvious flight from trouble, rang Brad Harris at Milford Haven to ask for news of the boy.

Reg, coming into the day room to look for him, found Frank sitting with tears in his eyes, saying over and over again: 'The poor kid . . . the poor kid . . . what'll he do now?'

'What's happened?' demanded Reg, who had also seen the account on telly.

Frank brushed a furious hand over his eyes. 'Danny Ross got killed on the exploration rig three days ago, before the kid got there – and that fool Brad Harris told the boy, and let him run off again without a word . . .'

Reg swore. 'Anything we can do?'

'Only tell the authorities what we know . . .'

'Will the two pilots be in trouble?'

'I shouldn't think so . . . it was my responsibility. . . . We all thought we were helping the kid to reach his father. . . . How were we to know?'

'And the tanker skipper?'

'Same thing . . . he can take who he likes on his own ship. . . . He thought he was helping, too. . . . Besides, at least he got the boy to Milford Haven and Brad Harris – the fool!'

'He was only doing his best – ' said Reg, mildly.

'Everyone was!' Frank sounded bitterly upset. 'That's the trouble. . . . Where will the kid go to now, I wonder?'

He got up and paced the room. 'I ought to have known,' he said. 'I felt there was something wrong . . . but I couldn't put my finger on it. . . . To think I let him go on that hopeless wild goose chase . . . Danny Ross's boy – and I was no help to him at all!'

'Oh come,' said Reg, trying to calm him down. 'You did your best for him, too . . .'

'My best!' snorted Frank. 'Sending him down to a blundering fool like Brad Harris! How *could* he tell the boy news like that and just let him go – ?'

'He didn't mean to,' said Reg, being fair. 'It was all a dreadful mistake. . . . But I think Johnnie will come back when he's ready – '

Frank stopped his pacing and looked at him. 'Do you? Why?'

'He's a brave kid . . . he can't run away for ever . . . he's not made like that. . . . He's got more than a bit of Danny in him . . . you saw that yourself.'

186

'Yes, I did.'

'Well then, he'll come back – when he's ready . . . I'm sure of it.'

'By God,' said Frank, 'I hope you're right!'

Dessie, when some of the news came filtering back, was all for dashing off to Middlesbrough and Aberdeen and Sullom Voe at once, if not sooner. But Sergeant Mackay patiently followed up the bits of news and the phone calls and finally reached Brad Harris himself.

But when they heard about Danny Ross's death, and how Johnnie had vanished again, this time no-one could hold Dessie back. So Maggie and Bill Hamilton decided to take her with them in Bill's car and drive straight to Milford Haven. Johnnie couldn't have got far. Maybe they would hear of more sightings of him soon, and then they could pick him up themselves on the way . . .

'In any case,' said Dessie, speaking urgently to the Sergeant while the others were not listening, 'you can't let him be picked up by the fuzz. He'd be terrified. . . . You're the ones he's running from. Don't you know that?'

Sergeant Mackay looked at her. 'Yes,' he said. 'I am afraid you are right.' But in spite of this, he still thought they were wrong to go dashing off with no clear plan in their heads – but somehow he could not bring himself to blame them.

Maggie had insisted on taking leave of absence and delegating all her other work while the search for Johnnie continued. She couldn't rest till he was found.

Julie Cass – or Ross, as it turned out – decided to stay with the children in the house, and refused to go to see the Company officials. They could write to her, she said. And anyway, so far they seemed to have done nothing but harm.

187

Dessie raged at her and Maggie offered to stay and look after the children, but she was adamant. 'I didn't like the Company then,' she said, 'and I don't like it now. It took Danny away, didn't it? And now it's killed him, hasn't it? Why should I go and see them?'

'They might have some money for you,' said Maggie, being practical.

'Money?' said Julie. 'It won't give Johnnie back his Dad, will it?'

This was so outrageously unfair, that Dessie exploded. 'You didn't do much about that either, did you?'

'No point in refusing money,' said Bill Hamilton sturdily. 'It might help Johnnie to get well . . .'

Julie turned on him. 'Got to find him first, haven't we?'

Dessie shouted at her furiously: '*We?* What are you doing about it? You wouldn't even tell us his Dad's name until we threatened you! And now you won't even come to look for him . . . what's the matter with you? Don't you care what happens to him?'

Julie shrugged. 'He's gone off before . . .'

'But never for as long as this,' said Maggie. 'It's more than a week now . . .'

'He's been all right so far, hasn't he?' Julie sounded unexpectedly pert and cocky. 'Got all the way to Scotland and back, didn't he? I think he's done all right on his own, so far!'

'Yes, but Julie, now – now that he knows his father is dead –'

'He'll come home,' said Julie flatly. 'Nothing else to do, is there? He'll come back, now there's no Dad to run to . . .'

Maggie stared at her, astonished by the sudden bitterness in her voice. After all this time, and with the news of his death still only a day or two old, she was still jealous of Danny and his hold on the boy's imagination. . . . Was that part of the trouble? Had that been behind it all along?

'Come on,' said Dessie. 'It's no good talking to *her*. Let's get going!'

While they were climbing into Bill's car outside the Welfare Office, a pink-faced tornado almost as fierce as Dessie rushed up to them. 'Wait!' it panted. 'I'm coming with you!'

Maggie found to her utter amazement that she was staring into the hot, flushed face of Sister Ruth from the Convalescent Home. 'Sister Ruth!' she said weakly. 'What are you doing here?'

'Helping to look for Johnnie!' said the nun, pushing her coif out of her eyes and straightening her ruffled habit with a little, impatient twitch. She saw the doubt in their eyes, and rushed on into most uncharacteristic rapid explanation. 'Sister Augustine said I could. . . . She said I was no good to her as a nervous wreck . . . she sent you a message . . . she said if he needs to rest, and if he wants to come with Dessie, she'll have them both for as long as they like. . . . She'll find room for them somehow. . . . He might need – he might need a place to – I mean, *respite!*'

'Yes,' said Maggie grimly. 'He might!'

'And I wasn't any good at anything when I heard the news, I just couldn't concentrate. . . . It's never happened to me before . . . it was most – most upsetting. But Sister Augustine said – ' her own voice sounded amazed still at what Sister Augustine had said to her, 'she said discipline was all very well in an ordered life, but Johnnie's *wasn't* ordered, and I needed to do something active! And if I thought I could help, I should go. . . .' She stopped for breath, and then, looking from one to the other, suddenly decided to speak directly to Dessie. 'You see, he might – have you thought – he might refuse to come home – even if we found him?'

There was a stunned silence.

Sister Ruth plunged on. 'He was looking for his father, remember. . . . I can't help thinking . . . he might want to ask. . . ? I mean, someone outside might be. . . ? Maybe, he would feel he could trust me. . . ?'

Dessie nodded. 'He might.'

'I mean – ' Sister Ruth looked suddenly flustered. Then she took a deep breath and the nun's carefully acquired armour of discipline and serenity suddenly returned to her. 'I might be able to reassure him . . . in a way that you could not . . .'

She was still speaking directly to Dessie. And Dessie understood her perfectly.

'Yes,' she agreed. 'You might.' She turned to Maggie and added in a brisk voice: 'She'd better come . . . we might need her . . .'

So the five of them set off together in Bill Hamilton's car to drive to Milford Haven. They were an unlikely group – a social worker, a self-employed artist, a thirteen-year-old girl and a rebellious, almost incoherent nun. . . . But they got on remarkably well.

In Milford Haven, Brad Harris received them kindly and anxiously in the Company offices, repeating all he had already told Johnnie and the police about Danny Ross's death, and all he could think of about Johnnie's reaction to the news and his sudden disappearance.

'I was only gone a minute,' he said, sounding upset and angry with himself. 'I just went to get him some tea – he looked so white, and he seemed to be on the verge of passing out. . . . I suppose I shouldn't have left him . . .

but I had no idea he'd just rush off like that. . . .' He paused and looked helplessly at Maggie. 'I know it sounds callous – the way I did it – but the boy was so insistent about knowing the truth. . . . He was not the kind of boy you could lie to, somehow . . . and I had no way of contacting his mother – not then.'

Maggie nodded and spoke gently: 'I'm sure it wasn't your fault. . . . Something was bothering Johnnie anyway – that's why he went away in the first place – '

'Besides,' said Dessie with perfect certainty, 'he'd want to be by himself – after news like that he'd just have to cut and run . . .'

They all looked at her in surprise.

'Yes, but where to, Dessie?' asked Bill Hamilton, remembering how she had been the one who knew about Danny Ross and the oil-rig . . .

Dessie shook the hair out of her eyes and answered in a dreaming voice: 'Nowhere in particular . . . nowhere special to make for, now. . . . He'd just look for somewhere quiet and go to ground . . .'

'What was this about a dog?' asked Bill.

Brad Harris rubbed a hand tiredly over his eyes. A man was dead and it was his responsibility, and they talked about dogs! 'Oh yes . . . little dog on a lead. . . . I talked to the crew on the *Marie Lou* . . . Get-Lost they said he was called.' A faint smile twitched his mouth.

Dessie laughed. 'I know *him*! He's a little stray, used to plague the life out of Johnnie in the Park. . . . Soft with animals, Johnnie is . . . always was. . . .' An extraordinarily sweet smile of remembrance lit her face for a moment.

'Then he won't just abandon the dog?' Bill was half-smiling, too.

'Oh no!' She sounded horrified.

'So . . . it shouldn't be too hard to trace a small boy tramping about with a dog.' Bill was thinking aloud.

'What I don't understand is,' Brad sounded as distressed as ever, '*why?* What was wrong about all that dreadful business with – er – Big Joe, was it?'

Sister Ruth, who until now had remained silent, suddenly spoke in a strange, quiet voice: 'Sometimes . . . even the most innocent bystander feels responsible for a tragedy they can't prevent . . .'

Brad Harris looked at her. 'Yes,' he said heavily. 'Yes, indeed. . . .' And he thought of Danny Ross, lying dead under half a ton of rock in thirty fathoms of ocean . . .

The silence continued, until Maggie broke it deliberately with practical matters. 'I managed to get this out of Julie Cass,' she said, producing a marriage certificate and Johnnie's birth certificate, 'if it helps . . . to tidy up loose ends . . .'

Brad Harris nodded. 'There will be financial arrangements. . . . I think Danny left something to the boy . . . it'll all be at his bank. We'll see to it . . . and there'll be Company compensation too, of course. . . . Not that money can compensate for a father,' he added bitterly.

'It might help the boy's future, though,' growled Bill, offering comfort.

While they were wondering what there was left to say, there was a knock at the door and in answer to Brad's summons, a burly seaman came awkwardly into the room.

'Jack Davies, sir, off the *Marie Lou* . . . known as Tonsils Taffy – even the boy knew me as that! I – I brought this to show you, sir. He gave it me, see. . . . Thought it might tell you something, isn't it?' He held out Johnnie's drawing for them all to see.

Bill Hamilton pounced on it. He gazed, growing stiller and quieter with every moment. 'This is – *beautiful!*' he breathed.

'Beautiful it is, look you,' agreed Tonsils Taffy warmly. 'A marvel with a pencil, that boyo was. . . . Magic, he called it, and magic it was!'

Bill looked from the drawing to Tonsils Taffy's brown anxious face and said: 'Tell me about it . . .'

So the Welshman told them. . . . He explained about David of the White Rock, and how the boy had listened enraptured, clearly hearing every word and every note . . . and he recounted, sadly, how he had left the boy on the verandah waiting for Mr Harris.

'So hopeful he was,' Taffy sounded as distressed as Harris, 'waiting to see his Da. . . . Tragic it is. . . . Is there anything I could do to help, like – seeing as I got to know him, look you. . . ?'

Bill smiled at Taffy and reluctantly gave him back the drawing. 'Keep it safe,' he said. 'I believe it will be valuable one day. . . . Look at the way he handles light! The boy draws like an angel!'

Harris stirred in his chair and asked in a driven voice: 'Tell me once more where you went after you left Johnnie at my house?'

'Back on board, sir . . . I went back along the jetty. . . . She was off-loading, see. We were standing by to disconnect . . .'

'So you'd have seen him if he and the dog had come along the jetty?'

'Oh yes . . . couldn't miss him, see? Besides, we'd have asked him if he'd found his Da. . . . Interested, we all of us was, see?'

Harris nodded.

'In any case,' added Tonsils Taffy, reminding him, 'he wouldn't have been able to get past the security gate without one of us, would he?'

'So he couldn't have gone out towards the jetties. . . . Where on earth could he get to in so short a time?'

193

'Hard to say,' said Taffy slowly, trying to visualise it. 'He might nip off down the road, look you. But then one of the jeep drivers would have spotted him. . . . Not many things you could hide behind up here, is it? Or he might have got a lift from a passing tourist . . . been done before, hasn't it?'

They all agreed it had been done before.

'I'll tell my mates to keep a look-out, see? But he's probably a few miles away into wild Wales by now, isn't it?' His voice had longing in it. He, it was clear, would love to be with Johnnie away into wild Wales. 'The Black Mountains, now . . .' he said in a voice of dream, 'you could stay lost there . . . for a long time . . .'

Then he seemed to realise that such a statement wasn't very reassuring. He gave them a lopsided grin that was a mixture of shyness and embarrassment, and made for the door. 'I hope you find him soon,' he said. 'He's a good boyo . . . one of the best. . . .' He was just going out of the door, when he suddenly turned back and added, as if compelled to speak: 'A boyo as brave as that . . . coming all that way . . . he'll be all right, see? He won't let a little bit of wild Wales defeat him!'

The people left behind in the room were a little shaken, but Dessie nodded to herself as if she agreed with him.

Maggie got to her feet and was just saying: 'Well, I suppose that's all we can do for the moment . . .' when the telephone on Brad Harris's desk rang shrilly.

'Yes?' he said. 'Yes. Of course. Send him in.' He looked up at Maggie. 'It's the engineer, Frank Gibbs, from Aberdeen. . . . They've sent him over to talk to you . . . in case it helps at all . . .'

Frank came in, looking as anxious as his firm, steady face would allow. He shook hands with Maggie and Bill, and then, after a small hesitation, with Sister Ruth and Dessie.

'It was my fault,' he began, 'I ought to have had more sense. . . .' And then he poured out the whole story, and how he and Danny's friends had only wanted to help. 'He had so much pluck . . .' he said. 'We were all tickled to death . . . hitching up like that with his dog . . . and he said . . .' his face clouded and he looked from Maggie to Sister Ruth in distress, 'he said . . . his mother knew . . .'

'Yes!' said Dessie, her mouth set in one hard line, 'she knew all right. . . . She knew where he was going . . . and she knew why, too. . . . But she wasn't saying!'

Frank's open face cleared. 'I didn't think the boy was a liar,' he said. He looked helplessly from one to another. 'I'm – we were all terribly sorry about Danny. . . . He was a good bloke . . . one of the best . . .'

One of the best, thought Dessie. That's what Tonsils Taffy said about Johnnie. And he is! A surge of warmth and determination swept over her. Johnnie would be found! He *must!* He was too good to waste!

'I only wanted to say,' began Frank, awkwardly, 'when you find him – I've got a bit put by – so have most of us – if the boy needs help . . . we'd all like to chip in. . . . Seeing we knew Danny and all . . . we all of us kind of took to Johnnie, somehow . . .'

He stood there, red-faced and embarrassed, until Dessie suddenly ran over to him, put her arms round his neck and gave him a large, impulsive hug.

'Thanks!' she said. 'I think you're smashing!'

At this, everyone laughed, and the tension was broken.

They spent a bit more time trying to plan a way to widen the search. Frank had to return to Aberdeen on the next helicopter flight across. But Brad Harris promised all the assistance he could muster. They knew they had to wait now, for someone else to report in about a glimpse of a wandering boy and a dog. . . . But all the same, they none of them wanted to give up and go home . . .

'I think we'd better spend a night somewhere over here,' said Bill. 'There might be some news tomorrow. And we could cover more ground.'

'Oh yes!' agreed Dessie. 'There are lots of little roads we could drive along . . .'

'And we could ask in the village shops,' added Sister Ruth. 'He's bound to need some food sometime.'

Maggie said nothing. She was seeing in her mind's eye a small boy trudging the lanes with a dog at his heels . . . a boy who was scared to come out into the open even to ask for food from a local shop. . . . She was afraid that Sergeant Mackay's publicity campaign might have done Johnnie more harm than good . . .

'Come on,' said Bill. 'We'll go and find somewhere to stay . . .'

Later that evening, he and Maggie went for a stroll along the lanes beyond the farmhouse where they were all staying. It was a friendly place, and the farmer's wife had heard all about Johnnie.

'Sad it is,' she said. 'A lovely boy like that . . . let's hope he's found soon . . .'

Dessie and Sister Ruth set off one way, not having much hope, but determined to keep looking. Bill and Maggie went the other way, equally unhopeful but equally unable to keep still.

Presently, Bill put a hand on Maggie's arm and drew her to a halt. It was a beautiful late spring evening, with a westering sun gilding all the hedgerows, a clear sky overhead, and all the birds of Wales singing their hearts out.

They stood quietly together, looking over a green

valley, and Bill watched Maggie's face as he spoke to her, and wondered if he was speaking too soon . . .

'I want to ask you something . . . and I don't know how . . .'

She smiled a little but did not turn to look at him. 'Try.'

'You've never told me . . . about the *Mrs* Fraser situation?'

She looked into his candid, troubled eyes and spoke simply, without constraint. 'There's no mystery. I was married. He died of cancer, very young. . . . I nursed him through it . . . and since then I've plunged into work rather extra hard, that's all . . .'

He rubbed an anxious hand through his springy grey hair and sighed. 'I'm sorry, Maggie dear. . . . I don't know how to say this. . . . Have you ever thought of – of fostering kids yourself?'

'They wouldn't let a single person foster –'

'Exactly!' He sounded both triumphant and shy all at once. 'So – supposing – just supposing, mind – you and I decided to get married?'

She had turned towards him completely now, wide-eyed with shock.

'No,' he said, pleadingly, 'don't speak yet – let me finish. I know I'm at least fifteen years older than you – and sitting about in Parks painting trees is rather a suspect occupation! But . . . but I am what's called a Respectable Artist, and I do make a reasonable living! I know you would want to go on with your career, too. . . . But – but, Maggie, we could take Dessie . . . and maybe they'd let us have Johnnie. . . . There's so much we could do for them. . . . Do you think they'd consider it? Or would they let him go back to that feckless girl who won't lift a finger to help him? Think of it, Maggie! He could get his ears put right . . . and then go to the right school and get some real education. He's so bright, you know, and so wonderfully teachable! Maybe I could – we could help him with his drawing, and get him to art school when he's ready . . . if he wanted it, that is –'

'Hold on!' said Maggie, laughing. 'You're taking my breath away!' Then she grew grave. 'In any case, he wouldn't desert those kids of his, you know . . .'

'Well, he could see them often enough. Every day if he liked. Besides,' he added slowly, 'hasn't he deserted them now?'

Maggie looked very troubled. 'I know. That's just what I can't understand.'

Bill nodded. 'There's probably a perfectly good reason – in his mind at least. . . . Don't worry so!' He grinned at her and added, cheerfully: 'Stop changing the subject, woman!' He put a strong arm round her and hugged her close. 'You don't need to be told I care for you, do you?' he asked, whimsically. 'I have done since the first day I walked into your office!' He looked suddenly unsure. 'But of course – I know I'm not much to write home about!'

'Who says?' Maggie was smiling again, with sudden tenderness. She thought seriously, he is already the rock I lean on. . . . Already I turn to him for help in any emergency. . . . He is good and kind, and he has the imagination and insight of an artist . . . and I really do believe I've begun to love him already . . .

'Just let me get this straight,' she said severely. 'You want to marry me so that we can have Dessie and Johnnie to foster? What happens if the authorities refuse?'

Bill smiled. 'I still want to marry you . . . and I suppose . . . there'll be other Dessies and Johnnies . . . over the years.' He looked at her with unexpected shyness and added hesitantly: 'And – I suppose – we might have kids of our own?'

198

'I'm getting on a bit,' she said, grinning. 'Thirty-three this birthday.'

'Rubbish!' said Bill. 'A mere chicken. I'm forty-eight!' He watched the setting sun slide behind the hill and make a glory of Maggie's unruly hair. She was really very pretty, especially when she blushed, he thought . . . and when she stopped looking so anxious. . . . He had a great and urgent longing to solve all her problems for her – to find Johnnie – to put everything right – to make her life entirely happy and entirely perfect.

'Nothing is ever entirely perfect,' said Maggie gently, perfectly understanding him.

'You're uncanny!' he said, and kissed her.

When Maggie emerged, rosy and smiling, he held her by the shoulders and said: 'Well?'

She lifted one hand to touch his face, with quiet re-assurance.

'Yes, Bill . . .' she said softly, 'yes. . . . But let's wait . . . till Johnnie is found . . .'

Johnnie had no very clear recollection of how he got out of the chair and down the verandah steps onto the drive, and no deliberate plan to hide or disappear. He simply knew he had to get away . . . he had to come to terms with this new knowledge about Danny Ross alone and in his own time. . . . Also, he knew confusedly that he must be out of the way before people started to ask questions and to find out where his mother was. . . . Or ought he to tell them where she was? They might be able to help her. . . . But she had always insisted that she didn't want anything to do with Danny, and he must never find out where she was. Well, Danny wouldn't ever find out now. . . . Johnnie shook his head, trying in vain to clear it . . . he couldn't think straight just now . . . he was too shocked and upset. . . . It was as much as he could do to stop shaking and keep the ground from heaving under him . . . Danny Ross was dead. . . . What was he to do now?

But before he could decide anything, Get-Lost took a hand. He saw a cat. Up till now he had been the most obedient and docile of little dogs – only too anxious to please. But cats were old enemies. He used to chase them in the Park at home . . . and the silly things always went up trees and spat defiance at him. . . . Now, without hesitation, he launched himself across the drive like a streak of black and white lightning, barking furiously, and the black cat fled away before him in through a tangle of bushes at the back of the flower-bed and out on to the red sandstone cliff beyond. . . . The lead Johnnie had been holding was yanked from his hand, and he ran frantically after Get-Lost into the darkness of the shrubbery. Once the other side, he saw the little dog tearing down the cliff in hot pursuit of the black cat that was running fast with its lissom body flattened to the ground like a panther. After them plunged Johnnie, tripping over a root as he went and grasping desperately at trailing ivy and small bushes to save himself from falling headfirst down the shallow cliff. He managed to check his wild rush a little, but even so he could not stop himself from running on down the cliff on to the reddish shingle below, where a large school party were just assembling to go back to their coach after a picnic on the beach.

'Get-Lost!' he said. 'Stop it! Bad dog!' and caught at the trailing lead as Get-Lost skidded round the pebbles, still trying to catch the elusive cat. But that intelligent animal had gone behind the party of school children and quietly escaped back up the cliff while no-one was looking.

'Come here!' said Johnnie, and pulled the dog down

200

beside him. He meant to sound even crosser, and even lifted his hand to give Get-Lost a well-deserved tap on the nose. . . . But somehow he couldn't. He smiled instead and said in a croaky, uneven voice: 'You're a terror!'

'Come on!' said a loud voice that was not at all croaky, close to his ear. 'Don't dawdle. We're waiting! What're you dashing up and down the cliff for? Honestly, rounding up a crowd of kids is an absolute nightmare! Hurry up, and keep in *line!* The coach is going!'

Astonished, Johnnie hurried up. Get-Lost kept very close to him, knowing he had been rather wicked and not sure what kind of punishment might be on the way.

The party of children crunched over the pebbles to the sea wall and the road opposite the yacht club. Johnnie kept behind them, but the Voice went on saying: 'Hurry up!' at frequent intervals close behind him, so he kept on going. He noticed that the old men were still sunning themselves on the benches outside the yacht club doors, just as they had been when he arrived on the *Marie Lou*, and one or two others were busy mending nets and boats. He suddenly longed for Tonsils Taffy and the *Marie Lou* and the endless quiet seas between Sullom Voe and Wales. . . . It had been safe there . . . safe and peaceful . . . and he was travelling to see his father. . . . He didn't know then that Danny Ross was dead . . .

'Come on!' said the Voice. 'Stop gawping! You've seen the Refineries and the tankers. What more d'you want? These are only little boats. . . . We're going to Pembroke Castle now. Get in!'

Bossy Voice turned out to be a harassed teacher in a thick tweed skirt and sensible shoes, with far too many children to deal with and no very clear idea as to who they all were. She was sturdy and grey-haired and not unkindly, but at the moment very fussed, and she called over the heads of the children crowding into the coach to a plumpish young man who was at the other end of the party.

'Have you got all your lot?'

'I think so!' came the reply.

'Better count them! They're like quicksilver. . . . Sure to leave someone behind!'

The children boiled in and out of the coach doorway like ants. Johnnie slid on to the coach next to a bunch of chattering boys and kept very quiet. He was used to keeping very quiet at school – and in the playground. Get-Lost kept very quiet, too, huddled under the seat by Johnnie's feet.

The coach set off up the winding hairpin bends from the little bay to the main road, on to the turning for Pembroke Dock and across the new bridge to the Castle. At the other end, the party all trooped off, still chattering and laughing, and went to have a look at the great stone mass of Pembroke Castle.

Johnnie and Get-Lost lagged behind, meaning to go off on their own as soon as the coast was clear. He still couldn't think straight. It wasn't possible to take in all that had been said to him by Brad Harris at Milford Haven. . . . He wanted, desperately, to get away by himself into the green countryside where it was quiet and he could let himself remember it all . . . but here, in Pembroke town, it was all bustle and noise.

'Come along!' said the Voice again. 'Don't hang about. Keep with the rest, these roads are dangerous. . . . Honestly, who said you could bring a dog? You know very well pets aren't allowed on outings – I'm sure Mr Jones didn't say you could. . . . Well, did he?'

Johnnie only vaguely heard the stream of questions. It was about Get-Lost, though, he followed that.

'He followed me,' he said with truth. 'Couldn't help it.'

202

'Well, it's too late now. You can't exactly take him home, can you? Keep with the others, now, and when you get back in the coach, keep that dog out of sight under the seat or something. . . . I don't know what the driver will say – '

She went on past him, still scolding. It was just like school. He was used to hearing a stream of incomprehensible instructions he couldn't hope to obey . . . and he couldn't escape her beady eye at the moment. There was nothing else to do but follow the others round the Castle and into the coach . . .

He didn't see much of the Castle. He had a confused impression of thick stone walls and lots of steps, solid round towers and arrow-slit windows, and high battlements. . . . When he looked down the steep sides, there was mirror-like grey-blue water on three sides with a couple of swans and some ducks on it, and green grass and ivy and a thick wedge of trees at the foot of the grey stone flanks of the Castle. . . . It was very high, and the ground and the water looked very far away . . .

He felt very strange and light, as if he was not really there at all. . . . It was like some awful waking dream that he couldn't get out of. No-one spoke to him – except in a kind of collective shout, herding them all together – but he kept on walking round with the others, round and round the stone walls, and Get-Lost trotted along beside him, behaving decorously among the crowds of visitors.

At last, they were all shepherded back into the waiting coach down in the car park below the main street and the high Castle walls. Get-Lost was hidden quietly under the seat at the back, and Johnnie sat staring out of the window, wondering where they were going.

It occurred to him then with a sudden jolt of fear that he had no idea where he wanted to go now. . . . Ever since he had set off from home, he had been sure of his direction and his purpose. He was going north – north to see his Dad – and he had managed to go north, too. A long, long way north, past Scotland and the North Sea and on to Sullom Voe . . . and then down again, all the way south to find his Dad at Milford Haven . . .

But now? There was no Danny Ross any more. No-one to tell him where to go next . . . or what to do. . . . It didn't really matter where he went . . . so long as he stayed away . . .

He saw the busy docks and grey waters of Pembroke Dock disappearing on his left and the straight road beginning to take them up into the green hills of Wales. He didn't care . . . he was too tired to care . . . anywhere would do . . .

The coach stopped next at Llandovery, in the little tarmac square by the ruins of the castle. There were playing field and swings beyond, and still further beyond that, the steep wooded hills of wild Wales began. Behind the nearest hills, higher ones rose up and flowed away in dark curves and steep bare slopes and secret valleys towards the Black Mountains and the edge of the Brecon Beacons. . . . On the other side of the little town, still more wild hills rose up tall and green and lonely . . . the jumbled roofs and squares of the little town seemed to sit snugly in the curving arms of the hills. It was safe and cheerful and bustling with ordinary, everyday life . . . but beyond it, the wild wilderness stretched for mile on mile. . . . A boy could get lost there very easily. . . . Johnnie looked out at the hills and suddenly loved them. He longed to escape into their green, empty spaces where he could be quite alone . . .

He waited until the party had been collected, harangued about getting lost or climbing the castle walls which were dangerous, and then dismissed with half an hour to spend eating ice creams and playing on the swings in the playing fields until the whistle blew.

'And mind you're back by then!' yelled Bossy Voice. 'We've got a two-hour drive back after this. . . . Don't stray too far away!'

He watched the two teachers turn away to get a cup of tea from the kiosk on the corner, and then he and Get-Lost went swiftly in the other direction. In a short while he came to a little river with a stone bridge over it. He crossed the bridge and went on up a small road into the green and dappled shadows of the woods . . .

'What happened to your boy with the dog?' said the bossy woman teacher to her colleague.

'What boy?' asked the man.

They both turned round to look down the road towards the coach. But there was no-one there. There was no boy with a dog in the playing fields, either.

'Well, I don't know!' exclaimed the woman. 'I must be seeing things!'

'With this lot, I'm not surprised!' said the man, and laughed.

Johnnie and Get-Lost had already left the town behind them, and were walking away up into the hills along the little road from the bridge. It had now become a narrow, leafy lane, which wound on in wide circles up the side of the hill . . .

It was a relief to be alone . . . but he still didn't dare to stop. . . . He felt that if he stopped he would want to lie down and weep . . . and he couldn't do that. A boy of his age didn't do that – especially not a Company Boy . . .

He walked on. It had been a long and confusing day already, and the light was beginning to fade from the green hills. He began to worry a little about Get-Lost. They would have to sleep somewhere, and the little dog hadn't had anything to eat since a very early breakfast on the *Marie Lou* before they docked. . . . Nor had he, come to that, but he didn't feel hungry. . . . Could they just sleep out somewhere, curled up under the hedge? Or would it get too cold in the night? He guessed that little dog had often slept like that before – but supposing it poured with rain in the night. . . ?

He was still worrying vaguely about this, when he saw a curious dark shape behind the thicket of trees above the bank that sloped upwards on one side of the lane. It was a funny shape – rather like a house, only it was much too small. . . . He stopped in the lane and looked up at it. Get-Lost put his head on one side and gazed enquiringly at his master. 'Where do we go from here?' he seemed to say.

Jonnnie moved on a few paces, and then found a little steep path leading up the bank between two leaning hazel bushes. He climbed up it, grasping at roots and thin branches to keep his feet from slipping, and Get-Lost followed him. He didn't need to clutch at anything.

At the top of the path there was a tangle of bushes and nettles, a cluster of bluebells and rose campion growing so thickly that he could scarcely avoid treading on them, and a small gap in a prickly holly hedge. He squeezed through, and so did Get-Lost.

They stood looking round them in the deepening dusk, and found themselves in an overgrown wild garden, and the dark bulk they had seen was indeed a house – a tiny thatched summerhouse at the end of the garden's uncut lawn. Johnnie was enchanted. He had never seen a house so small or so pretty. It had two tiny windows, latticed, though one or two panes were broken, and it had a small green-painted door which stood open lopsidedly hanging on one hinge. The ancient thatched roof overhung the walls and was supported on graceful pillars made of solid pine trunks, making a wide verandah round three sides of the little house. The fourth side stood with its back to the holly hedge which acted as a windbreak.

Greatly daring, Johnnie went up the two crumbling steps on to the rickety verandah and peered in through the door. There was an old horsehair sofa inside, with some of the stuffing coming out, and two shabby wickerwork armchairs with faded cushions on them . . . there was even a dusty, cobwebby rug lying on the sofa, and everything felt dry to the touch and smelt of leafmould and moss and ancient, flaking wood. In one corner there was a little old bamboo table, and in another there were two folded up deckchairs with rotting canvas. . . . But it was warm and dry and cosy, and it felt like home . . .

'Look, Get-Lost,' he said. 'Our new house . . . d'you think we dare stay here?'

Get-Lost thumped his tail hopefully. It wasn't for him to say.

The only thing we haven't got, thought Johnnie, is water. . . . Maybe I'd better look for some before it gets quite dark. Tin-Can-Charlie said we always had to find water first . . . and I've got a water bottle . . .

He followed the path that led away from the summer-house along the edge of the overgrown lawn and found that it sloped gently downwards with banks of pale, late narcissi nodding at him in the dusk as he went. . . . At the bottom, there was a small stream flowing into a perfect oval lily pond.

Johnnie filled his water bottle, and the tin dish for Get-Lost, and quietly made his way back to the summer-house. But having done that, he could go no further and do no more.

A sense of awful desolation came over him. He was

alone now, and he had no plan in his head – no future. His search had ended in failure. Danny Ross was dead . . .

Silently, he flung himself down on the old broken sofa and lay face downwards with his head buried in his arms. . . . I must think, he said, I must think what to do . . . but he could not think. . . . He could only remember that laughing face in the photo, and the sound of a voice that he would never hear again . . .

Get-Lost knew something was wrong. But he didn't know how to help. For a little while he sat watching, but at last he climbed up on to the sofa, and thrust a consoling head in between Johnnie's folded arms . . .

A hand came out and clutched him . . . but Johnnie did not speak. Instead, at last, the tears came – slowly at first, and then in a torrent. Johnnie was done now, and there was no-one to see his grief. . . . He wept his heart out for the father he would never know. . . . Get-Lost tried to lick the tears away, but he did not know how to stop the gasps and shudders that racked his master. . . . In the end they ceased, and Johnnie lay still . . .

Presently, as the darkness grew around them, both the boy and the dog fell into healing sleep.

Johnnie was woken by the sound of a voice shouting. He couldn't hear it very well, but it seemed to be coming from the garden beyond the summerhouse, and it seemed to be shouting 'Help!'

He sat up, listening intently. Get-Lost was listening, too, with his head on one side, ears cocked, and eyes bright with interest. Johnnie got up and went to the door and looked out. . . . Yes, there it was again, a voice insistently calling 'Help!' It wasn't low enough to be a man's voice, or high enough to be a girl's . . . it was sort of old and croaky – or that's what it sounded like.

208

He stepped out into the dewy morning and went in search of the voice. Every so often he had to stop to listen, because his ears were bad and muddled this morning, and he could not easily distinguish direction and distance. But Get-Lost could, and he ran on ahead, barking his idea of reassurance that he and Johnnie were coming to deal with the emergency, whatever it was.

Johnnie came round the corner to where some shallow steps led down to a lower overgrown lawn edged by a straggling box hedge which shielded the sloping path from view. . . . Here he stopped and stared. For the owner of the voice was an old lady, dressed in old-fashioned heathery tweeds and at this moment lying upside down in a wheelchair that had toppled sideways down the slope.

He ran across to her and began to struggle to tip the chair back on to its wheels with her still inside it. Then he stopped, remembering that she might be hurt and to move her might be wrong.

'Are – you – all – right?' he asked, bending over her anxiously.

'Of course I'm all right, boy!' she retorted. 'Get me up! The plaguey thing tipped over, that's all. . . . Get me out of here!'

He heaved and pulled and struggled until the chair came upright suddenly and settled back down on its wheels with a sickening bump. He wondered if the old lady would be badly jarred by it, but she seemed unperturbed. He settled her back into the chair, straightening her skirts and the small tartan rug that she held clutched in one gnarled hand.

'Where to?' he asked, with his hands on the wheelchair handles.

'Don't be silly, child . . . back to the house, of course. I can probably do it myself, except I'm afraid the wheels may be bent. Push it forwards a bit and let's see . . .'

Johnnie pushed it forwards. It went smoothly enough, though something seemed to be dragging it back. He bent down to examine it, and found that it had a brake rather like the one on the bicycle he used to borrow from Mr Patel for the paper round. It had somehow got jammed on, and he gave it a kick with his foot so that it sprang back, releasing the chair into an easy glide . . .

'That's better,' chirped the old lady. 'Much better. . . . Come along, boy, don't dawdle!'

Johnnie came along, reflecting that life seemed to be full of bossy ladies ordering him about. But all the same, there was something about this old lady – something strong and indomitable and snapping with good sense that he rather liked.

They followed the path which grew broader as it came up to the house, and turned into a sweep of grass-ridden gravel in front of the four long windows and wide-open door which made up the south face of the house. Through the open door he could see a hall inside, and a curving staircase leading up to a kind of gallery with doors opening off it. The hall was tiled in black and white squares, and there was a narrow stained glass window half-way up the stairs that cast pools of colour on to the chequered hall floor below.

The outside of the house was grey stone and slate, heavily overgrown with ivy, and at its back was a thick belt of dark trees, mostly tall pines and yew, with one splendid cedar which seemed to stand guard over the house and keep the weather at bay. . . . Behind the trees rose the steep, wooded hills, and still beyond them, higher scrubby slopes leading up to real bare mountain foothills . . .

And around the house was this tangled, gentle garden – a riot of untended flowerbeds and knee-high grass and wild garlic and bluebells blooming in happy profusion wherever there was space to breathe. . . . Johnnie thought it was absolutely beautiful . . .

'In here, boy,' said the old lady, and Johnnie pushed her into a long sunny room with a dining table at one end and a grand piano at the other, and along one wall a sideboard standing in front of an open hatch to the kitchen. Johnnie was a practical boy, and he could see at once that the room was laid out so that someone in a wheelchair could manage things on their own . . .

'After that,' she said, 'I need something stronger than tea. . . . Can you find the brandy? On the sideboard over there . . . and a glass.'

Johnnie found the bottle labelled 'Fine old liqueur brandy' and beside it a couple of round balloon glasses. He brought one over with the bottle and offered them to her. But the old lady's hand shook so much that she couldn't pour, so Johnnie took it away and poured some out for her.

He waited patiently while she drank it, watching in a strangely adult way to see if she looked better. . . . In truth, something odd was happening to him. He had, for as long as he could remember, been used to doing things for other people – the kids and Mom, the tea to get and the washing to do, the paper round for Mr Patel. . . . He hadn't thought about it at the time, but this last week when he had been on his own, he had missed the sense of belonging that all these chores had meant. . . . He had felt lonely and centreless, without any particular tasks to be fulfilled. . . . He had missed the kids more, of course, than the washing-up. But they all seemed to be mixed in his mind with warmth and companionship and such family life as he could manage to make for the kids in between the rows with Big Joe and his mother's evasive tactics of running away from trouble. . . . During the week of travelling, of course, he had had the picture of his Dad in his mind, and the need to find him had driven him on. . . . And even when he missed his family badly, he told himself that it was for the best and he was doing the right thing, and his Dad would be able to put everything straight and help all the family. . . . But now – since yesterday – there was no strong motive driving him on, and nothing to make him feel useful or needed by anyone . . .

And here was this old lady, clearly needing help from someone, and seeming quite glad he was there . . .

He found himself looking into a pair of very bright, very perceptive black eyes which were summing him up with a kind of humorous, twinkling shrewdness.

'Well, boy –' she said. 'I'm Emmaline Lucas. Who are you?'

'Johnnie.'

'Is that all?'

'Johnnie . . . Ross.' After all, he was still Danny's son, and still proud of it. . . . He didn't know yet that people all over the country were looking for him.

'I see.' She looked at him attentively. 'Had any breakfast?'

He shook his head.

'Neither have I. Can you boil an egg?'

'Yes.'

'And make tea and toast?'

He nodded, smiling a little.

'All right then. Kitchen's through there. Usually have mine on a tray by the window. Sunnier. Better make it two eggs each. Don't be long. I'm hungry!' She put her hands on the wheels of her chair and spun herself round, and then moved with surprising speed over to one of the tall windows where the sun was streaming in and making a bright path on the faded green carpet.

Johnnie went into the kitchen and stood looking round. A fridge. That would have eggs. Bread? In the white bin marked 'Bread' of course. And there was the electric toaster, on the working top beside the electric kettle. . . . Tea? There was a black tin with Chinese figures on it standing beside the kettle . . . yes, tea. A strange, scented tea he had not met before. . . . It smelt lovely. Butter and milk in the fridge. What kind of stove? Electric. Yes, he could manage all that. He found a saucepan and filled it with water at the sink . . . then he remembered Get-Lost and gave him a bowl of water, too. . . . He liked working in this kitchen. It made him feel quite at home . . .

In a little while, they were sitting opposite each other, the old lady and the boy, with the little dog curled up on the rug at their feet.

'Very nice,' she said, and nodded at him briskly.

He had time to look at her now, and he saw that she had a thin, pointed face and a high rather noble-looking forehead with her white hair swept back in a straight mane that glinted with silver in the sun. Her mouth was longish and mobile, with a definite quirk of humour at the corners, and she sat straight in her chair with a stiff, upright back. It was only her legs beneath the tartan rug that had clearly decided not to work any more.

'I could do with you about the place,' she said, looking at him with her head tilted to one side as if considering the matter deeply. 'Staying long?'

Johnnie hesitated. 'Might be . . .'

'Why aren't you at school?' she shot out.

He looked at her, and then began to laugh. 'It's holidays. . . .' And that was true. So it was. It seemed funny to him all of a sudden, and he went on chuckling.

The old lady was smiling, too. 'Well, I could certainly do with a hand . . . though I don't often fall upside down in my wheel chair!' She lifted a gnarled hand to pat her hair into place. 'Had a companion, you know. Silly creature. Went off last week. . . .' Her eyes snapped fire at him. 'Not that I needed her much! I can cook, you know – when my hands aren't too stiff!' She grinned as if to mitigate the fierce gleam in her eye.

'I can cook too,' said Johnnie slowly. His voice came out a bit gruff and strange, and he saw her look at him sharply, but she said nothing. It didn't occur to him that he could hear her dry old voice quite clearly, without having to struggle to understand her . . .

There was silence in the room. To Johnnie it felt strangely peaceful. Outside, the sun was making the wild garden look like a green and golden paradise. . . . How he would love to paint it, like the Painting Man did, with a great splurge of beautiful colours all across the canvas . . . he sighed. He missed the Painting Man . . . and Maggie . . . and Dessie . . . Dessie, most of all. . . . How she would love this place . . .

'Garden needs doing . . .' murmured Miss Lucas, half to herself. 'D'you like gardens?'

Johnnie nodded. The silence flowed again between them.

'Well?' The sharp old voice broke into his dreams.

He started. 'Yes?'

'Like to have a go?'

'Why not?' said Johnnie, and offered Miss Lucas some more toast.

There began for the two of them a curious, unacknowledged friendship, and with each day that he stayed, the relationship got deeper though they were neither of them aware of it.

Emmaline Lucas was an independent, solitary

214

woman, known to the few local villagers and hill farmers as an eccentric old lady who kept herself to herself and fiercely refused all offers of help. Some years ago, she had lost the use of her legs and taken to a wheel-chair. It didn't stop her being independent, though. She had bought herself a deep-freeze and an automatic car, and went once a fortnight to Llandovery to do her shopping. She had also acquired a series of companions, none of which had stayed long, finding the large rambling house and garden too remote and too desolate to bear. They also, according to Emma Lucas, found the idea of work too much to bear, and one by one she sent them packing with, as she said, their lily white hands unsoiled.

The old lady loved the house and garden. She had lived there a long time, and she knew every stone and every tree. When she was younger, she used to climb the hills at the back, and even went up to the tops of the mountains and the secret lakes in the valleys with her young brothers. . . . But they had all gone now, and only she was left, with a house that was too big and full of friendly ghosts, and a wild, unmanageable garden echoing with a host of childhood memories . . .

She also had, more practically, a dozen brown hens, two nanny goats called Ermine and Trudy though nobody saw the joke, and a belligerent billy goat called Billy the Kid. . . . Then there was Merlin, the old grey donkey who ate most of the grass and some of the flowers and was very partial to roses. . . . Emma was quite adept at milking the goats from her wheel-chair by now, and if Billy the Kid got fierce, which he did from time to time, she used to charge him with her chair, shouting abuse, and he backed off.

Before long she had shown Johnnie how to milk the goats and feed the hens and where to collect the eggs. . . . Merlin, the donkey, didn't need much atten-

215

tion in spring and summer while the grass was rich and long. He eyed Johnnie suspiciously at first, but after a day or two he accepted him, and even came over to have his ears rubbed when he saw the boy approaching. But even so, Get-Lost kept well clear of his heels.

To Johnnie, it was like a dream. . . . He had the run of this beautiful place . . . he had work to do, and food to eat, and somewhere of his own to sleep . . . and there were plenty of scraps for Get-Lost. For some reason, the old lady never asked where he came from, or where he went back to at night. . . . He supposed she believed he came down from the hillside village above them, and went back home after dark. . . . But, come to that, she never asked any questions at all . . . she just accepted that he came and went as he liked. . . . It didn't seem to occur to her, either, that a boy of his age ought to be in school. . . . Maybe, he thought, she had got vague about school and got terms and holidays mixed up in her mind . . . or maybe she just didn't bother to think about it . . .

However it was, he turned up in time to get her breakfast. He spent long hours in the garden, clearing and weeding under her instructions. . . . At lunchtime they both sat down to bread and cheese and strong cups of tea. Sometimes it was their own goats' cheese which she showed him how to make, and sometimes it was fresh local cheese from the travelling shop which came clanging round every Wednesday . . . and sometimes it was their own bread, too, when the baker's van forgot to call . . .

In the afternoon, the old lady slept, and Johnnie could do what he liked. He and Get-Lost explored the garden and the hills beyond, and if it rained they stayed snug in the little summerhouse, which Johnnie was slowly cleaning and fitting up like a real home. . . . Get-Lost had never been so happy, so well-fed and so free . . . nor had Johnnie.

At least, it was a kind of happiness. . . . But underneath there was a constant ache for many things. He wanted to know if the kids were all right . . . he wanted Dessie, and the Painting Man and Maggie. . . . He wanted, and knew he could never have, that elusive shadow Danny Ross, who could have told him what was right and taken away a load of guilt he still felt about Big Joe lying in a crumpled heap on the floor. . . . Mostly, he shut his thoughts away and simply got on with the task in hand. But sometimes, alone in the little summerhouse at night, he could not prevent himself from remembering . . .

Usually, at about six o'clock, he heard Miss Lucas calling him in to get the tea. Sometimes, she cooked things for him like sausages and bacon, and sometimes he cooked for her. . . . Only once he got awkward and refused to help – and that was when she got out a tin of baked beans. Johnnie went white and turned away. He remembered that day – the look of outrage and fury on Big Joe's face – the jerk of his elbow, and the cascade of hot beans on to his own feet . . .

'No,' he said. 'Sorry,' and his throat closed tight.

Emma Lucas did not press him. She was a very perspicacious old lady. Something was clearly very wrong with the boy, and she was not going to make things worse. Quietly, she put the beans away and got out a tin of spaghetti instead.

She had got used to the idea of high tea by now. Once, in earlier and more elegant days, she had insisted on afternoon tea in the drawing room, with wafer-thin sandwiches and the best Rockingham tea set. . . . And then, in the evening, she would change into a long skirt and sit at the polished mahogany table in her dining

217

room, opposite the companion of the moment, eating a well-served dinner. . . . But now, times had changed . . . the long sunny drawing room with its French windows to the garden was now her bedroom . . . there were no chattering maids in the kitchen, not even a twittering companion in the second-best bedroom. . . . Only one old lady, and one startlingly beautiful, silent boy. They ate together in companionable peace, after a day in the garden. And then there was the whole, long spring evening with its aching twilight to be got through. . . . The boy helped her there, too . . .

She taught him to play cribbage . . . and chess. Johnnie was surprisingly good at both, and could keep whole patterns and sequences in his head. . . . She also played the piano sometimes, and this Johnnie found enthralling. His ears were a lot better in these quiet surroundings, and he could mostly hear the notes . . . especially the deep bass ones. . . . Sometimes, when it got too tinkly (she was playing Chopin at the time) he lost the thread . . . but the strong, angry voice of Beethoven totally captured his imagination. . . . He could feel rages and storms, and sudden calms and smiling peace, and soaring towers and falling rain . . . high adventures and slow retreats . . . climbing dark mountains, and crossing wide seas, like the great ocean-going tankers from Sullom Voe. . . . It was all there, everything in the world he knew, and more besides . . . he was utterly enslaved.

Miss Lucas didn't believe in the telly, or the radio much. She said the outside world was a bothersome place, and she'd rather forget it. . . . But she did have a good record player, and this opened even more windows on to strange horizons. Johnnie discovered that not only Beethoven could take him on tremendous journeys . . . all kinds of people could . . . particularly someone call-

218

ed Vaughan Williams (he read the name on the label) who seemed to understand about wide airy spaces and could conjure up great skies full of sailing clouds, and their darker shadows moving on quiet hillsides . . .

'Yes, he understood this kind of country,' said Miss Lucas. 'Brought up in it . . . Gloucestershire has hills and sky and wide spaces, too. . . . You can grow with him . . .'

Johnnie grew.

It was a day or two before Johnnie dared to ask for two other things. One of them came up naturally, for it rained hard while he was gardening and his clothes got very wet. He had left Frank's furry parka behind in the summerhouse, not wanting to ruin it in the rain and mud of the garden, so the rain just went right through to his skin. He came into the kitchen shyly, dripping at every corner. Get-Lost simply shook himself and lay down near the Aga cooker. But Johnnie just stood there, not knowing what to do.

'Better have a hot bath, boy,' said Miss Lucas. 'Catch your death.'

'Can I?' His eyes grew round with hope.

'Of course. Hurry up. I'm cooking tonight . . .'

Johnnie turned to go, and then hesitated. 'Could I . . . borrow the washing powder?'

'Take it. Like a clean child, meself. . . . Don't be long.'

Johnnie literally wallowed in luxury. . . . He had never known such a bath, or such a bathroom. It was a big, draughty room with the same black and white tiled floor as the hall. The bath was old-fashioned, roomy and panelled in mahogany, with brass taps. The lavatory was like that too, square and boxed in with mahogany, with an ornate brass handle on the chain . . . and the wash-basin had brass taps, too and a pattern of green ivy leaves all round the top. Johnnie was entranced. . . . He had been able to wash in the little cabin on the *Marie-Lou* – but this steamy space and limitless hot water and soap was wonderful. He had a sudden, sharp twinge of anguish, remembering the kids and wondering who was doing the washing for them now. . . . Was little Kevin struggling to do it all alone?

Then he got absorbed in scrubbing himself and his clothes clean. Get-Lost had insisted on coming into the bathroom with him, and finally Johnnie plunged him into the soapy water, too. When he got out, and the dog got out, there seemed to be a lot of water on the floor, so he set to and mopped it up, naked as he was. It wasn't until he had finished, that a sudden thought struck him. He had washed everything he possessed, including Mr Patel's trousers and jersey . . . and he had nothing else in the world to wear.

After a moment's thought, he tied the towel round himself and went downstairs. A bedraggled, somewhat mystified Get-Lost padded down after him. He stood in the kitchen doorway, looking helplessly at Miss Lucas, and said: 'I'm sorry. . . . I haven't any more clothes . . .'

She looked up from the stove and smiled. The boy seemed like some kind of visiting angel, thin and flame-like, with his white skin and damp gold hair – and those deep, visionary eyes that saw so much. . . . The folds of the towel hung like a carelessly draped white robe, as if the wind of his flight still faintly stirred them . . .

'Beautiful . . .' she murmured, and then fixed him with a beady black eye. 'Second door on the landing. My brother's old room. . . . Chest of drawers, and a wardrobe. Find yourself something . . . may be a bit big . . . never used now . . .'

Johnnie retreated up the stairs. He laid his hand on

the knob of the second door on the landing, turned it and went in. The room was quite large, and contained an old white bedstead with brass knobs, a heavy mahogany wardrobe, a small desk and a large chest of drawers with brass handles. The walls were white, and covered in pictures of sailing ships – ships of all sizes and ages and styles. . . . Johnnie was amazed that there could be so many kinds, and went closer to look. There was a model of a sailing ship standing on the chest of drawers, with all its sails and rigging still intact. . . . He fingered it lovingly and let his hand run along its smooth curving sides . . .

In the drawers he found a bewildering array of clothes . . . so many, he didn't know how to choose. But at length he found some pants, and a shirt that didn't look much too big, and a blue pullover with a hole in one elbow. In the wardrobe he found various pairs of trousers, old-fashioned and baggy, but one pair of thin grey ones almost fitted him, especially when he turned-up the bottoms. . . . There was a belt already threaded through the slots, and he tightened it round his slim boy's waist and felt better.

He went to look at himself in the glass, and saw a strange pale boy with damp gold hair and large rather frightened eyes looking out at him. The blue of the jersey made the eyes look bluer than usual. . . . Who am I? he thought. Am I still Johnnie Ross? After a moment, he went downstairs and stood hesitantly in the doorway.

Emmaline Lucas caught her breath. It might have been Lance, her brother, standing there – except that he had not been quite so fair or so beautiful . . .

'You look very nice,' she said. 'Come on. Food's ready.'

When they had finished eating and Johnnie had cleared away, he asked about the ships.

'Yes, Lance loved sailing ships . . . made some good

models, too. . . . Interested, are you? There's a book in the library. Think you can find it? Let me see . . . third shelf on the left, half way along the wall by the window. . . . It's a big book with a blue cover and gold lettering, called *Sailing Ships of the World* . . .'

Johnnie stood looking at her in a puzzled way, he had heard most of the instructions, but he didn't know where the library was. . . . He thought a library was a red-brick building in the town where they had books and a counter with little tickets and rubber stamps . . .

'Well, boy – what's the matter?'

'Where – is – the – library?'

'Bless me, I've never shown you, have I? Haven't you peeped in on your own, then? Most boys would!' She grinned at him. 'Down the hall, door at the end. . . . Can you remember what I said?'

'Yes,' said Johnnie.

He went along the hall, and opened the tall white door at the end. He went into the room and stood staring. He had never seen so many books all in one room – shelf after shelf of them from floor to ceiling, all in neat orderly rows – some with old brown leather bindings, and others with crisp gold lettering, some large, some small. . . . And all, he thought, filled with words and pictures, and things he ought to know . . .

At last he moved forward, remembering his instructions, and put his hand out towards the book on sailing ships of the world which was there, as she had told him. . . . And it did have a blue cover, and the letters were gold, as she had said. . . . His fingers brushed over it, but for some reason that he could not understand they came to rest round the next book on the shelf and drew it out. . . . The cover was blue as well, but this was a tall thin book, full of coloured prints – and each successive picture had the most marvellous colours and mists and swirls of water and cloud and sunset and steam that Johnnie had ever seen. He stood there, transfixed, slowly turning page after page in wonder and sudden overwhelming love. This, this was how he wanted to paint – all these dreams and visions and cloudy washes of colour – beautiful beyond his wildest imaginings, and full of unending promise of unseen and half-seen miracles of light. . . . Oh, this was looking into heaven itself!

He stood there so long that at last Emmaline Lucas came to find him, swinging into the room with a swish of her wheel-chair. She stopped when she saw him standing there lost and dreaming, and her voice when she spoke to him was more than usually gentle. 'Well, boy? Can't you find it?'

He turned a blind face to her, and held out the book, saying in a strange, shaken whisper: 'Who – paints like this?'

She glanced at the open page, recognising at once that bloom of light behind the mists. . . . 'Why, boy, that's Turner. Don't you know a Turner when you see it?'

He stood looking at her intently, interpreting her words to himself with careful attention. 'Turner?'

She came nearer in the chair, and took the book from him gently. 'Here. "The Fighting Temeraire" – that's the most famous one. Lance loved that one – see the ship . . . and the fire in the water? He loved it because of the gallant old ship. . . . But Turner just loved London – see this one? That's just the Thames . . . and what about this? Steam and speed . . . see the old steam engine? D'you like that one?'

Johnnie nodded, speechless. She put the book back into his hands and said: 'Take it away and look at it. . . . Keep it if you like. . . . I'm a stupid old woman. I didn't realise you liked books . . . you can borrow any you like . . .'

He gazed at her. '*Any* of them?'

'Why not? Nobody else wants them. . . .' She looked at him curiously. 'Do you like painters? Do you paint yourself?'

He seemed to hesitate. 'I – can draw – a bit. . . . I haven't any paints . . . here . . .'

She nodded. 'Have you been drawing, then?'

'A bit.'

'Show me!' she commanded.

Johnnie looked troubled. 'I shall have to – have to – fetch them. . . . They're – outside . . .'

'Well, go on then. Fetch them!'

Maybe, as Johnnie still hesitated, this was the moment when Emma Lucas began to suspect that Johnnie did not go home to the village after dark. . . . But if she did, she said nothing and asked no questions – only repeated her command impatiently: 'Fetch them, boy – I want to look at them!'

So Johnnie went down to the summerhouse, with a newly fluffy, dazzlingly black and white Get-Lost prancing beside him, and got his drawings out of the dry, dark corner where he had put them one by one since he came. He took them carelessly in his hand and ran back to the house and laid them on Miss Lucas's rug-covered knees.

There was one of the house – four-square to the hills, with the dark trees behind it and the ivy climbing up the walls, and a flood of welcoming light from the door. . . . He already knew how to use light – instinctively – and from the shadowy outlines of the house and garden this sudden outflow of radiance seemed to spell shelter and safety and warmth. . . . That was how Johnnie saw it. . . . There was one of old Merlin, the donkey, looking grey and wise, with one ear cocked forward in enquiry and the other laid back as if twitching a fly away . . . he had an intelligent spark in his liquid dark eyes and almost a smile curving the sides of his soft muzzle, and his coat was rough and thick and furry. . . . It was clear that Johnnie already loved him – it showed in every line. Then there was one of the garden – a wild tangle of trees and unpruned rose bushes, a gentle wash of grass and flowers, and among them Get-Lost, looking out with joyous excitement from his new domain . . .

Last of all, there was a portrait of Emmaline Lucas herself . . . erect and indomitable in her chair, her eyes bright with challenge, her high forehead with its springing wing of white hair held upright like a defiant banner . . . the face, lined and aged, but alert and full of determined strength, and a faint hint of a smile at the edges of that straight, uncompromising mouth. . . . It was a powerful and revealing portrait, and she was astonished at the boy's observation and understanding. . . . Why, he knew her! He knew all about her! And he had made her seem quite tall and brave, sitting there in her wheel-chair, with the light on her face and the shadows behind her . . .

'Why, boy, you're a Rembrandt, not a Turner!' she exclaimed, pleased by the power of his drawing.

'Rem – ?' he asked, haltingly.

'Rembrandt, child. He painted people . . . he loved people . . . and he used light like you use it. . . . Look, I'll show you . . .'

She got out Rembrandt and showed him. Johnnie fell in love all over again. 'But if you want to paint like Turner, you want water colours first,' she said. 'They're softer. . . . Let me see . . . I had some somewhere . . . let's go and look . . .'

So it was that the second thing he wanted to ask for – books to read, all the books he could possibly want – was given to him without asking. . . . And the third thing, which he had not even dared to think about – paints and brushes and limitless piles of unused sketching blocks, the way to get down all this glory around him in colour – was granted before he even began to long for it . . .

In the evenings now there was a gentle kind of routine. They played a game. He read a book. Miss Lucas played the piano. . . . Sometimes she asked him what he was reading. He always showed her the book, but he rarely said much about it. He found it hard to talk anyway – the words went so fast and so sweetly by in his head when he was reading – and so painfully slowly when he was trying to say them aloud. . . . The old lady seemed to understand this, and only smiled and patted his hand and said: 'That's good. Worth reading. I'm glad you're reading that.'

At about nine o'clock, just as it was getting dark, Miss Lucas went to her room and prepared for bed. Johnnie had accepted her disability without question and never showed any sign of curiousity about it. But it occurred to him that she must have difficulty getting in and out of bed, and in and out of her clothes. . . . And where did she wash, if she couldn't get up the stairs?'

But one evening he went on reading after she left the long dining room which was where they spent most of their time in the evenings, and presently he heard her calling him.

'Johnnie? Are you still there?'

He went to the door of her room and looked in. Miss Lucas was sitting on the edge of her chair beside her bed which was a wide divan that looked fairly easy to get into. She had put on a dressing gown over a stiff frilled white nightdress, and she looked frail but still undaunted by anything – not even the awkward gap between her wheel-chair and the bed. . . . He noticed as he came forward that at the end of the big drawing-room there was an open door into a little cloakroom with a shower . . . so that's it, he thought. She manages in there – all alone. The thought troubled him somehow. . . . He came nearer to the bed.

'Yes, Miss Lucas?'

'Could you make me a hot drink tonight, boy? Ovaltine, I think. . . . You'll find the tin on the shelf by the stove . . .'

He nodded. Then, greatly daring, he asked: 'Do you – want a hand into bed?'

For a moment he thought she was going to be angry and shout at him. But then she suddenly seemed to be reassured by something in his face. She actually laughed. 'Good idea. I am a bit stiff tonight.'

Johnnie crossed the room to her side, and without another word put his arms round her and lifted her quite easily and gently on to the divan. She felt light in his arms, and her bones seemed brittle and small, like a bird's. . . . He slid the covers over her knees and propped the pillows behind her. Then, being naturally tactful, he went away very quickly to heat some milk for her hot drink.

When he brought it to her, she was smiling and seemed undismayed by having to be helped into bed. But he noticed that her hands shook a little as she took the cup, and that she slipped two white pills into it before she drank.

'You're a good boy, Johnnie,' she said. 'A great help. . . . Get along now, child. I'm quite all right . . .'

He smiled at her with sudden radiance – with such an upsurge of love and reassurance that she was dazzled.

'Good night, Miss Lucas,' he said.

After this it seemed that an extra barrier was down. Emmaline Lucas had admitted that the body was a frail thing and there were moments when it let her down. . . . Johnnie understood this, and though he made no comment whatsoever, he watched her now with care, and knew without being told when she was tired or needed extra help. She showed no embarrassment at having a boy of twelve look after her needs and bring her hot Ovaltine in bed. . . . And Johnnie showed no surprise either. They both accepted the situation, and took each day as it came, not worrying about the future.

At least, if Emmaline Lucas worried about the future, she did not say so. . . . Maybe, in the dark hours of the night when she was alone in the house, she did sometimes wonder what would happen to her when she got too incapacitated to manage alone. . . . Maybe she even wondered what she would do when the boy went – for he would surely go in the end. They all did.

And Johnnie, also alone in the dark night, sometimes lay awake and worried about the kids and his feckless Mum . . . and whether Maggie Fraser, the Welfare Lady, was really looking after them. . . . Was Kevin trying to do the cooking and keep the baby quiet? Had Mum stayed home with them, like a proper mother, or had she gone off again? Then his thoughts would stray to the Painting Man who had understood how he saw things better than anyone. . . . Did he miss him sometimes in the Park? And was Dessie worrying about him and wondering where he was? If she *was* worried, was he right to stay away? He never came to any conclusion about this. . . . It haunted him and lay like a heavy ache on his heart – together with the awful sense of guilt that he had been responsible for what happened to Big Joe. . . . Was it his fault? He supposed it must have been. . . . Sometimes the ache grew so heavy that he could no longer lie in bed, and he would get up and wander out into the darkened garden, with Get-Lost at his heels . . .

The cool grey shapes of the trees calmed him, and the feel of the damp grass under his bare feet was strangely soothing. . . . Here, the world was quiet and untouched by human violence or human grief. . . . He could not put into words what he felt, but the anxious busy thoughts in his head seemed to grow small and unimportant. . . . All that mattered here was that things should keep on growing gently and sturdily, without hindrance, in the dark wilderness of the dew-laden garden . . . nothing else seemed real . . .

Sometimes, when things felt really bad, he would talk to Get-Lost in the dark night watches. He would sit hunched on the grass, hugging the little dog close and say: 'What shall I do, Get-Lost? Do you know?' And Get-Lost would lean close, as dogs do, and try to lick his nose, and do his utmost to be a comfort. . . . Once or twice, Johnnie even talked to old Merlin standing patiently under the trees, knee-high in grasses. The old donkey would prick his ears and Johnnie would clasp him round his grey furry neck and lean his head close and whisper things into those black velvet ears. . . . And then Get-Lost would feel left out of things and pretend to find a rabbit or a fox in the garden . . . and Johnnie's blue mood would give way to laughter as he tried to chase Get-Lost in the dark and prevent him barking loud enough to wake Miss Lucas . . .

He loved the garden. Whether at night or by day, he loved it almost as passionately and as intimately as Miss Lucas did. He felt he knew every root and twig . . . every leaf and every flower. . . . He had never had a garden to look after before . . . now, under the old lady's instruction, he learnt how to clear the weeds from the buried flowerbeds and disentangle the half-smothered roses and train them over the ancient iron pergolas across the paths. . . . He cleaned the little lily pond out and cleared it of choking weed, and found two fragile water lily plants and some golden marsh marigolds struggling towards the light . . . and he even found a few shy fish hiding under the reeds . . . and one small newt. . . . He learnt how to use a scythe on the long grass, and how to bundle the sweet-smelling cut swathes into trusses for Merlin to eat. . . . He learnt how to plant out seedlings into his newly-turned earth, holding the small green plants in his fingers and feeling the warmth and security of the brown earth as he piled it up round them and settled them safely in the sunny borders . . .

The garden, being so isolated and so untended, was alive with birds. Sometimes he heard them singing to him, their high clear voices penetrating the fogs and echoes of his ears with perfect clarity. . . . Sometimes he did not hear them so clearly but he could see them all round him . . . their wings flashed at him in the sun . . . and there was a robin who came to watch him dig and even hopped on to his spade . . .

He was continuously amazed and enraptured by this new green, living world around him. . . . He worked in a kind of dreamlike state of wonder and tranquillity. . . . He felt he never wanted to leave this enclosed, enchanted paradise . . .

Miss Lucas watched him grow brown and strong in the sun and wind and soft Welsh rain – and she smiled. He reminded her continuously of her young brothers – lost now in deeps of time like her own sunladen childhood. With Johnnie and Get-Lost running about the mossy paths, it was like being young again.

One day she took Johnnie with her in the automatic car and drove to Llandovery to do some shopping. He helped her into the driver's seat and stowed her chair away neatly folded beside her, noticing the way the car was designed to accommodate the folded chair and to make it easy for a disabled person to drive. All the knobs and levers were within hand reach, and close to the steering wheel there was an extra knob which opened the nearside door so that the chair could be pushed out on to the pavement ready for the driver to climb into. . . . Miss Lucas hardly needed Johnnie to help her, but all the same she seemed glad that he was there, and Johnnie himself was delighted to be going with her.

He and Get-Lost climbed in the back, and Miss Lucas turned round and grinned at them both. It felt like a party. He watched with attention as she manipulated the car with its automatic gears and drove down the leafy lanes with great precision and confidence. He had expected her to be a bit vague and unsafe, but she wasn't at all. She drove cheerfully into the little market town and parked neatly in the old market square behind the main shopping street.

'Here we are!' she said, quite gaily, and released the catch of the door.

Johnnie unfolded the chair and helped her into it. They left Get-Lost on guard in the car, and went off to look at the shops.

The little town dreamed in the sun. The cobbles under his feet round the old Market Hall felt warm and worn with age. The town was busy and friendly, and nobody seemed in a hurry. He could hear the sound of sheep baaing in the market stalls on the other side of the street, near the ruined castle. Above the Market Hall, the clock in the octagonal tower chimed the hour. Johnnie's observant artist's eye took in the curve of the old stone arches under the Market Hall building, and the uneven lines of the houses on the north side of the square. They all looked a little crooked, as if they had sagged a bit and then settled comfortably into old age. . . . Johnnie's fingers itched to draw them. There was an old black and white pub tucked into one corner which looked even saggier and sleepier than the rest . . .

He began to push Miss Lucas in her chair across the cobbles towards the main road and the rows of shops.

'Johnnie,' said Miss Lucas, 'I owe you some wages. . . . What do you want to do with them?'

Johnnie looked astonished. 'Wages?'

'You've earned them, boy. You've worked hard. . . . Isn't there something you want to buy?' She was smiling up at him, almost rogueishly.

Johnnie smiled back. As usual it made the recipient blink. 'Could I – get some – thick – paints?'

'You mean oil paints – yes. I know a shop . . .'

They bought paints and brushes and a block of canvas-paper on which to experiment, and one good canvas, as Miss Lucas said 'For your next masterpiece!' Laughing together, they left the shop, Johnnie pushing the chair, Miss Lucas carrying the parcels.

Then she said: 'What about a new jersey – instead of that one with holes? After all, it's your own money!'

So they bought a new jersey which Miss Lucas insisted must be as bright a blue as the old one – and a pair of sandals because Johnnie's old shoes were becoming deplorable. After that, they bought some stores for the house, and some more pills from the chemist, and finally Miss Lucas said: 'Now let's have a Welsh tea in town before we go home!' and directed him to her favourite café.

On their way back to the car, she said over her shoulder: 'You haven't bought much for yourself. . . . Isn't there anything else you want?'

Johnnie thought. Then he said shyly: 'I could – get a ball – for Get-Lost. . . . But I've got some money . . .'

She nodded, clearly respecting his independence. She let him settle her back in the car and then pointed across the street. 'The chemist is a pet shop, too . . . you can get a ball there . . .'

Johnnie ran across the road and into the shop and chose a small, shiny red ball for Get-Lost. On the way back he saw in the little jewellers shop along the street a small blue butterfly-wing pendant in the front of the cluttered window.

'How much is it?' he asked, wondering if Mr Patel's money would be enough.

'A present, is it?' asked the woman behind the counter, also wondering if the boy's money would stretch to it.

He nodded. 'For Miss Lucas,' he said, with pride.

'Your auntie, is it?' said the woman, her lilting Welsh voice reminding him sharply of Tonsils Taffy. 'Make a lovely birthday present . . . look at that blue, now . . . like the sky, isn't it?'

Johnnie agreed. He even murmured it aloud: 'Yes . . . like the sky . . .'

'Well now,' she said, head on one side, 'seeing as it's *special* – 'She turned the label over and looked at it, 'it says two pounds here . . . but that was before the Sale . . .'

'Sale?' asked Johnnie, looking at her with large anxious eyes.

'Indeed, yes,' said the woman, utterly overthrown by those eyes. 'The Sale. Half price now, see? So how would a pound suit you?'

Johnnie's vivid smile broke out like the sun. He handed over Mr Patel's pound, and received the blue pendant in a small silver box. . . . The woman was still blinking in a dazed way at the smile long after he had left the shop.

When he got back to the car he got in the back with Get-Lost and showed him his red ball. Then he leant forward and laid the little box on Miss Lucas's knees. 'For you,' he said, and sat back very small, feeling suddenly shy.

The old brittle fingers seemed to fumble a little as they opened the box, and then there was a silence. It went on so long that Johnnie was alarmed and leant forward again to see if Miss Lucas was all right. She was holding the blue pendant in her hand, and she was looking very bright-eyed and strange.

'Miss Lucas?' he said. 'It's all right . . . it's only a present . . .'

She turned to him then, and sniffed and rubbed a fierce hand over her eyes. She could not tell him that long ago, on her fourteenth birthday, her father had given her just such a pendant of the same glorious blue . . . her first almost grown-up jewellery to wear with her first long white dress. . . . And how young and carefree and joyous she had been then, and how light her feet had been in the dances. . . . Instead, she managed a lopsided grin and said in a husky voice: 'It's simply beautiful, Johnnie. . . . Put it on for me . . .'

He fastened it round her neck and looked at the iridescent colour, flashing in the sun.

'Beautiful!' he agreed. 'Like the sky . . .'

The little search party at the Welsh farmhouse went sadly home on the third morning. They had drawn a blank everywhere. No-one had seen a fair-haired boy with a dog. . . . There wasn't even a whisper about him . . .

They weren't to know, of course, that Johnnie had reached the summerhouse in Miss Lucas's garden on the day he left Brad Harris at Milford Haven – two days before they even set out for Wales to look for him. . . . They weren't to know, either, that he was safe and reasonably warm and well-fed, and as nearly happy as a boy of his troublesome conscience could be. . . . All of them had anxious visions of a tired, cold child wandering in the dark, afraid even to ask for help . . .

'Do you think he is all right?' asked Maggie, looking almost haggard with worry.

'Of course he is,' said Dessie sturdily. 'I'd know if he wasn't.'

'But how will he survive? He only had two pounds on him to start with – and that was more than a week ago . . .'

'He'll manage. Johnnie's not stupid. . . . He'll find some work or something . . .'

'I can't understand why nobody's seen him!' said Bill, sounding upset and mystified both at once. He hated uncertainty and not being able to put things right for Maggie.

'Maybe they have,' said Sister Ruth, in a mild, thoughtful voice, 'but they didn't realise it . . .'

'We'll simply have to wait for news . . .' said Maggie, sighing. 'There's nothing else we can do.'

They drove back home, and Maggie promptly went round to see Julie and the kids. She found the children alone, with Kevin valiantly trying to get the tea.

'Where's your mother?' she asked sharply.

'Dunno,' said Kevin. 'Went off.'

Maggie was horrified. 'How long ago?'

'Yesterday. . . . Didn't come home last night.' He spooned some jam on to a piece of bread for Treesa. 'I give Benjy his tea,' he added.

Sighing, Maggie made hasty arrangements to put the three of them back into care . . . and as a temporary

235

measure, took them home with her. She only had a small flat, but they'd fit in somewhere.

'She'll come back,' volunteered Kevin, in his cool, seven-year-old voice. 'She usually does.'

Maggie looked at him in exasperated admiration. He didn't seem unduly bothered. What a life these children led – what crises they had endured so far, totally without complaint or surprise.

'When's Johnnie coming home, Miss?' he asked. There was much more concern and longing in his voice over his big brother, she noted, than over his casual mother.

'Soon, Kevin,' she said. 'We'll find him soon . . .'

A day or two later, a loud-voiced school teacher rang Sergeant Mackay from Abergavenny and told a tale about a coach party and an unexplained extra boy with a dog. . . . 'Didn't think it odd at the time,' said the Voice. 'Thought it was one of the other lot. . . . We did count 'em . . . but one was away sick and forgot to tell us, see? And then I saw this bit in the paper . . . could have been him . . .'

They counted back the days and found it must have been the morning that Johnnie left Brad Harris . . .

'And he got off at Llandovery and disappeared again?' asked Sergeant Mackay. He knew that Maggie's party had already enquired all over Milford Haven and the surrounding countryside and gone away empty-handed. . . . So had the Welsh police, whom he had already alerted. . . . All the same, it was worth a try . . .

Then a hesitant Welsh voice rang and said doubtfully: 'I don't know if it could be anything, mind . . . he was such a nice boy, see? Bought a silver pendant in my shop, silver and blue, it was. . . . Said it was for his auntie's birthday, isn't it? Told me her name, too. Miss –

Cross, was it. . . ? No, it wasn't that . . . there now, I've forgotten it. . . . Never did have a head for names. . . . Lovely eyes he had, and such fair hair . . . and a beautiful smile, see? Looked a bit like the boy that was missing, see?'

'Did he have a dog?' asked Sergeant Mackay, trying to disentangle fact from Welsh chatter.

'Dog? No . . . I didn't see any dog. . . . He ran across the road and got back into a car with the old lady. . . . I watched them go, you see. Curious, I was . . . and him so polite and good-looking, look you . . .'

Car? Old lady? thought the Sergeant. It can't be Johnnie. 'You're sure you can't remember that name?' he asked.

There was a pause. Then the lilting Welsh voice replied. 'No. Sorry I am. . . . It was something like Cross . . . I didn't catch it very clearly, really . . .'

'Well, thank you for calling,' he said. 'I don't think it can have been the boy we want . . .'

'Glad I am,' replied the warm, musical voice: 'I wouldn't want that lovely boy to be in any danger, look you. . . . But sorry I am your Johnnie can't be found . . .'

She rang off, and Sergeant Mackay sat by the phone for a long time in puzzled silence. Could it be? What would he be doing with an old lady and a car? Why would he be buying silver and blue pendants. . . . Where would he get the money?

No, he thought. It can't be. It must be a coincidence . . . all the same, he rang the Llandovery police and alerted them. They promised to look into it, but they sounded rather unimpressed.

Sister Ruth had returned to Bournemouth, still rebellious and still uncharacteristically upset. She had made Maggie promise that if there was any news she would instantly tell her, and she had announced belligerently to Sister Augustine that if Johnnie was found she would insist on being allowed to go and see him. . . . Sister Augustine sighed and agreed.

'You know,' she said kindly, trying to keep the note of reproof out of her voice, 'this is not exactly in accordance with the discipline of the Order!'

'I know,' agreed Sister Ruth, 'I never was much good at unquestioning obedience . . . maybe I ought to leave it. . . ? I mean, I still think the Order ought to make use of all our talents – such as we've got. . . . I'm a qualified teacher, and I do no teaching here. . . . You're a qualified nurse, and you do no nursing. . . . What are we doing here?'

'We are doing what we are told to do,' said Sister Augustine severely.

'That's just what I mean,' exploded Sister Ruth. 'And since I've been up in Blackbridge with Maggie Fraser, I've seen so much else that wants doing!'

'You know very well we do a good job here – '

'Yes, but anyone could do it.'

'Anyone could *not* do it. . . . The children who come here need very special care . . . you know that. . . . And they do sometimes need nursing – and they do sometimes need teaching!'

Sister Ruth looked contrite. 'Yes, that is true. . . . But it is all so . . . shortlived. . . . I would so love to feel that the children could have more permanent love and care . . . and my work could have more permanent results!'

'That's probably self-indulgence!' There was definitely a gleam of amusement in Sister Augustine's dark eyes.

'Probably,' agreed Sister Ruth. 'I'm an undisciplined, vain, self-centred woman!' She smiled, rightly assessing the gleam in those eyes . . . 'All the same . . . I'm afraid I may get even worse as time goes by!'

'We'd better get on with the tasks in hand then, while we can!' said Sister Augustine, and took Sister Ruth upstairs to help her sort out the clean linen for the dormitories.

Dessie had made a pact with Maggie Fraser. She would go back to the home where she had been placed in care, and she would go back to school, if she could be certain Maggie would take her along when Johnnie was found. She had no doubt at all that he would be found – in the end. And she was fairly certain in her own mind that he was not at present in any physical danger. . . . She thought she would know if he was . . . but she felt equally convinced that some heavy weight of worry lay on him. . . . There was a dark patch in her mind when she thought about him . . . Johnnie was alone and deeply troubled about something, and she ought to be there to sort it out for him.

In the meantime, Johnnie's kid brothers and sister had arrived at the home as well – and not for the first time, either. So she made it her own special self-appointed task to keep an eye on them and give them as much care and attention as Johnnie used to do when he was home. They were good kids, not at all tiresome – except that Benjy cried a lot, Treesa hid in corners and sucked her thumb, and Kevin was getting very thin and sad without Johnnie. She did her best to cheer him up, and said, every time he asked about his big brother: 'Won't be long now. He'll soon be back.'

She hoped it was true. Oh, most passionately and desperately, she hoped it was true. Sometimes in the night, in the long girls' dormitory, she would lie and remember the sea at Bournemouth, and how she and Johnnie had swum in silver that moonlit night . . . 'They can't take it away from you,' she had said to him. 'It's yours, see? For always . . .' And he had put a cool white pebble in her hand and murmured: 'Yours . . . and mine . . .'

She had the pebble still. She kept it among her few precious possessions in a cardboard box. . . . Sometimes, when the memory of that halcyon time got too strong to bear, she would take the pebble out of the box and put it under her pillow before she slept. . . . She would dream then of the sea, breaking gently on the dark shore in a line of silver . . . and Johnnie, running free along the sand . . .

Bill Hamilton watched the change in Maggie with something like despair. He didn't know how to help her, or what to say that was any comfort. Day by day she got paler and more haggard with anxiety, and her eyes held a look of bewilderment and distress that he longed to assuage.

'Where can he be?' she said, over and over again. 'How on earth is he living? Do you – Bill, do you think. . . ? Could anything awful have happened to him?'

Bill shook his head. Anything could have happened to him in a world as full of violence and trouble as this one – but he was not going to say so.

'No . . . I said before, he's resourceful . . . used to coping on his own. . . . He'll be holed up somewhere quite safe. . . . Probably doesn't even know we're worried about him . . .'

'You don't think . . . Julie might know where he is and have gone off after him?'

Bill hesitated. 'I doubt it . . . she's probably just gone off on a spree with some man.'

240

Maggie sighed. 'You're probably right!' Then she rubbed a weary hand over her face and added: 'I'm sorry, Bill . . . it's just that I feel so useless!'

'We can only wait, Maggie . . . and go on with our daily lives. . . . When he comes back will be the time to take action!'

Even so, he was thinking of the future, and quietly setting his house in order. . . . He collected up all his good paintings and sent them up to London to the art gallery that usually sold them for him . . . that should bring in some ready cash. . . . He also rummaged about in drawers and got out his old diplomas and teaching certificates from the Slade . . . he could always go back to teaching if they needed extra money. . . . Then he had a bonfire in his small back garden and burnt a lot of rubbish, including some of his worst pictures. But then he thought of Johnnie and took the old canvases off the fire and saved them. . . . The boy could always paint over them while he was learning . . .

After that, he gave away a lot of old clothes and sorted out his books and papers into extraordinarily tidy piles. He hadn't thought yet where he and Maggie would live – if they did get everything straight and decided to get married. . . . She had a nice flat, but it was too small. He had this unpretentious terrace house, but that was a bit small, too – if their plans were going to come to anything. . . . He decided to decorate the rooms with clean white paint. . . . At least it would sell better, if he moved . . . and he had to do something!

The truth was, Bill was as upset and strung up as Maggie about Johnnie. He had grown mysteriously fond of the boy, somehow – and found himself wondering constantly about his safety, his future, and the development of that marvellous talent of his. . . . That drawing of the Welsh singer on the tanker . . . he couldn't get it out of his mind. It was so vivid and so . . . ecstatic somehow. What he would give for a talent like that himself! He was a first-rate craftsman – a good, steady run-of-the-mill working artist. But Johnnie had a spark of original genius that he had never had. . . . It was up to him, therefore, to help it along in every way he could. . . . As soon as Johnnie was found. If he was found . . .

But he wouldn't let himself think like that. Be positive. That was the strong thing to be. He picked up the phone and dialled Maggie's office.

'Maggie,' he said, 'stop brooding, and come out to lunch.'

'How did you know I was brooding?'

'I can hear it all across town,' he said, laughing. 'I'll pick you up in ten minutes. All right?'

'All right,' agreed Maggie, sighing. She admitted, ruefully, that she was always sighing, just lately!

'And by the way,' added Bill, smiling into the phone, 'did I ever tell you I love you?'

Maggie laughed. 'Oh Bill! Not now!'

'Why not now? Everyone needs reminding now and then that someone loves them!' He rang off, still smiling.

Yes, thought Maggie, the warmth of Bill's voice still with her. But with Danny Ross dead, and Julie gone off somewhere, who is there to remind Johnnie that someone loves him?

A few days after the expedition to Llandovery, Johnnie brought his first oil painting to show Miss Lucas. He had spent a long time looking at the Turners and Rembrandts in the library, and the way they handled light obsessed him. He saw the garden anew, with light brimming behind each leaf and frond of hillside bracken. . . . He saw the clouds above the hills, rimmed with light, and their shadows moving across the sunlit flanks of the mountains – like the music of Vaughan Williams. . . . He saw the light behind Merlin's grey fur, making a fuzz of dim radiance round his shaggy head, and the way the sunlight picked out bits of Get-Lost's fluffy coat and made him look quite silver and sparkling . . . and how even the goats, chewing peacefully in the sunlit grass, had sudden points of brilliance about their long white coats . . .

When he had looked at all this for a long time, he decided that bright sunlight was too difficult at first, so he chose a rosy evening at sunset, when all the colours had a dreamlike muted glow about them. He set Miss Lucas in her chair at one side, with one hand stretched out to Merlin's head which was peering down at her from a golden-green wash of orchard grass. . . . Even the three goats were there – vague white ghosts among the lush grasses – and so was Get-Lost, eagerly chasing an imaginery rabbit into the shadows. . . . A great cascade of creamy pink blossom foamed on the old apple trees in the orchard, and the grass was awash with pink campion and silvery lady's smocks. Behind Miss Lucas, the long windows of one end of the house just caught the setting sun and glowed crimson-red – and above the flowery landscape, the sky bloomed with all the soft colours of sunset and cast a gentle reflection of rosy light on to Miss Lucas's upturned face . . .

It was a picture of love – with every stroke of Johnnie's brush he was saying: 'I love this place . . . I love this old house and this rambling wilderness of a garden . . . I love the orchard full of ancient fruit trees. I love old Merlin and the goats living quietly together in this enclosed, forgotten place . . . I love little Get-Lost, playing with the shadows. . . . And I love Miss Emmaline Lucas, who presides over all this richness like a wise, calm old priestess in her sanctuary . . .' He did not put all this into words, of course. He didn't know enough words for it. But it was there on the canvas, in the creamy light-ridden surface of his painting, for all to see.

Miss Lucas looked at it for a long time. Johnnie thought for a moment that she was going to cry again, like she did over the pendant. . . . But instead she looked up at him in the end and smiled.

'It looks . . . enchanted somehow . . . like a fairy tale. Is that how you see it?'

'Yes,' He smiled back, and made a gesture with his hand, as if to enclose that enchanted garden in one sweeping curve of space. '. . . a perfect place . . .'

She was staring at him oddly. 'I believe you love it almost as much as I do, child.'

Johnnie nodded.

'All my life,' she murmured, 'all my long life, I've lived here . . . all my childhood and my youth . . .' She was talking to herself really, but her voice was gentle and clear. 'And in my old age, too . . .'

Johnnie said slowly, trying to put a difficult thought into words: 'You don't . . . always need years . . . to love something . . .'

'No,' agreed Emmaline Lucas, looking at the boy through a dazzle that was not only sunset. 'No, Johnnie . . . nor you do . . .'

He thought Miss Lucas seemed a little tired that night, and she went to bed early. But she did not complain about anything, and only asked for her now customary hot drink and her pills. . . . She also asked Johnnie to lift down an old cardboard box full of photos which stood on top of the chest in the corner.

'I want to look at my memories!' she said, smiling,

and then dismissed him gently but firmly. 'I have everything I need now, boy. Goodnight!'

Johnnie left her, and wandered down through the garden to the summerhouse through the falling dusk.

That night he dreamed that Get-Lost had found a fox near the hen-run and was barking his head off with outrage and alarm . . .

He woke suddenly, and found the little dog gone from his side. Faintly, the sound of urgent barking came to him over the sleeping garden. Was it barking? Or were his ears playing tricks?

He got up and went to look out. He could not see anything unusual. The garden lay quiet, the trees stood like grey ghosts under a fitful moon behind scudding clouds. But Get-Lost *was* barking – even his ears could hear him – he was certain now. And there was something more like terror than excitement in his sharp, shrill cries.

Johnnie moved down the path towards the sound, – and then he began to run. . . . For he had caught a whiff of something on the wind that was not the scent of flowers. . . . It was smoke.

He came round the corner towards the house, and saw a thin curl of smoke coming from the closed French windows of Miss Lucas's room. As he ran closer, he could see the red flicker of flames reflected on the ceiling through the windows. . . . He remembered suddenly that you mustn't open windows in a fire . . . it made the draught worse. . . . In any case, Miss Lucas always locked the French windows at night before she went to bed . . . and the front door. He tore round the house to the back door. He knew where the key was – on the nail behind the wooden beam in the dairy. . . . He had put it there himself when he went to the summerhouse that night. He reached up and took it down, his hand shaking with haste, and fitted the key in the lock and turned it. . . . The door swung open as he lifted the latch, and he raced through the kitchen into the hall.

Smoke was already pouring out under the drawing-room door, and he could feel the heat. . . . He thought: I've got to get her out . . . which way will be quickest? Then he flung open the door and burst into the room. A whoosh of hot air, smoke and flame shot past him into the hall. He could see Miss Lucas, not in bed but huddled in her chair asleep . . . or unconscious? The charred remains of the cardboard boxful of photographs lay smoking on the floor, close to the electric fire which was still switched on. . . . The curtain at one of the long windows was already ablaze, and so was the carved pine mantelpiece above the electric fire. The hearth-rug was smouldering too, and one of the big upholstered wing chairs was sending out clouds of acrid smoke . . .

Coughing desperately, Johnnie seized the handles of the wheelchair with the unconscious old lady still huddled within its arms, and swung it round, trying to think how to get her out. . . . The doorway was filled with heavy smoke by now, and the curtains behind it were already on fire. Across the hall, he saw a tongue of flame reaching out from the rug towards the oak treads of the stairs. . . . No good that way, then . . . the smoke would kill her, even if he could avoid the flames . . .

He rushed over to the second French window and turned the key in the lock . . . but the doors seemed stuck somehow . . . probably the heat had already made them warp and blister. . . . Seizing the wheelchair again, he took a stumbling run straight at the jammed doors to the garden, ramming them hard with the wheels of the chair. . . . There was a splintering crash and a sickening jolt – he hoped the bump would not hurt the old lady still further – and then with a sudden jerk the doors gave way, and Johnnie and Miss Lucas and the chair shot headfirst into the garden.

He picked himself up, vaguely noticing that one hand hurt him, and went to see how Miss Lucas was. She lay in a quiet, dark heap on the grass, but she was still breathing – though her breath came in strange gasps of pain because of the smoke.

She's alive! he thought. He picked her up in his arms and staggered with her further down the lawn away from the house. In case, he thought . . . just in case. . . . She'll be safe enough out here . . .

Then he remembered the telephone, and that he must summon help. The phone was in the hall, but not very near where the flames and smoke were. He could probably reach it.

He went back inside the drawing-room, and stopped to tear down the other pair of curtains before they caught fire and took the flames upwards . . .

Water, he thought. I could put it out if I had enough . . . there's a garden hose somewhere . . .

He went over to the bed and grabbed a blanket to wrap round his head, and then charged into the hall past the smouldering door curtain and the burning rug on the floor . . . I must get those out, he thought. . . . But telephone first . . .

He reached the table where the phone was and picked up the receiver. . . . For the second time in his young life he dialled 999 – and again said: 'Help!' But this time he added in a clear, lucid voice: 'Fire! Fire! Miss Lucas at Bryn House. . . . Quick! Fire! Ambulance! Miss Lucas at Bryn House. . . . She is hurt. Help!'

Then he rushed into the kitchen again and turned on the taps and filled all the pails and basins he could find. . . . While they were filling he went out into the shed behind the dairy and found a long length of garden hose. He dragged it into the kitchen and struggled to fit it on to one of the taps. . . . It would not stay on at first,

247

and kept slipping off in little spurts of water, but at last he got the spring clip fixed and the rubber tube stayed firmly over the jet of water from the tap. . . . He took the hose with him into the hall, and tried to play the water on to the spreading flames on the stairs . . .

All this time, he had forgotten about Get-Lost who had raised the alarm. . . . He supposed the little dog had run off again into the garden, afraid of the heat and flames . . . but now, to his horror, he found himself looking up into the terrified face of Get-Lost peering down at him from the corner of the banisters on the landing above the hall. . . . He must have fled up there when the fire spread across the hall, and retreated in panic from the approaching flames . . .

'Get-Lost!' he called. 'Come down! You'll be trapped! Come down!'

But the little dog was too petrified to move. The flames were below him, and creeping upwards. And as they crept forwards, so he backed further and further away . . .

'Oh!' said Johnnie, suddenly furious. 'You *stupid* dog!' And he laid the hose across a chair with the jet of water pointing up the stairs, pulled the blanket back round his head, and dashed through the small licking flames up the first flight of stairs . . .

Get-Lost uttered a wild yap of relief as Johnnie's hand reached out and grabbed him by the scruff of his neck.

'Stupid!' repeated Johnnie, no longer furious, but alarmed now at the speed with which the fire was spreading . . . 'Now, put your head in there – and don't look!' He pushed the dog as far inside the blanket as he could, and dashed back down the stairs. . . . The wood was very hot and crumbly, and one of the treads gave way as he ran. . . . But he got through, and tore out through the broken French windows on to the lawn, gasping and

248

retching, eyes streaming, his gold hair blackened with smoke and soot . . .

He found Miss Lucas still lying where he had left her. He put the dog down beside her, and, suddenly frightened by her stillness and the damp night air, he laid the blackened blanket over her and stooped to listen again to her breathing. It was steadier now, he thought . . . not so gasping. . . . But why didn't she wake up? He shook her a little and called her a couple of times, but she did not stir . . .

Then he looked back at the house and began to think. The firemen would soon be here. The ambulance would come, too . . . and probably the police. . . . All sorts of questions would be asked. He would be unable to hide the truth from them any longer. . . . He would be taken back home and told about Big Joe, and they would say it was his fault . . . and probably put him in prison . . . and he would disgrace all his family . . .

Well then, he thought, I must go away. I must go now. With Get-Lost. Before they come. It will be all right. They'll look after the old lady. They'll stop the house from burning down . . . I needn't stay any longer. . . . If I slip away now, they'll never know . . .

He actually turned away towards the drive and stooped to pick up the frightened, shivering little dog. . . . But then, something stopped him. He looked down at Miss Lucas lying so quiet and helpless on the grass . . . he remembered how light and fragile she had felt in his arms as he laid her down . . . I can't, he said. I can't leave her! I can't leave the house to burn down . . . or the garden, or the animals . . . I've got to stay and see that they are all right . . . I'm Johnnie Ross, and I can't run away any more. . . . Let them do what they like! I've got to stay!

A sudden wild frenzy of protective love blazed up

within him. He rushed back into the house, leaving Get-Lost beside Miss Lucas, and began frantically beating out the flames with a shovel, a broom, a poker – anything that came to hand. He poured water all over everything, – he ran madly to and fro, trying in vain to go faster than the fire. . . . At last, exhausted and blinded, he staggered out into the kitchen to collect another brimming bucket of water, and passed out cold on the wet stone floor, just as the clanging fire engine came roaring up the drive . . .

As the first fireman came running into the kitchen, Johnnie roused himself a little and murmured: 'Miss Lucas . . . in the garden . . .' Then, speaking very carefully and distinctly, he said: 'I am Johnnie Ross . . . I'm sorry I ran away . . .'

He woke in a white hospital bed, to a dazzle of sunshine. It made him blink, so he could not see very well. . . . He could feel, though. . . . Everything seemed to hurt . . . but he was clearly alive. . . . Then memory came flooding back and he tried to sit up. 'Miss Lucas?' he said – and then again, more urgently: 'Miss Lucas?'

There was a roaring in his ears rather like the fire, and he couldn't hear very well. . . . But a voice said slowly and clearly: 'Miss Lucas is all right . . . a bit of shock, like you. . . . But she's fine.'

'Fine?' repeated Johnnie vaguely. The room seemed to tilt and dissolve in a strange, pearly mist.

'Just fine!' repeated the voice.

Johnnie scarcely heard it. There was something he ought to tell them . . . but he couldn't think what it was. . . . 'Safe. . . ?' he murmured.

Before the voice could answer, he had drifted away again and the pearly mist closed over his head.

He did not know that the owner of the voice was Maggie Fraser, or that she sat there all that day, often with tears in her eyes, waiting for him to wake . . .

The next time he woke, he recognised Maggie and smiled. 'Hallo,' he whispered, feeling suddenly safe and glad. Then he thought about home and his eyes grew anxious. 'The – kids?'

'They're OK, Johnnie. Don't worry. Everything is all right.'

'Are they going to put me in prison?' he asked.

Maggie stared. 'Good heavens, no! What an idea! You're a hero, Johnnie, didn't you know?' Then she thought about the implications of that remark and decided to tell him about what had happened to Big Joe.

He listened intently, though his ears were still very buzzy since the fire, and then he repeated Maggie's words very slowly, as if to himself: 'Nobody's fault?'

'No, Johnnie. He was already very ill . . . it was nobody's fault.'

There was silence in the room for a while. Johnnie's expression was grave as he thought about it, but he didn't say any more.

At last, in sudden panic, he remembered his dog. 'Get-Lost? I forgot. . . . Is he. . . ?'

'Yes.' Maggie was smiling. 'He's all right, too. Dessie's looking after him.'

'*Dessie?*' His face lit with hope. 'Is she here?'

'She's here, Johnnie. She'll be in to see you later on. . . . So is your friend the Painting Man – but they'll come in tomorrow when you're stronger. . . . And Sister Ruth sends her love and says she's coming to see you soon.'

It was all suddenly too much for Johnnie. Miss Lucas

251

being all right – and the kids as well . . . the news about Big Joe . . . and Get-Lost being safe, and all his friends being here – Maggie and the Painting Man and Dessie – especially Dessie. . . . He turned his head away quickly to hide the tears.

'Go to sleep now,' said Maggie gently. 'You're worn out . . . it'll all keep till tomorrow.'

'Tomorrow . . .' sighed Johnnie, and fell asleep again.

In the morning, he insisted on getting up and going to see Miss Lucas. He found that his legs were wobbly and his feet hurt, and when he looked in the mirror, he saw that one side of his face was scorched red, and his hair had gone pale and frizzy at the edges. . . . But otherwise, the same dark blue eyes looked back at him and said: Who are you? I'm Johnnie Ross, he said. And I don't have to hide any more!

He found Miss Lucas propped up in bed, looking frail but as indomitable as ever. Her black eyes flashed a welcome even before she spoke, but she did not make any extravagant gesture or show any obvious pleasure at his arrival.

'Well, boy,' she said. 'Survivors, you and I! And they saved the house, thanks to you!'

Johnnie smiled. 'Are you . . . all right. . . ?'

'Me? What do you think? I'm tough, you know. . . . The smoke got me, that's all.' She put out a hand and drew him down on to the chair beside her. 'My fault, you know – the fire. Fell asleep in my chair. . . . If it hadn't been for you – ' She paused, and then gave his hand a friendly squeeze. He felt the dry, brittle fingers grip him with surprising strength and firmness.

'You're a good boy, Johnnie,' she said.

In the afternoon, Dessie came. She stood at the bottom of Johnnie's bed and pushed the wild hair out of her eyes, and began to chant softly:

'Johnnie Dumbo,
Hasn't got a crumbo – !'

and then, when she saw the smile begin in his eyes, flung her arms round him and gave him a huge, suffocating hug.

'You idiot!' she said. 'Frightening us all to death! I could kill you!' In fact she seemed likely to, her arms hugged him so tight. But they could not stop smiling at one another, and Dessie's strong hand held on to his brown one and couldn't let to.

'I kept the pebble . . .' she said.

'I want to show you her garden . . .' he said.

They looked at one another, still smiling.

'Plenty of time . . .' said Dessie.

The Painting Man came to see him last of all – and when he came he was smiling and full of brisk instructions.

'Come on, now. You can get dressed. The car's waiting.'

Johnnie looked at him, wide-eyed. 'Where are we going?'

'To take Miss Lucas home, of course. . . . Back to Bryn House . . . will you like that?'

The boy's face was pale with hope. 'Is it . . . fit for her . . . to live in?'

The Painting Man nodded cheerfully. 'Yes, it is. We've fitted up the other room – the dining room, I think it is. . . . There's rather a smell of burnt wood, and the hall and the front room will have to be re-decorated, and the stairs will want renewing here and there . . . but we can manage . . .'

'We?'

'We're all going to stay a bit and put things straight. . . . Isn't that what you want?'

'Yes!' said Johnnie. 'It is!'

When the car reached the house and Johnnie got out, a small black and white streak launched itself across the drive straight into his arms. Get-Lost was not the pristine dog he had been after that wonderful Day of the Bath. . . . Half his fur was singed a dirty yellow, and the other half was blackened with smoke and soot . . . but he was still the same, crazy, excitable, devoted little dog, and he did his best to lick Johnnie's face clean away in his delight at having him back.

Miss Lucas seemed undismayed by the journey, and they settled her in the dining-room, where she sat regally in her wheelchair and looked almost back to normal, if a shade more fragile than usual.

Johnnie looked at her anxiously, and said: 'Are – you – all – right?' remembering suddenly how light and frail she had felt in his arms as he carried her out of the fire.

'Of course I'm all right, boy!' she retorted. 'Go and show Dessie the garden . . . I know you want to.'

He was a little astonished at how much Miss Lucas knew. . . . But he went obediently and joyously, hand-in-hand with Dessie out into the tangled wilderness that he loved. Little Get-Lost, determined never to let him out of his sight again, padded after him like his own shadow . . .

They went first to look for Merlin, who was standing disconsolately in the orchard, not knowing that his friends had returned.

'There he is!' said Johnnie. 'Doesn't he look sad?' He ran up and put his arms consolingly round the old donkey's

254

furry neck. 'Hey, Merlin . . .' he crooned into one black velvet ear. 'Hey, old furry-face, did you miss me?'

The old grey head nodded and tossed in reply, and the soft lips nuzzled at Johnnie's face.

Dessie stood watching him, smiling a little at this affectionate reunion, then she too went up to Merlin and began to scratch his ears.

'I was – so – afraid – ' began Johnnie.

'About the animals? You knew I wouldn't let anyone touch them – '

'I didn't know . . . you were here!'

They looked at each other and laughed.

'I thought –' began Johnnie again – but it was all too hard to say, and anyway Dessie probably knew . . .

'You thought the old lady would die – and the house would burn to the ground – and the animals would all have to be destroyed . . .' she said. 'I know. Well, she didn't, and they weren't! *I've* seen to that! Come on, let's go and see the goats.'

Johnnie followed her, unable to think of a word to say. When they had inspected Ermine and Trudy, while keeping a wary eye on Billy the Kid who might be jealous, they went to look at the hens and collect the eggs. Dessie seemed quite at home, and even knew where the hens' grain was kept and gave them a handful to keep them quiet.

'How – ?' began Johnnie for the third time.

Dessie grinned. 'Your old lady – Miss Lucas – she woke up sooner then you did, see? She told us what to do!'

Johnnie grinned back. 'She – usually does!'

They wandered away again into the wild garden dreaming under the sun. . . . By dappled paths and grassy banks and small rough thickets of unpruned rose bushes, they made their way down past the lily pond until they came to the little summerhouse. They stood side by side looking up at it for a moment, and Dessie saw how the small verandah had been swept and tidied, and the trailing white sprays of the Russian vine had been neatly cut back round the flaky blue door . . .

Shyly, Johnnie led her up the steps and inside the tiny hexagonal room. The junk had all been cleared away . . . the old horsehair sofa had a fresh blanket on it, and the two wicker chairs had been brushed clean. . . . The rickety bamboo table had been mended, and Johnnie's painting things were stacked on it, with his drawings left in a tidy pile beside them.

'Is this where you've been sleeping?'

He nodded.

'Lovely!' said Dessie. 'All on you own!' (That was the one part of being 'in care' and in the home that she disliked . . . that long dormitory with never any privacy or any place of your own.)

Johnnie wished suddenly that he had a stove and some cups and then he could have made tea for Dessie in his own small house. Tin-Can-Charlie would have managed somehow. . . . Perhaps, he thought wistfully, one day, Miss Lucas might let me. . . . I could easily collect enough things to bring down here . . .

'So quiet,' said Dessie, standing by the door and looking out over the garden. 'It feels . . . as if nothing bad could ever happen here . . .'

'I know,' agreed Johnnie. 'Enchanted, Miss Lucas said. . . .' He wanted, urgently, to show Dessie the painting he had done for Miss Lucas. . . . But it had been up at the house . . . maybe it had been lost in the fire . . .

Dessie turned back and silently took Johnnie's hand and led him out again into the green and golden peace of the garden. She knew that Johnnie was thinking he was going to have to leave this lovely place and the stern old lady, Miss Lucas, and he was terribly torn at the prospect. . . . She could feel the sadness in him growing at every step.

'D'you remember the sea?' she said.

He nodded.

'All yours . . . remember?'

Again he nodded, with tears in his eyes. He remembered everything – all too well. But he could not speak just then . . .

In the converted dining room Miss Lucas sat upright in her chair, refusing to be tired.

'I have things to do,' she said. 'My lawyer is coming – about the fire insurance and so on . . . and I should like to talk to you two. . . .' She looked from Maggie to Bill and smiled. 'But it can wait. . . .' Her eyes caught a flash of movement in the garden beyond the window – Johnnie and Dessie running hand-in-hand along the overgrown paths . . .

Miss Lucas sighed. 'He loves this place, you know,' she said. 'Did I show you his picture?'

'No,' replied Bill, feeling a trifle dazed by her quick changes of thought.

'Over there! Behind the piano . . . I hope the fire didn't get to it.' She pointed a commanding finger.

Bill went over and fetched the canvas out into the light and stood looking at it. . . . He was silent so long that Maggie came up to look over his shoulder.

'Astounding!' he murmured.

'It was his first attempt at oils,' said Miss Lucas. 'Only bought them three days before. . . . I'd been showing him Rembrandt – and Turner. He loved Turner. . . . But anyway, that's what this place means to him – and to me!'

Bill saw the passion behind the strokes of Johnnie's

brush – the soft rose-and-gold bloom of the garden at sunset and the matching glow of rosy light on the old lady's face as she looked up at Merlin's head silhouetted against the sky beyond . . .

'Extraordinary . . .' he said. He found himself absurdly moved by what he saw. There was such power and such love behind it.

'Yes, well – ' said Emmaline Lucas, 'you say you care about the boy . . . I think you'd better take care of this.'

Bill, hearing something strange in that dry old voice, looked up sharply and met a pair of very shrewd bright eyes that were fixed on him with demanding intensity.

'Yes,' he said, answering far more than her actual words, 'I will.'

It was a day full of comings and goings. The lawyer came and was closeted with Miss Lucas for a long time. The insurance assessors came. The local builder came to talk about repairs. And, touchingly, a procession of villagers came, offering vegetables from their gardens, flowers, home-made cakes, help in the house, help in the garden, clean blankets and curtains in case the others were too smoke-damaged to use – and a host of other suggestions, including an offer to scrub out the sooty rooms and clean the windows.

Miss Lucas saw them all, sitting erect and alert in her chair, and thanking them one by one. It was strange, she reflected, that she had lived in that house all her life and the villagers had never been very friendly – till now. An emergency and one brave small boy had brought down all the barriers.

In the evening, when everyone had gone, Miss Lucas announced that she was going to bed early, and requested that Johnnie should bring her usual hot drink to her room.

Johnnie had been wandering about all day with Dessie, in a haze of relief, joy and sadness which he could not understand at all. He was filled with delight to be back in his beloved garden and to find that the animals were safe, and to be able to show Dessie all the places he most loved. . . . But over all this glory there hung the faint shadow of parting – and some darker foreboding which he could not quite dispel. He knew he was going to have to leave Miss Lucas. People did have to go away – back to the world where they belonged. He was Johnnie Ross now – a responsible boy who would have to take decisions. There were the kids to look after – there was his Mom who never could manage to make a go of things somehow . . . and there was Maggie who kept saying he'd got to go back to hospital and get his ears put right . . . and the Painting Man who said he'd got to learn to draw. . . . And there was Dessie, who supported him in everything he did, and who never asked for anything, but who looked at him with eyes of hope . . . a hope which he did not know how to answer . . .

He took the cup of Ovaltine carefully into the library, and found Miss Lucas perched on the edge of her bed, looking very frail and tired.

'Shall I help you in?' he said, and once again lifted her quite easily in his strong young arms.

Miss Lucas laughed. 'Young Lochinvar,' she said.

Johnnie didn't understand, and she didn't explain. But when he had put her carefully down in the bed and pulled the covers over her, she said: 'Sit down, Johnnie. I want to talk to you.'

Obediently, he sat down beside her, looking into her face with attention so that he could follow what she was saying.

'A few things to tell you, boy,' she began, and sipped thoughtfully at her Ovaltine before she went on. 'I've

259

lived in this house all my life . . . always loved the place, as you know. . . . You love it too, don't you?'

Johnnie nodded. This scarcely needed saying.

'Last few years, though, as I got stiffer, I got very lonely . . . never saw anyone, really, . . .' She looked at him over the top of her cup. 'Till you came along . . . made the place feel alive again . . . running about the place . . . like my young brothers. . . .' Her voice became softer, full of dreams. Then she seemed to recollect that she was talking to Johnnie, and she smiled at him with more than a gleam of mischief. 'We had some good times together, boy, didn't we . . . you and I?'

Once more, Johnnie nodded. He couldn't for the life of him see why any of this needed to be said.

'I wanted to tell you – it's meant a lot to me, having you here – I'm a very lucky old woman . . .'

Johnnie interrupted her. 'I am lucky, too,' he said. And smiled.

That brought Emmaline Lucas to what she wanted to say. She drew a long, tired breath and tried to marshall her thoughts.

'Yes, Johnnie. I think you are. You've got some good friends. . . . Maggie and Bill are – steady sort of people. You can trust 'em. . . . And Dessie – ' She grinned at him, once more full of mischief. 'Dessie'd fight dragons for you!'

Johnnie grinned back. Far down in his mind he could see a small, bright, clear picture of Dessie standing squarely on her two sturdy legs, waving a sword at an incredibly fierce, fiery dragon. . . .

'You also have your painting, Johnnie. It's important to have something bigger than yourself, you know – you won't stop, will you?'

'No,' said Johnnie. And then, very clearly, 'I couldn't.'

She nodded and reached out a hand to pat his. 'That's good. That's what I wanted to hear. . . . Life is very rich, Johnnie, d'you see? . . . lots to do . . . lots to be. . . . You've got to learn all sorts of things. . . .' Her old, light voice drifted a little. Then she returned to him, resolutely precise. 'I want you to promise me that you'll get those ears seen to – and go to the right sort of school They can teach you how to cope with *everything*. *Everything*, do you understand?'

'Yes.'

'Promise?'

'Yes.'

Her eyes snapped fire at him. 'A promise is a promise, Johnnie Ross!' She paused, her thoughts drifting away again. 'Life isn't all sunsets and apple-orchards,' she murmured, looking out at the darkening garden. 'I sometimes wish it was!'

Johnnie gazed out at the garden, too. He understood her. He could see, very clearly, his mother and the kids sitting round the kitchen table – the unwashed dishes in the sink and the floor he would have to scrub . . .

'But,' he said, straining after the right words, 'the sky's still there – '

Unexpectedly, the old lady's eyes filled with tears. She grasped his hand very tight in her bony fingers and said unevenly: 'Of course! It's always there!'

There was silence between them for a while, and then Miss Lucas said: 'The night of the fire – you stopped running away.'

Johnnie waited.

'From now on, d'you see, Johnnie – you can take decisions – on your own. You're growing up, boy. . . . Your father, Danny Ross, was a brave man, by all accounts. Good at his job. Reliable. Cared about his friends. And you're like him. Understand?'

Dumbly, Johnnie nodded.

'Head of the family now, boy. I shall rely on you to make a go of it. . . . Proud of you!'

Johnnie sighed. Then he blurted out what troubled him most. *'I don't want to leave you.'*

Emmaline Lucas smiled. 'You won't, boy – that's what I'm saying. Wherever you go – whatever you do – you're Danny Ross's son, so he's still there. And you're my friend – so I'm still there. Understand?'

It was a difficult thought. Johnnie considered it carefully. 'Yes,' he said at last. He suddenly remembered Dessie's gift of the little glass snowstorm and the tiny figure in a silver space suit. . . . 'Inside the glass . . .' he said, obscurely.

'Exactly,' said Miss Lucas, as if she understood him perfectly. 'Safe enough – you and I . . .'

They looked at one another, smiling. Then Miss Lucas handed him her empty cup and said briskly: 'That's enough talk for tonight! Now I'm going to sleep!'

Johnnie stood up.

'Miss Lucas – ' he began, and stopped.

'Yes, boy – ?'

'Thank you.'

She didn't misunderstand him. She nodded contentedly and lay back and shut her eyes.

'Goodnight, Miss Lucas,' he said, very softly.

'G'night. . . .' Her voice was drowsy. Then her eyes flew open, fierce and indomitable. 'I shall be watching, mind.' She said.

Johnnie tiptoed away.

In the morning, he woke very early. He and Dessie had been allowed to sleep in the old summerhouse, since the weather was mild and gentle. . . . Dessie was still

262

asleep, wrapped in her sleeping bag, lying on some cushions on the floor. He stepped over her, carefully, and went outside.

Nothing stirred. He wandered on into the dew-laden garden and stood looking out towards the hills where the sun was rising. It was very quiet. A blackbird was singing, high up in one of the old apple trees . . . he could just hear it. . . . The colours of the flowers and the wet grass were silvery and muted . . . the world seemed drenched in light . . . drenched in peace . . .

I love this place, he thought . . . and wandered on . . . till he came to the little sloping path down to the neglected lawn where he had first found Miss Lucas. He stood there, remembering. Almost, it seemed to him, he could hear her imperious voice calling to him across the sunlit garden. For it was sunlit now – suddenly the whole sky was awash with colour, and the sun leapt up in a dazzle of brightness from behind the hill . . .

'You're my friend – so I'm still there!' said Miss Lucas, from the sunrise.

It was there that Maggie found him. But when she told him her news, she fancied he did not seem surprised.

'She died in her sleep,' she said. 'Quite peacefully. You must not be too sad, Johnnie. She was an old lady, in a lot of pain. She had lived a long time and had a good life. . . . And at the end, she was very happy.'

'Yes,' said Johnnie quietly. 'I know.'

He was quiet all that day – and quiet at the funeral. There were things to do, arrangements to make – people to see. He helped with them all – and Dessie silently took his hand and helped to see him through.

But at last it was over, and Maggie called Johnnie into the empty library and said: 'I have a lot of things to tell you.'

Quiet still, he stood looking from her to Bill, and back to Dessie who stood beside him, staunch and silent as ever.

'What things?' he asked.

Maggie glanced at Bill for reassurance and then began. 'First of all, Johnnie, Miss Lucas has left this house to you.'

Johnnie stared, waiting in silence. Almost it seemed to Maggie that he was listening to other words than hers.

'There is some money, too,' she went on. 'Not a lot – but enough to keep this place going for a few years. . . . She says in her instructions that she would like – '

'I know what she would like,' said Johnnie. He looked round at the shelves of books, and at the garden beyond the windows. 'A lot of kids could live here,' he said slowly, thinking it out. 'But it would need – ' He looked from Maggie to Bill. He was suddenly too shy to suggest it.

'Yes,' agreed Maggie. 'I know what you are thinking –' She did not look at Bill. 'But there are other considerations, Johnnie. You have been made a Ward of Court now. Miss Lucas arranged that for you – and you are in my care until everything is sorted out.'

Johnnie smiled. 'I'm glad,' he said simply.

'There will also be some money from the Company – from your father's firm. They have arranged for it to be put in trust for you – '

'Why not my Mum?' asked Johnnie, puzzled.

There was a moment's silence. Then Maggie said gently: 'Your Mom has gone off again, Johnnie. . . . We don't know if she'll come back or not . . . but in any case, Kevin and Treesa and the baby will be kept in care now – they can't be pushed around any more.'

Johnnie nodded.

But Maggie saw his face, and added, still gently: 'She

264

couldn't really cope, Johnnie. It wasn't her fault . . . it was just all too much for her. Do you understand?'

He nodded again. He understood all too well. She had never been able to cope, his Mum. She was like a child – just like Kevin and Treesa and the baby – lost and muddled and helpless, with her long bright hair and her frightened eyes . . .

He sighed. He remembered Miss Lucas's old, clear voice saying 'Head of the family now – *proud of you.*'

'I couldn't stay here,' he said in anguish, knowing he was throwing away everything he loved. 'Not without the kids – I'm all they've got now.'

This time, it was Maggie who sighed and nodded.

'And me!' said Dessie, sounding fierce and angry and sad all at once. 'I'll help look after them – '

Johnnie turned on her the full radiance of his smile. He did not speak.

'Now, look here,' said Bill, breaking into the silence in a practical, cheerful manner, 'there's other things to decide, too. Your ears, for instance. They've got to be done – and we've got to find that extra special school. You must learn *everything*, Johnnie. *Everything* they can teach you!'

'Yes,' agreed Johnnie. 'I know – ' He looked confused for a moment – sad and tired and confused. A small boy uncertain of the future – with too many weighty decisions to take.

'Would it – would this place – work as a – a home?' he asked. 'Could we – ?' He couldn't finish it. His eyes were big with hope. But it seemed a lot to ask. He stared out at the garden. A sudden longing for its receiving quietness assailed him . . .

'If you went to your special school, you could come here for the holidays,' said Bill. 'It would only be for a while – till you were ready for your senior school . . .'

265

'And – Dessie? And the kids?'

'There are quite good schools nearby,' said Maggie, speaking slowly, almost reluctantly.

'You could all go there together in the end – ' added Bill.

'But – ' said Johnnie, looking from one to the other helplessly: 'Do you – want to?'

Maggie hesitated. Did she? Wasn't it too big for her? An enormous undertaking – and a commitment for which she was not yet ready – a commitment to Bill as well . . .

'I don't know . . .' she said slowly. 'There's a lot to think about – ' She found herself looking into Johnnie's anxious eyes. . . . Somehow she could not refuse to answer that look. 'I suppose – we could try. . . . But it's your decision, Johnnie. She left it all to you . . .'

Johnnie shut his eyes. 'I – I want to think – ' he said, and ran out of the room into the garden.

They looked after him in consternation. But Dessie said sharply: 'Leave him be! He'll be all right!' And she went away too, out into the garden. But she did not follow Johnnie. Not yet.

Behind her, Maggie and Bill stood looking at each other anxiously.

'What is it?' said Bill, laying a hand on her arm. 'Why are you afraid?'

'It's so big, Bill. . . . Such a huge responsibility . . . other people's children. . . .'

'*Our* children,' corrected Bill.

Maggie was silent.

He looked at her with sudden deep tenderness. 'Are you having cold feet about me, too? Is it because of your first husband?'

266

She sighed and shook her head. 'Alan? No. It's not because of him. . . . At least, in a way it may be. . . . You see, Bill, we were such children ourselves then . . . we were so in love, and life was so beautiful. . . . Everything seemed entirely right . . . we both had a good future . . . and then – in a year he was dead.' She turned away from him to look out at the garden with unseeing eyes. 'At the time, I thought I would never want to feel anything again . . . you know how it is with grief. . . . But gradually you come out of it. . . . Work was my salvation – and it still is now. . . . The kind of problems I have with people like Johnnie make my own personal life seem very unimportant somehow . . .'

'But it isn't, Maggie.' Bill's hands were on her arms, urgently turning her towards him. 'Your life is important, too . . . and your own private happiness. . . . You're still young – '

'Bill, I don't know if I *can* feel enough. . . . I don't know if I even want to – '

'Rubbish!' said Bill, smiling now. 'I've watched you over these weeks of anxiety over Johnnie. Of course you can feel! And I thought – I had begun to hope – you felt as I do. . . ?'

Maggie looked at him miserably. 'I do, Bill – I think . . .'

'You *think?*' He laughed, and then suddenly stooped and kissed her very hard. 'How does that feel? Wouldn't you miss me if I'd gone?'

Her eyes went wide. 'Gone? Where?'

But the expression in her eyes had told him what he wanted to know. He wasn't really frightened now. All the same, he felt he had to explain it carefully.

'Maggie dear – if you won't marry me, I don't think I can hang around and watch you not allowing yourself to feel. . . . I'll just have to go away . . .'

Panic seized Maggie, and she gripped his arms, recognising at last what was happening to her. 'I do believe – I can't do without you!' she said, and her smile as she looked up at him was suddenly luminous and shy.

'That's better!' smiled Bill. 'That's what I wanted to hear! Now we're getting somewhere. . . .' He added another determined kiss to confirm it. 'So – are you still terrified of this suggestion of Miss Lucas's?'

'Terrified!' agreed Maggie, unable to help smiling too.

'But – you will take the risk?'

'I – I suppose I'll have to – ' She still sounded slightly appalled by all the implications. 'That is, if Johnnie decides to go ahead . . .'

'Please,' said Bill, his voice full of longing. '*Please*, Maggie . . . it's worth a try . . .'

'There's so much at stake . . .'

'Of course!' said Bill. 'Of course there is! But you were never a coward!'

Oh yes I was! thought Maggie. I've been a coward for a long time now. . . . And this thing with Bill frightens me most of all . . .

But all at once she saw how vulnerable and anxious Bill looked in the midst of his pleading, and she knew that she couldn't bear to make him unhappy any longer. . . . Coward or not, she was going to have to take on all this responsibility, and somehow make a go of it, for Johnnie's sake – and make Bill happy as well . . .

'All right,' she said at last. 'But we don't know that any of this will be allowed to happen. . . . There's an awful lot to be decided first . . .'

'Don't worry so!' said Bill, hugging her close. 'We'll work it all out. . . . There's bound to be a way round everything if we try! Let's go and find Johnnie before you change your mind!'

Arm-in-arm, they wandered out into the garden. . . .

*　　　*　　　*

For a few moments, Johnnie ran headlong down the sun-dappled path. He wanted to get away – to think – to decide. . . . But he wanted to get away, too, from the sudden awful weight of grief that now assailed him.

He hadn't wept for Miss Lucas – not a single tear. While there were things to do and people to see, it hadn't been possible. And anyway, he wasn't sure if he wanted to weep then . . .

But now – when the full knowledge of her kindness and foresight came to him – the realisation that all this lovely wilderness was his, if he could only use it right – he was suddenly defeated. He didn't want it without Miss Lucas. It belonged to her. He couldn't bear it all alone . . .

Stumbling, he ran on until he came to old Merlin leaning his grey head over the orchard wall.

'Merlin!' he gasped. 'Oh, Merlin! I miss her so! Do you miss her too?' And he buried his face in the rough grey fur of Merlin's shaggy neck and sobbed his heart out.

He stayed there a long time alone. But at last he grew calm. He understood now what he must do. He had to grow up. He had to make himself qualified for the future Miss Lucas had offered him. . . . He knew what path he must take . . . not always the quiet paths of this sunlit garden . . .

He looked round, remembering the old, clear voice saying: 'Safe enough, you and I . . .' and found himself looking straight into Dessie's anxious eyes.

'Goodbye, old Merlin,' he said, and put his arms round the patient donkey and hugged him hard. 'I'll be back!'

Then he held out a hand to Dessie and drew her close. 'I mean – *we'll* be back!' he said.

269

Fontana Paperbacks: Fiction

Fontana is a leading paperback publisher of both non-fiction, popular and academic, and fiction. Below are some recent fiction titles.

- ☐ SO MANY PARTINGS Cathy Cash Spellman £2.50
- ☐ TRAITOR'S BLOOD Reginald Hill £1.95
- ☐ THE KREMLIN CONTROL Owen Sela £1.95
- ☐ PATHS OF FORTUNE Susan Moore £1.95
- ☐ DAYS OF GRACE Brenda Jagger £1.95
- ☐ RAVEN William Kinsolving £1.95
- ☐ FLOODGATE Alistair MacLean £1.95
- ☐ FAMILY TIES Syrell Leahy £1.95
- ☐ DEATH IN SPRINGTIME Magdalen Nabb £1.50
- ☐ LEGION William Blatty £1.75
- ☐ A CROWNING MERCY Susannah Kells £1.95
- ☐ BLIND PROPHET Bart Davis £1.95
- ☐ ALL THINGS IN THEIR SEASON Helen Chappell £2.50
- ☐ A CRY IN THE NIGHT Mary Higgins Clark £1.75
- ☐ SUNRISE Rosie Thomas £1.95

You can buy Fontana paperbacks at your local bookshop or newsagent. Or you can order them from Fontana Paperbacks, Cash Sales Department, Box 29, Douglas, Isle of Man. Please send a cheque, postal or money order (not currency) worth the purchase price plus 15p per book for postage (maximum postage is £3.00 for orders within the UK).

NAME (Block letters) _____

ADDRESS _____

_____